A Very Small

Price to Pay,

Sir

A Josh & Ellingham story

Dennis Talbot

Dedication

To my grandchildren

Evie, Emily, Jason, Jack, Oscar, Josh, Joey & Olly

Acknowledgements

To Lisa, who read the first draft and encouraged me to publish.
To Irene, who read the amended version and did the same.
To my wife Pauline who carried out the final proof-read.

THANK YOU

ISBN: 978-1656-9871-81

This is a work of fiction.
Names, characters, places and incidents originate from the
writer's imagination. Any resemblance to actual persons, living
or dead, is purely coincidental.

First Published in 2014 by
OLYMPIA PUBLISHERS as
"A Small Price to Pay, Sir"

1

The last person I wanted to see, that day of all days, was Jane Barrington-Ross, and there was no mistaking it was she. Even on a busy pavement, at the hundred yards or so she was away, her carrot hair and the bouncy way she walks. No, no chance of mistaken identity. For a short time we had been engaged to be married, a thing I was all in favour of at first but within a few days it became clear that she was a bit too hot to handle; always coming up with harebrained schemes, to drop yours truly deeply in the soup. Although our hearts had cooled, we still admired and respected each other on a different plane. We eventually had a difference of opinion on my mode of income; she thought I ought to get a job and I thought I oughtn't. With me to decide is to act, and as at that instant I just happened to be alongside the side entrance of one of those large department stores, it was the work of a moment to disappear inside.

Once inside, I realised my mistake. I had rushed headlong into the local branch of that large conglomerate, the *Thre'penny & Sixpenny Store*. It was, however, well populated, mostly with the lower orders of humanity making it easy to mingle and so, I suppose, it suited my purpose well enough. Keeping an eye on the entrance that I had used to see if said Jane B-R had followed me in, I made my way between aisles of personal and household goods, all at prices that made you wonder how they could possibly be of the slightest use. However there seemed to be enough takers so who am I to pass judgement, never having used an egg timer or a hairnet.

A large crowd was assembled around some sort of demonstration and since this seemed to be a suitable place to make myself inconspicuous I worked my way into it. A not unattractive girl, if only she had realised that her particular shade of lipstick made her look as though she had been sucking a beetroot; and none too carefully at that, was giving sway about a new miracle household cleaner or some such thing. Being as I was now well into the crowd, and noting that this girl could hold an audience, I thought I might as well see what was on offer. I suppose she must have noticed me moving my way through the throng and took it that I was more than usually interested in the product she was promoting. At any rate she spoke directly to me.

'You sir, you look like a man who knows a good thing when he sees it. Come and try "Kleeno" for yourself. See how easily it removes these baked-on stains. Come sir try for yourself, prove to these good people all the claims for "Kleeno" are true.' And as she beckoned me forward, a voice from somewhere behind me said,

''E wouldn't know a baked-on stain if it leapt orf the pan and bit him.'

''S'right', said another voice, 'bet 'e's got a butler what does that.'

Laughter ensued and much joy and merriment was gained at the expense of yours truly. I recognised that the only way to extract myself from what could possibly be a long entanglement was to make a purchase, and without delay; I plumped for the large economy size, which incidentally set me back two shillings and four-pence: *Thre'penny & Sixpenny Store* forsooth. I extracted myself from those present and made my way towards the main entrance on the high street, deciding to abandon my purchase on the way. With this intent in mind I stopped, at random, to appear to look at one of the items on display, which by ill fate happened to be ladies nether garments. I moved quickly on when the young lady behind the counter gave me a rather funny look. Nearby were some men's gloves in some sort of cheap patent leather, in sizes large, medium and small. Deciding that these would do quite nicely as a suitable depository for "Kleeno", I lingered a moment or two and tried a couple of pairs on as though I was interested; then deftly walked away bereft of the brown paper bag containing the said miracle substance and made fair headway towards the main entrance. Shortly before I got there I felt a restraining hand at my elbow,

''Scuse me sir', it said, and turning I was confronted by a stout, round faced man in a dark grey uniform, the peaked cap of which had clearly been made for a man with a smaller head than it's present wearer. Or perhaps it had shrunk and his lords and masters were too mean to replace it, which ever it was he was looking at me with eyes that said what are you up to my lad. These store detectives, floor-walkers or whatever they call themselves are often retired policemen and bring to the job the suspicions gained over a lifetime; dealing with un-savoury characters and I suppose those suspicions die hard.

'You left this behind you sir,' he said, with an even more piercing look.

'Oh so I did, thank you so much. Forget the old head if it were loose, what?'

3

I felt in my pocket and gave the man the two pence change from the half-crown I'd tended for the blasted stuff. Not that a half-crown would make a huge dent in my finances but one hates to be out of pocket needlessly.

Outside, horror of horrors, there was Jane, hands on hips looking directly at me.

'You were avoiding me you miserable young oik,' she said, her hazel eyes flashing.

'Oh hello,' I said, trying to hide my embarrassment at being found out.

'Oh hello yourself, you were weren't you?'

'Sorry?'

'You were avoiding me, no use denying it; I know a quick nip into a convenient doorway when I see one. Very hard to hide when you're six foot tall you know. No matter, there's something I wanted to see you about,' she said, her face softening into a bright smile.

My heart sank to my neatly polished brogues.

'Oh, erm, I see,' I said or some other equally tentative phrase.

'Buy me lunch and I'll tell you all about it.'

I had intended to lunch out in any case; and to be fair dining with Jane is a not unpleasant experience. Since there was a good quality hotel just across the road and I was feeling a bit peckish anyway we repaired there and were conducted to a table by the window. We passed the usual pleasantries as we sat looking at the menu.

'How's that father of yours,' she asked, 'still making motorcars?'

Perhaps I should explain, my father does indeed make motorcars. Not him personally you understand, he owns a factory near Oxford and turns out a hundred or so a month. Quite a sensible man my father. He had already noticed by the time I was about ten, that anything more technical than a pair of scissors was quite beyond me and therefore kept me as far away from the manufacture of motorcars as he possibly could. His idea then had been that I should go into law but I showed even less legal ability than I did mechanical skill; he quickly withdrew me from that venture. He now makes me a monthly allowance plus a goodly dollop of shares in the company which are doing quite nicely thank you, and there matters rest to everyone's satisfaction. Except of course, as stated earlier Miss J. Barrington-Ross had not quite seen it that way.

'Yes, still making the monthly quota,' I replied. I asked about her family and received confirmation that all was indeed well.

'Joshua,' she said and paused, turning a ravishing smile and twinkling hazel eyes on me.
I have to admit it was those eyes and that smile that had first set the spark of love in the old heart. My heart skipped a beat then sank back into the brogues again. I'm always known as Josh by all and sundry, and when *Joshua* comes out something pretty awful is almost always about to follow. My father has a brother and two sisters, and my mother, who at the time of which I am writing had passed away six years ago, had three sisters, so I am stuck with five aunts, plus an extra one by marriage, all of whom are likely to call me Joshua just before pointing out some shortcoming in my actions or character. Or tell me that they require me to do something completely unfit for human consumption. So the heart sinking into brogues routine is a fairly common one.

'Joshua,' she said again, 'there's something I need you to do for me.'

'Jane old thing please don't take this the wrong way, I'm always ready to be of service as you know but I'm awfully busy just at the moment.'

'Awfully busy my foot you wouldn't know awfully busy if it jumped up and bit you.'

I could see it was set to be one of those days big on things jumping up and biting me.

'I am busy, I've absolutely oodles of things that need doing; and at this very moment in fact.'

'Name one,' she demanded.

And there of course she had me.

'Oh, OK,' I said, 'spill the beans and make it snappy. The waiter will be here for the order any second.'

'My Uncle Rothwell -,'

'Who?'

'Do be quiet whilst I explain Josh.'

'Sorry.'

'Uncle Rothwell my mother's brother is very keen on flowers. He has a garden second to none, but his real love is roses.'

'Understood.'

'Walter Thomas the famous rose grower has told him that he has grown a new rose and wants to name it in my uncle's honour.'

'Yes I've heard of that.'

'It's a great accolade. Uncle Roth is over the moon.'

'I can see that he would be but where do I come into this?'

Before I could find out, the waiter arrived and the conversation had to be shelved for a while. Amid much licking of the pencil and repeating everything we had said, *I suppose you have to get these things right; after all, too often I had been given one thing after ordering another, so I think he was just making doubly sure he had got it right -* we resumed as he wended his weary, baggy trousered way to the kitchens or wherever it was he wended his weary, baggy trousered way to.

'Your Uncle Rothwell's rose,' I reminded her.

'Yes I know, he's over the moon…'

'You already said that.'

'Josh, button it or I'll bean you with the peppermill.'

A nod's as good as a wink as they say. That, together with the size and construction of the peppermill, meant that I indeed buttoned it.

'Uncle Rothwell has asked to see the rose before it's unveiled, if that's what you do to roses. The long and the short of it is they won't let him.'

'Understandable both ways, he wants to see it; they want it as a surprise for the world. Where then, as I asked before do I come in?'

'You my dear Josh, are going to get hold of one of the blooms for him.'

'Get hold of one of the… how?'

'Steal it, of course!' and she said it with a sweet smile, and without any visible prick of conscience.

'Me – No, no, no – not likely old thing. I get cold feet if I forget to buy a platform ticket, no sorry forget it; absolutely not on the cards.'

'Joshy?'

'Don't Joshy me, rely upon it, it isn't going to happen.'

'But it's such a small thing to ask.'

'Ha.'

'Do just this one little thing for me?'

7

'I won't do it; besides I know nothing about roses, how would I know I had stolen the right one?'

'Ah there I have a plan, you get them to show it to you.'

'If they won't show it to your uncle why on earth would they show it to me?'

'Well it's like this.'

I don't know what it is about Miss Jane B-R, but I came away from our luncheon having agreed to have a go at her plan. As we were leaving I was again presented with the large economy size "Kleeno" that I had cunningly, or, at least, thought I had cunningly, left behind one of the table legs. I thanked the waiter for his diligence and gave him a sixpence for his trouble; bringing the grand total of investment in "Kleeno" to three bob. I wondered if I could obtain shares in the blasted stuff, after all if it is half as good at cleaning as it is at sticking like glue to the purchaser it has to be a gilt-edged winner.

'Still as forgetful as ever I see,' she said giving one of those condescending half-smiles that women always reserve for these occasions, to save them having to keep saying "typical man".

'Yes, nothing changes,' I said to save a long explanation about "Kleeno".

I gave her a peck on the cheek by way of goodbye and we went our separate ways.

I returned to my original plan for the day, and a pretty difficult one it looked like being. The night before the day I'm telling you about, if you see what I mean, I had attended a cocktail and dance evening at my club. You've perhaps heard of it; The 'Straw Boater' by the Royal Theatre. Anyway, as I said I had been to the said party and had noticed a rather charming young lady; the club is normally a male only establishment but on cocktail evenings the rules are relaxed and members are expected to bring a lady guest. Having been let down at the last minute by the lady I had invited due to her getting engaged the night before, and thinking people might see it as bad form to be escorted to unknown destinations by strange men, if you get my meaning, I had reluctantly gone unaccompanied. The young lady, the other young lady, the one I had noticed at the club, was always just out of reach. Strangely, as I moved toward her she seemed always to be moving away; that and the fact that I was constantly being accosted by friends and their escorts and being expected to chat, our paths never managed to cross and so I never actually got chance to work my considerable charms upon her. I did however, by deft questioning of those I spoke to, find out that it seemed she was something of a mystery woman. All I could establish was that her name was Elizabeth or "Liz" and she had been the guest of one of the newer members that no-one seemed to know much about. Then quite suddenly about ten-thirty she had gone from our midst.

Desirous of finding out more about her to allow me to make her acquaintance I made my way to the Straw Boater to see what, if anything, could be gleaned from the signing in book. It was about three fifteen by my watch as I climbed the steps of the club. The place was a hive of activity; but not club members - members of the constabulary. I found myself sidelined for a while by the fuss and had to wait for several minutes before Walters the club commissionaire made himself available.

'Good afternoon Mr Tolson sir - sorry about the delay,' he said.

'Good afternoon Walters, what on earth's going

on?'

'It seems that a very expensive fur stole went missing from the cloakroom during last evening's party sir; all of the staff seem to be under suspicion.'

'Not you surely Walters?'

'Thankfully I was not on duty last night sir, but we've all been interviewed.'

'It's about last night's party that I'm here.'

'I see sir, how can I be of help?'

'I'm trying to track down a young lady who was here last night and a quick look at the signing in book might provide the necessary information.'

'Can't be done sir I'm afraid, the police inspector has taken it for evidence.'

'Nothing to be done then for the moment. Any idea when it's likely to be back in circulation?'

'Not too long I hope sir, I understand that one of the young policemen is making a detailed copy of all the evening entries; when he's finished I would hope it will be returned.'

'Do me a favour Walters, you've got my phone number somewhere, give me a ring when you get it back, leave a message with Ellingham if I'm not in.'

'Certainly sir, will there be anything else.'

'No thanks - no point hanging around for a quiet drink with this lot climbing all over the furniture. I'll head off to the old homestead.'

'Before you go sir, Inspector Jackman has requested to have a word with anyone who was at last night's party sir. I believe you said you were there sir?'

'No reason to deny it, Walters; lead on let's get it over with.'

'Very good sir, the inspector is this way,' and he

led me into a small room behind the reception desk.

'This is Mr Tolson, Inspector, he was at the cocktail party last night.'

'Ah, sit down please Mr Tolson. I wonder if you would mind answering a few questions?'

I said I didn't mind and told him as simply as I could all that I could remember; which was of course very little; my mind had been preoccupied with this mysterious Liz. He thanked me and took my address and telephone number in case he needed to speak to me again, and I was on my way.

'Good day then sir.' Walters touched his forelock - I think it's called - as I left.

'Good day to you Walters.'

With the adequate allowance my father gives me I am able to rent a rather nice flat in one of those modern buildings with built in underground car parking, in one of the better parts of the dear old metropolis, and also employ a valet, Ellingham, though he prefers to be called a gentleman's personal gentleman, a more upbeat term it seems. I arrived back home shortly before five o'clock having walked from the club and stopped for a haircut on the way. The sound of my key in the latch alerted Ellingham as it always does and he appeared as I opened the door.

'Good afternoon sir, I hope you have had a pleasant day.'

'Yes, if a bit perplexing, Ellingham. By the way I have something that might be of use to you.'

He opened the brown paper bag.

'Kleeno, sir?'

'Yes, no doubt you will be able to find some good use for it.'

11

'It is a product new to my acquaintance, doubtless it will be of interest to compare it to my existing cleaning agents, thank you sir.' He looked at the large economy size as one might look at the present of a dead rat; and pretty unprepossessing dead rat at that, then said -

'I'm sorry to hear that your day has been perplexing, anything I might help with sir?'

'Could be, Ellingham, could be.'

But before I could put him wise to the situation the doorbell rang.

'Better see who's there Ellingham, we'll talk later.'

'Certainly sir.'

He quickly placed the large economy sized, in the corner cupboard by the front door, giving me a moment to make myself scarce in the sitting room then opened the door.

'Miss Barrington-Ross, sir.' He looked across the sitting room at me, with slightly raised eyebrows; he disapproves of Miss J. B-Ross.

'Thank you Ellingham, that will be all.'

'Might I enquire, will Miss Barrington-Ross be staying to dinner sir?'

I looked across at her enquiringly.

'Just a flying visit, no dinner for me, thank you Ellingham.'

'Thank you Miss, sir?'

'That's all for the moment thank you Ellingham,' and he was gone.

Twice in one day is getting a bit strong for Jane's company I don't mind telling you, and this latest intrusion could only mean some new twist to my affairs that would no doubt age me a good few years, and probably send me grey-haired and gibbering, to an early grave before it was over. And such damned near proved to be the case.

'Josh – they've put the thing under lock and key.'

'Come again?'

'The rose; they've locked it away.'

'Oh well that's it then old thing, sorry I can't help, damned hard to steal something from behind a locked door, Um?' I could see I had not convinced her.

'You don't think a little thing like that is going to stop us do you?'

'It may not stop you but it puts me right out of the picture, count Joshua Tolson out of the scheme or plan. Sorry old thing out of the question.' How could I have put it much plainer than that?

'It just needs us to be a bit more devious and resourceful that's all.'

'How do you mean, devious and resourceful?'

'I've got it all worked out…'

And by Jove she had too, and a nifty little plan I have to admit – hard to see how it could fail; except fail, of course, it would, as sure as eggs-is-eggs as soon as it involves me. However, I agreed to give it a shot and she buzzed off.

I was aware that Ellingham had appeared in the room; he makes just sufficient noise on the parquet flooring to announce his presence.

'Ah, Ellingham, where were we?' I asked.

'You had suggested that there was perhaps some matter in your affairs to which I might be of assistance, sir.'

'Indeed, Ellingham and it concerns Miss Barrington-Ross.' He raised his eyebrows ever so slightly again.

13

'Fear not Ellingham, love is not re-kindled; love is dead as the dodo. This concerns her Uncle Rothwell.'

'Ah, Lord Westcott, sir.'

'Good lord is that who he is? Do you know him then Ellingham?'

'I only know of him, sir, having never met the gentleman. He is, I believe, something of a rose fancier. Indeed, I understand that a new variety of rose is to be named in his honour.'

I was astounded by the man's knowledge.

'How on earth do you know all this?'

'I like to think I am abreast of general affairs sir, one never knows when it might be of use.'

'Well it could be of use right now, it's about that bally rose that I have the problem, Ellingham.'

'I see sir, might I enquire the nature of the problem?'

'Indeed you may, Ellingham.'

And I proceeded to put him wise to my predicament. He listened quietly to the outline, slightly raising those eyebrows again from time to time, then when I had finished he said -

'The plan Miss Barrington-Ross puts forward could prove a problematic one sir, if the rose grower asks you to prove your identity you could well be found out.'

'You think they would?'

'With an item as newsworthy in the horticultural world as a new rose, sir, I feel that they could well take the most stringent precautions before allowing anyone to see it. After all, sir, for all they know you could be, what I believe is called, an industrial spy – or someone from a rival organization intent on sabotage sir.'

'It seems an impossible task without forged

papers then, what?'

'That could well be so sir. Might I enquire why you feel it necessary to do this kindness for Miss Barrington-Ross, sir?'

'She's an old chum, Ellingham, one likes to do little favours for old chums.'

'Indeed, sir.'

'Think on it, Ellingham; give it your best.'

'I will give your problem a good deal of thought, sir, though I fear as yet I cannot see an answer.'

Ellingham is a wonder worker on many levels; not only is he more than adequate in his domestic duties, he can also see his way through the most perplexing of problems. Although he doesn't always create the exact outcome wished, he has, so far at least, always managed to extract yours truly without devastating damage, and at the same time created a situation generally beneficial.

'Anything else happen whilst I was out?' I asked.

'The new car was delivered as you expected, sir.'

You will I'm sure remember me telling you that my father keeps me well away from the manufacture of motorcars. Though he has found a way that I can be of enormous use to him and the factory. He provides me with a new car every six months or so; recognising that that period in my hands equates to many years of normal use. He positively dotes on me breaking them, using me as part of the research and development department. He reckons that I can find a weakness in design that would cost him thousands on a test rig. I'm not altogether sure whether I like to be thought of in those terms, but it does mean that I'm always in the very latest Tolson car. This one would be his newest creation the Mark 14 Super Sports.

'Best be nipping down to the garage and taking a look at this new steed, what?'

'I fear that is not possible, I took the liberty of returning the vehicle sir.'

'Returning it Ellingham; why?'

'I did not feel that the colour which the factory had supplied fitted your image sir.'

'The colour, what's wrong with the colour?' I asked, getting a bit hot under the collar.

'It had been supplied in a very brash combination of reds sir.'

'That's right, that's what I ordered bright red with plum coloured wings.'

'You *ordered* that particular colour combination sir?'

'Yes that's what I asked for; it's the very latest in fashion. It's quite the rage Ellingham.'

'Indeed sir?'

'Indeed so Ellingham, get on to the factory first thing in the morning and get the bally thing returned.'

'Do you not think that a more sedate grey or possibly black would be more fitting to a gentleman in your position sir?'

'No I do not, Ellingham, get it back.'

'I was merely thinking sir, that when you make your not infrequent visits to you father's friends and your relatives in the country – is the impression that particular shade of vehicle would make, exactly the image you would wish to portray; sir?'

'Yes it jolly well is! And don't think I can't see through your little plan Ellingham; you feel it is not fitting for *you* to travel in my new car because of the colour. If that's the case you can jolly well walk or travel by train –

get it back Ellingham and without delay,' I said, and I rather think I stuck my chin out at the fellow; I meant it to sting what?

'As you wish sir.'

And there the matter closed.

Ellingham is a man of many talents, as I have already intimated if that's the right word, not the least of which is his ability to create the most melt-in-the-mouth meals. So much so that more than one of my many aunts has tried to wrest him away from me. Thankfully the man is totally loyal to the young lord and master and continues to create said meals for me on a regular basis. Well up to his usual standard, the one he had just provided was over, and as I sat drinking my after dinner coffee the phone rang. And Ellingham answered it.

'Your club sir. Walters wishes me to inform you that the guest book is once again in his possession. Do you wish to converse with him sir?'

'No, no need, just thank him from me if you would Ellingham.'

'Certainly sir,' and he went to hang up.
When he returned I said,

'I'll be nipping off to the Boater in a couple of ticks, should be about an hour or two.'

'If you won't be needing me then in the mean time, I am in the midst of reading "War and Peace" sir, a most enlightening book to which I would like to return, if that meets with your approval.'

'Ye gads Ellingham, you find "War and Peace" enlightening?'

'Indeed so sir.'

'Well read away then my good fellow, though I never got past the first two pages.'

'Quite so sir.'

I entered the club to find it bereft of the local rozzers and most of the members as well.

'Where is everybody Walters?'

'There is a special evening at the senior executive club sir, I rather think most of the members will be there, sir.'

He was probably right; most of the members' male parents would be members of the above club and no doubt expect their offspring to show their face. Having been to several of these occasions myself in the past they had my deepest sympathy.

'You were requesting to look at the book sir,' he said extracting said volume from below his counter.

'If you'd be good enough to sign yourself in, it's all yours sir.'

'Thank you Walters, ten minutes should tell me all I need to know, I'll take it into the smoking room if that okay?'

'I see no reason why not sir, I'll collect it should I need it.'

It didn't tell me as much as I would have liked. The young lady had indeed been entered as the guest of one of the members; but here's the perplexing thing the member's name entered in the book is Manson, John Manson; her name is also Manson, odd. They can't be husband and wife since it is a requirement of membership that all of the members are single and male; resignation from the club on marriage is one of the rules. Brother and sister that must be it, my needle sharp intellect had solved the problem. Could it be that they both lived at the same address? An enquiry with Walters as to the membership details of this John Manson could prove of use. I returned with the book to the front desk. Walters was just dealing with another of the members, a chap I thought I had met briefly somewhere before; a fellow an inch or so taller than me but a bit less wiry and athletic, wearing one of those combinations of beard and moustache that makes you look as though you are talking through a hairy doughnut. Anyway, Walters was glad of the book's return since it allowed him to complete the necessary formalities.

'Hello, Joshua Tolson isn't it?' This other fellow said as he signed the book, surprising me by his memory.

'Yes that's right,' I said, 'though I'm sorry I know your face but I can't remember your name.'

'Manson, John Manson, we've never been properly introduced and all that rot but someone pointed you out at last night's party. Said you were a good egg and the right sort of company, yer-know.'

This was of course an amazing coincidence, which nonplussed me a bit; and it's never easy to reply to that sort of flattery, so suppose I probably said something along the lines of –

"Oh, ah, I see, care for a drink: Then we can put matters straight, what?"

'I'd be delighted, I can see you've business with Walters so I'll be in the smoking room when you're available.' I nodded and off he went.

'I trust the book gave you the necessary information sir.'

'Walters if I was to tell you what I now know you would be totally amazed.'

'Glad to be of service sir.'

I tipped the man two shillings; one likes to keep on the right side if these people and Walters is one of the old school, service is all. Strictly speaking I suppose the book is confidential so I showed my gratitude.

'I'll be in the smoking room with Mr Manson if I'm needed Walters.' I said.

'Very good sir, and thank you sir.' He broke a brief smile as he slipped the two-bob into his waistcoat pocket. I nodded and wandered off to what was likely to be a very interesting conversation.

The smoking room was all but deserted and my new acquaintance had commandeered two leather chairs at the fireplace; not that there was a fire of course - at this time of the year it's replaced by a rather attractive Chinese screen. He sat with his legs crossed and I was able to see that he was wearing a pair of those rather nifty shoes from America with the white leather panels let into the sides; not perhaps the height of fashion at the moment, but damned pretty, don't you think? I remember wondering what the effect would be on Ellingham should I be bold enough as to purchase a pair. Deciding that the red and plum coloured Mark 14 Tolson Super Sports was probably enough in the way of domestic disharmony for the moment, I shelved the project.

As you can imagine, after the initial pleasantries the conversation turned to the missing fur, and when Dawson shuffled over to take our drinks order, he's eighty if he's a day by the way, and rumour has it was purchased with the ground-rent, we quizzed him to find out the latest posish.

'I was not on duty last night gentlemen. I find the rough and tumble of the cocktail evenings a bit too much for me these days, I think it's all that raucous music from the dazz band - so I can only tell you as much as I have been able to ascertain from the other staff,' he said.

'It's *jazz* band by the way – but tell us what you

can, that'll do nicely Dawson, spill the beans,' I said.

'Very good, Mr Tolson - it appears that one of the ladies at last night's party checked into the cloakroom a rather expensive fur stole, mink I believe gentlemen, but when she came to leave the fur was gone. It appears that someone, presumably one of the ladies, used a duplicate ticket to obtain it.'

'No chance it was a mistake then?' asked Manson.

'It seems not sir – it suggests a deliberate act of theft. The ticket that was used to retrieve it being as I said an exact copy of the correct one.'

'One of the members then?' I suggested.

'No,' said Manson, 'as Dawson has said it would have to be one of the guests; a lady. A man collecting a fur stole would be rather memorable, what?'

'Good lord, you're right.' I said.

'If that will be all, I'll be getting your drinks gentlemen.'

'Yes thank you Dawson,' and he shuffled off.

'Nice old fellow, getting on a bit to be still working, must love his job, what?' said Manson.

'I think it's what keeps him going, I should imagine they have probably provided him with a room high up somewhere in the rafters to save him having to travel here each day,' I said.

'If so, the stairs must cause him a problem.'

'There is a sort of service lift somewhere out at the back, but how far up that goes I've no idea.'

At this point Dawson returned with our drinks, most of them still in the glasses, and I enquired about his domestic arrangements.

'I have a small but very comfortable little room on the third floor sir, the lift goes up to the second floor and if a take my time I can make the flight of stairs to the third without too much effort. I am quite comfortable, gentlemen, and enjoy still being involved in the camaraderie of the staff.' he said. 'Will that be all, gentlemen?'

'Yes, thank you Dawson.'

'Ring if you need anything else gentlemen,' and off he shuffled.

We resumed the subject of the fur stole.

'There must have been the best part of seventy females at the do last night, it could have been any one of them,' I said.

'Begging your pardon, old chap, but I think we can take it that our own guests are above suspicion.'

'I came alone, my guest was unable to attend at the last minute and I was unable to get a replacement at short notice. But I meant nothing derogatory as to your own guest, of course. It's just that a lot of those young ladies must be fairly new acquaintances to the member entertaining them, if you see what I mean?'

'Quite, I'm sure that's so; thankfully I can vouch one hundred per cent for mine, she's my cousin,' he said.

One more bit of information for the Tolson investigation. So I said -

'Ah, was she the pretty girl in the blue dress?'

'Yes, did you see us come in?'

''S'pose I must have done. She is rather memorable, what? I say no disrespect and all that.'

'None taken old chap, you're quite right she is a bit of a looker, I say would you like to meet her?'

'Rather, I think she might be just my type.'

'Steady on old chap, wait till you've met her, what?'

22

We laughed and I gave him my telephone number, and we chatted about this and that for half an hour or so. As I bid him my farewell, he went off to the billiard room.

I got a taxi back to the old abode, arriving there at about ten fifteen. Ellingham as always heard my key in the lock and was there almost as I closed the door.

'Good evening sir,' he said taking my coat, 'is they're anything you require?'

'I'd like a nice cup of tea and the evening paper, Ellingham.'

'I have the kettle on the hob in anticipation of your return, it will be with you shortly sir.'

'Bring me the pot and all the bits and pieces then if I fancy another cup I needn't disturb you again.'

'It is no disturbance sir, however I will do as you request. You will find the evening newspaper on your chair in the sitting-room sir.'

'Ah, right-ho Ellingham.'

And sure enough there was the very paper as stated. I flopped myself down to flick through the thing, I'm not one of those people who must have a pristine copy of my chosen rag, and Ellingham at my request will pencil a ring around items he feels would be of interest or importance to me. Tonight he had marked a bit about one of my friends being had up for drunk in charge of a motorcar: a bank robbery at the very branch I use, and some financial news from the other side of the Atlantic, all of it interesting but hardly earth-shattering on a personal basis. And by the time the tea had arrived, I had settled myself to a leisurely perusal of the rest of the issue.

Then there, right in the middle of page two was an item that made me sit up and take notice, it read:

Miss Elizabeth Manson, daughter of the late Sir Archibald Edward Manson who spent his life in the service of his country in Africa, has returned to this country recently to extend the work her father started; helping the children in small outlying villages to gain proper schooling. She will be arranging various fund raising events and talks and hopes to build and equip several small village schools and provide qualified teachers. Readers who might like to donate to this worthy cause can send their cheques to us here at the 'Bugle' made out to 'Schools in Africa.'

What a girl, what a girl.

2

I don't know if you find it the same but I often find a good night's sleep can present the answer to the problem that has had you scratching your head the night before. Well such was the case. The problem of J.B.R.'s rose was solved and no need to pinch one. I simply present myself as one of those high-class photographers from the monthly magazines, one of those very expensive colour ones, and take a colour photograph of the damn thing; simple. If I point out to the aforesaid Walter Thomas, rose-grower, that publication date is well after the public announcement of the rose what could be the problem?

I lay mulling the scheme, or plan, over in my mind when Ellingham tapped on the door heralding my morning cup of tea. He waited a moment then entered.

'Good morning sir, your tea. You may be able to already smell that I have taken the liberty of frying bacon and your favourite sausage for breakfast. I can however provide something different if you would prefer.' He was right, I could smell them, and damned good they smelt too.

'Bacon & s will do very nicely, Ellingham.'

'If you wish I could accompany them with a fried egg, sir?'

'Accompany them with two fried eggs if you would, there's a good chap, the old brain has been working on overtime all night and needs replenishing.'

'As you wish sir, though current thinking is that

too much fried food, especially eggs, is not good for the general health, sir.'

'Well current thinking is not currently thinking straight. Not good for the general health indeed, tosh, I say, tosh, to current thinking. Current thinking will soon be telling us that cigarettes are bad for the general health what?'

'There is already indeed a lobby of thought that smoking cigarettes is injurious to the health in many ways sir, it has been suggested...'

I cut the man off.

'Current thinking and lobbies of thought are nothing but killjoys. Two eggs Ellingham and get cracking.' I smiled and rather think I gave a merry chuckle, pleased with my little quip.

He drifted off back to the b and s and presumably two eggs and left me to continue mulling over my plan. Photography is something I do know a little about, having dabbled in it a bit; clicked the odd shutter or two, don't yer know? The latest colour techniques are a bit on the costly side but would get yours truly nicely off the hook with J. Barrington R. So I saw it like this, make a plan of action.

Firstly: Locate and buy suitable colour camera.

Secondly: Get a roll of colour film.

Thirdly: Go to rose grower and talk him into letting me take the picture.

Simple. Never underestimate the three-point plan.

The sausage, bacon and two eggs had been consumed, the last nibble of toast had gone the same way and I had settled in my chair with the first gasper of the day. Ellingham entered and proceeded to clear the table.

'You'll remember I asked you to think on my

little problem?'

'Indeed so, sir, but as yet I am afraid nothing has presented itself as an adequate answer.'

'Worry no further Ellingham, I have the answer. It presented itself the moment I awoke.'

'I am pleased to hear it. It is often the case with those thing that trouble the mind sir,' he said continuing to clear the table.

'I'll give you the gist of my thinking, and you can point out any flaws in my plan.'

'As you wish of course, though it is hardly my place to criticize your plans or actions, sir.'

'Nonsense; listen, absorb and comment. To good or ill, tell it as you see it, you will not offend.'

'Very well sir, if it is your wish, I am as the current saying goes "all ears".'

I laid my plan before him adding the finer points to put the final gloss to my little brainchild. And I'm damned if the blasted man didn't shoot the whole thing down in flames.

'I fail to see exactly how you will convince the grower that you are who you say you are. You will also need a considerable amount of professional equipment to convince the person that you are indeed from a quality magazine. And finally...'

'Enough Ellingham, you go too far.'

'I am sorry if my observations displease you sir but there is one further observation which I feel is pertinent to the issue.'

'Well I do not wish to hear it. Pertinent or not, you take too much upon yourself. I expected support and get only the big put down. "One further observation", I say "one further observation" forsooth. You go too far, be gone about your business my good man.'

'If you are certain you do not wish me to put my fears into words sir?'

'Go, be gone.'

'As you wish sir.'

I was as you can guess a bit miffed with the man pulling a perfectly good plan like that to pieces no doubt to satisfy his own ego, it's not good enough. At this point the doorbell rang and presumably Ellingham answered it for he entered a few moments later to announce that the Tolson Mark 14 Super Sport had reappeared.

'The mechanic wishes to explain a few new technical details to you if you are so disposed sir?'

'Oh lor' more complications, always making life more difficult. Why do they do it Ellingham; change, change, change – change for the sake of change; that's what I say it is, why *do* they do it?'

'I am afraid I could not say sir, though no doubt it is seen within the industry as striving for a state of mechanical perfection sir,'

'Tell him I'll be there in a brace of shakes, just need to comb the teeth and clean the hair, and all that.'

'Very good sir.'

Well there she was in all her glory, the reddest of red on the bodywork, the plummest of plum on the wings, just the right amount of chrome and a black mohair fold-down hood. The finest, prettiest little two-seater money could buy. I don't know if you are like me; but I always have to give my latest steed a name; no problem choosing one for this baby; "Ramona" sprang straight to mind. She would forever be "Ramona" - and more importantly, for the time being at least, she was mine.

'Mornin', Mr Tolson, sir,' said the mechanic.

28

'Good morning, it's Petters isn't it?' I said, for I recognised the chap.

''S right sir, I got to show yer a few things, what's a bit diff'ent to yer old one.'

'O.K. fire away, I'll do my best to take it all in.'

'Ter start wiv, there's one more gear,' he said.

I have to say I have always found three gears more than enough of a handful.

'Four gears?'

''S right sir, perhaps if you was to sit in the driver's seat and I can explain how you selects 'em.'

I did as he suggested and over the next quarter of an hour or so, and three or four turns around the block, I have to say I rather got the hang of the new fangled animal.

'I wonder sir, would yer be kind enough to run me back to the factory?'

'My pleasure Petters old chap, my pleasure.'

And a pleasure it indeed was for I was already deeply in love with the beautiful Ramona. As requested I dropped the said mechanic back at the factory and as courtesy required poked the old bean around my father's door, only to find that he was in the design department discussing yet another innovation to the Tolson range.

'Give him my regards please Miss Morgan,' I said.

'Of course Mr Tolson, is there any message?'

'No; just popped in, in passing yer know.'

We smiled and I was on my way. Miss Morgan is a lady with a bright smile, in her late thirties, who must have been a *twenties flapper* and seemed never to have grown out of the fashion. I don't know if you are aware but there is actually a car manufacturer of the name of

Morgan; out Malvern way and I've always wondered if she was acting as a sort of spy for them. Anyway, no doubt my father knows what he's doing, I suppose she might be one of those double agents. I went back to the flat, arriving just in time for a late morning coffee.

I entered the jolly old abode with a merry tune upon the lips and a lightness of the heart. Ellingham is always very aware of my mood and quick to assess its cause.

'I take it you are pleased with the new vehicle sir?'

'You may take it that such is the case, very much so.'

'I am pleased to hear it sir.'

'It's got four gears, and do you know what, there's something to help you get quiet gear changes between third and fourth gear.'

'So the mechanic led me to believe, the feature you refer to is I understand called synchronous meshing sir.'

'That's right, that's what he called it, do you know it's near impossible to get the gears wrong.'

'That, if I may say so sir has been a fault that has much marred your driving in the past.'

'How right you are Ellingham. Much as it grieves me to admit it, as ever you have put your finger on the crux of the matter. But rest assured bad gear changes are a thing of the past. They are I am sure; dead history.'

'Most pleasing sir. Without wishing to change the subject your morning coffee is ready will you be taking it in the lounge sir?'

The kitchen in the old palace whilst not large, sports an adequate table and four chairs, this is however

Ellingham's domain and I treat it as such not wishing to encroach on his work or privacy; I always ask before I enter.

'I'll take it in the kitchen with you if that's all right? I've much to tell you about the new steed.'

'Certainly sir, most agreeable,' and he led the way.

'Getting back to the car,' I said, as I sat down, 'the brakes are a dream. Very powerful and efficient; stop you on a sixpence, don't yer know.'

'That would seem to be a little optimistic if I might say, I fear the laws of physics would not quite agree with your interpretation sir.'

'Then the laws of physics have it all wrong Ellingham, the bally things lift you out of the seat; nearly had the mechanic chappie through the windscreen the first time I tried them.'

'That is indeed an improvement worthy of careful consideration sir.'

'You can see what these development chaps are after; these things, contrary to what you may believe, are a sort of striving towards mechanical perfection; not just a case of change for the sake of change you know?'

'I believe I have heard that said sir.'

Before we could discuss the Super Sports further the telephone rang and Ellingham excused himself to go off and answer it.

'Mr Joshua Tolson wishes to converse with you on the telephone sir.'

That's not me you understand, couldn't phone myself, what - but my Uncle Josh, I was named after him.'

'Did he say what about?'

'I did not enquire sir.'

31

This was likely to take some little time so I took my coffee to the instrument and stood it on the small tablemat, on the aforesaid corner cupboard reserved for such occasions. As I picked the thing up, Ellingham arrived with a kitchen chair and a knowing nod.

'Uncle Josh, hello, how are you?' I asked as I seated myself.

'Fine, fine, fine, the old leg's still playing me up from time to time don't yer know; can't believe it's over twenty years since I fell off the blasted horse and it still plays me up. I'm getting a touch of gout in the other foot, that somehow seems to be giving me neck problems, doctor thinks it must be the way I'm lying in bed trying to get relief from the pain. Still get terrible indigestion if I eat later than nine-thirty, but that's nothing new. He tells me, er, the doctor that is, I've got to look after the old ticker but they always tell you that at my age I'm told. Poked m'self in the eye on the top of a damned cane in the greenhouse a week or so ago and the damned thing won't stop weeping; blasted painful too I don't mind telling you. Your Aunt Evie says I'm going either deaf or senile or both, then she walks away from me whispering just to lay it on a bit yer know. Cut m'self shaving this morning, blood everywhere, but still among the living yer know. The quack; cut the plaster off the other day of course so the old arm's on the mend. Thanks for kind wishes and the tobacco by the way. So yes, fine, fine.'

Uncle Josh is what's known as accident prone, so I knew that my polite enquiry as to his state of health was likely to lead to this extensive catalogue of his ailments but one has to follow the civilized conventions what.

'Glad to hear you're back to form uncle. What did you wish to speak about; not that it isn't always a

32

pleasure to speak with you of course.'

'Speak to you, oh yes I rang you didn't I? Your aunt says you are to come down to The Willows this weekend; won't take no for an answer.'

The Willows is the rambling old house in deepest Gloucestershire where my Uncle Josh and Aunt Evangeline live. It was built, so my aunt reliably informs me, about the time that Napoleon was coming to the fore: there's twenty or so bedrooms plus room for the staff. When I went there as a boy there was also a working farm, but little by little over the years it's been rented out to local farmers; all that remains is about forty acres of gardens and woodlands. It's a most beautiful spot, but my heart sank. These commands from on high generally mean that my aunt has some dastardly plan for my future, which will make me wish that I had decided to take the summer on a far-flung isle.

'Sorry dearest uncle but it simply can't be done – much too busy at the moment what with one thing and another.'

'Friday in time for dinner, that's what she said, so see you then.'

'Uncle you don't understand, I ...'

He had rung off. Aunt Evangeline's wrath is her least likeable characteristic and, coming very easily to the fore, not something to be taken lightly. So it seemed that in less than four days I would be off to The Willows, and the prospect left me about forty degrees short of overjoyed; barely even joyed at all in fact.

'We're off to The Willows on Friday Ellingham, in time for dinner.'

'Indeed sir? I will look forward to it.'

'Oh you will, will you – I wish I could say the

33

same; oh well, I suppose it's a chance to give the fiery steed an outing what?'

'You seem a little put out by the prospect of the visit sir?'

'Indeed I am Ellingham, I fear my aunt has some dirty work afoot and as ever it seems to me that I'm the one it will all go sour on.'

'I'm sure all will turn out for the best, sir.'

'I wish I shared your optimism. Better start to decide what to pack.'

'I was all ready mulling the matter over in my mind sir.'

There is a little man on the High Street, a photographer of some repute to whom I have taken my custom on a number of occasions. He's one of those people, salt of the earth as they say, who always manages to look as though he has become addicted to being run through some sort of heavy machinery or perhaps pulled backwards through a hedge and forgotten to say stop. He seems to have taken scruffiness to a new level; he could lecture on the subject. However, my request for advice on the best camera to suit my needs was dealt with most efficiently; and after all the man is a photographer, not an adviser on gentlemen's sartorial elegance.

'Your own camera, if you still have the one you purchased from me last year will be capable of producing good quality colour photographs. However if as you say you wish to look professional I have an idea that could well be just what you are looking for,' he said.
And by Jove it was.

'Before I opened this little shop sir, I had spent a number of years as a press photographer, freelance you understand, but supplying photographs to the top magazines,' he said

'You don't say.'

'I do indeed say sir, and what is more I still have the camera I used, couldn't bring myself to sell it. And I won't sell it now, but you can borrow it provided you agree to take great care of it.'

'I say that's jolly decent of you, would you really lend it to me?'

'Not only that sir, I'll give you a few minutes instruction on how to use it.'

I have always thought that the world is stuffed much fuller with the milk of human kindness, if you can indeed stuff milk, than most people think. And this man Harold Betts rather proved my belief. Within a few minutes he had me pulling focus, taking light readings and adjusting exposure settings on a rather ancient, but very professional looking camera. I thought it only fair to explain why I wanted to look professional. I swore him to secrecy then gave him the low down.

'Then maybe this will be of assistance,' he said and, feeling in his wallet, handed me a press identity card. 'Just couldn't throw it away, part of my life for twenty years.'

'Thank you, most kind and I promise to take the greatest care of everything. I'm hoping to get the pictures this afternoon.'

'Take my advice sir, always take at least two pictures on different exposures, that way you cover for most eventualities.'

'Good advice, I'll do that. If I can get the film back to you before you close how soon can I have the photos?'

35

'Colour takes a good bit longer than black and white, but lunch time tomorrow, say one thirty to be certain.'

'That will do very nicely.' I loaded the camera and its accompanying tripod and flash bulbs and lots of other bits-and-bobs into the car and off I zipped to the establishment of Walter Thomas, Rose Grower, some twenty miles away.

"Ramona" went like a dream; the highways and byways of merry England flashed by and I had a song in my heart, if not actually on my lips. Just before three o'clock I pulled up outside the establishment of the aforesaid rose grower. This consisted of a bungalow building which seemed to serve as his home: tacked on to the side was a lean-to kind of structure which seemed to carry out the combined duties of sales office and tool store. Various other buildings were dotted around an extensive area in which rose bushes in differing stages of flowering and a multitude of colours stood in regimented rows. I turned the car around in case I needed to beat a hasty retreat and parked it in a small area just inside the iron gates and stood there bewildered by the huge array of roses, how on earth could anyone know which was which?

However the show must go on and I started to unload the camera and tripod and associated equipment.

'If you's the photographer chap, you's a bit early. Mr Thomas 'as 'ad to go out but says I'm to show yer the rose, if 'e's not back.' Turning, I was in the presence of an elderly man with a stooping stance and a weather tanned face, no doubt the result of many years ministering to the needs of roses. His hands as you would expect were gardener's hands, grubby with soil and dirt in the fingernails. He wore a red tartan style shirt and his

36

trousers were tied at the middle with a necktie that had seen many more years in its present duties than ever it had around his neck. In short a man used to honest toil over a lifetime dedicated to growing roses, or some similar occupation.

'Er, oh, um, er yes I'm the photographer.' I said, a bit bewildered as to how this chap could be expecting me, though clearly he was.

'How do I know you's the photographer chap?' he asked.

I waved a cheery hand at the equipment.

'Anybody, can 'ave a camera,' he said.

He had a point of course and one that's hard to dispute. He stood there sucking his teeth and rubbing his hands on a muddy sack secured as an apron kind of thing by the aforesaid necktie. I showed him my newly acquired press card, he looked at it and gave it back to me. Whether he could read it or not I don't know, but it seemed to satisfy him and he led me to a part of the rose nursery which seemed to have been newly fenced off from the rest.

'There yer is,' he said, 'the rose to top all roses and bein' presented to that toff bloke end o' the month.'
I remember thinking, double six, first shake of the dice, what?

'So this is Lord Westcott's rose?' I asked just to make doubly sure if you get my drift.

'Aye, that's the one, lot o' fuss if you asks me, but I just grow 'em. Leave yer to it then, if yer need anythin' I'll be over in that corner; after I've been behind that shed for a quick pee – when yer gets to my age yer f'rever in need of a pee.' He left me feeling that I had been favoured with just that little bit too much information.

37

Still a bit bewildered I set up the camera and came upon my first problem; the bally rose kept moving about gently in the breeze. I found a bit of stick lying about and used this to prop the rose steady, but no matter how I placed it, it always seemed more prominent in the viewfinder than the blasted rose. The battered old son of the soil reappeared after a while and I asked him to hold the thing steady for me. The poor chap clearly had a hand not best suited to steady anything, and even he admitted that the thing was moving less without his help and so eventually he tottered off again. I fiddled around for a while and eventually the breeze dropped and the rose stood fair and square in the picture. I used up all twelve frames of the film, taking the rose from three different angles and with differing exposures. Happy I had done the job justice I was packing up when a black car pulled into the entrance and drove up to the bungalow and the occupant, a stout man in his late forties disappeared inside. Taking this as my cue to cease to be among those there gathered I walked briskly to the jalopy and loaded my equipment. Too late: the stout fellow, who I took to be W. Thomas in person was coming out of the bungalow and heading straight for me. Tricky, what?

'Afternoon young fellow, got a good picture?' He held out his hand. 'Thomas,' he said. I took his hand. and said -

'Thompson, but with a 'p' - if you see what I mean,' I replied. You'll note the quick thinking and the use of a pseudonym, I think that's the word I mean. 'Yes I think I've done it proud.'

'No need to remind you of the need for secrecy, I'm sure Mr Lennon will have got you posted on that one. When that picture goes in the catalogue it'll cause a sensation in the rose world, I hope the colour film will do it justice.'

Ah, so that was why they were expecting me; but before I had twigged that there must in that case be another photographer about to arrive there he was arriving; a chap on a battered old motorbike and sidecar, with the legs of a tripod clearly poking out of the top. I had the feeling that this could turn decidedly nasty, unless I was damned lucky.

'Two of you, does it take two of you?' asked Walter T.

'Never seen him before in my life,' I said, 'he must be an impostor.'

'Or what if you are, ah?' He looked at me very strangely, turned on his heel and shouted to the old fellow with the stoop and the waterworks problem. 'Did you check this feller out?'

'Beg `y pardon, Mr Thomas, sir?'

'Did you check this photographer chap out?' he yelled

'Aye sir, `e got a press card an ev'ythin',' the old fellow yelled back.

By this time the motorbike chappie had arrived on the scene, switched off the engine and taken off his helmet and gloves and was standing around looking a bit bewildered.

'Press card, ey - come on show it young feller me lad.' I produced it and handed it to him.

'I thought you said your name was Thompson?'

Lummy – wrong name on the card, time for some quick thinking.

'That's right, Harold Thompson-Betts, I prefer to use just the Thompson.'

'Um, I see,' he said, and he looked at me in a quizzical sort of way for a few moments.

I gave him the benefit of the Tolson innocent smile. It seemed to satisfy him for the moment, since he returned the card.

'Right then who are you?' he said turning to the newcomer.

'I'm David Plymm, Mr Lennon sent me to photograph a rose for your catalogue, if you're Mr Thomas?' he said still looking bewildered.

'Show us your press card then in that case,' said W.T. with a twitch of his head that said get out of that one.

'Don't need one I'm a photographer, I do weddings and portraits and things, don't need no press card for that. Oh and if he's supposed to be a press photographer I for one don't think he is.'

'Oh yes, and why would that be then?' asked W. Thomas.

'Don't ever remember seein' a press photographer in a brand new Tolson car.'

He had a point of course and a damned good one at that. It was becoming an afternoon big on good points, and so I was in the car and away before they could stop me. Planning you see, turning the car around just in case it might save a nasty situation. The striving for mechanical perfection at Tolson Cars had seen "Ramona" equipped with an electric self-starter, you just prod a button with your clutch foot, and as if by magic the engine bursts into life. Just before I turned out on to the road I looked back in the old, or in this case rather new, rear-view mirror to see W. Thomas jumping up and down and shaking his fist. I put a bit of a spurt on I can tell you. If you're going to make a get away, make a *fast* get away

40

that's what I say and the fair "Ramona" was just the car to choose in those situations.

I arrived at the emporium of Harold Betts a few moments before he closed and returned his camera and other stuff.

'Did the camera and card do the trick, Mr Tolson, sir?' he asked.

'Everything went to plan. Well perhaps not everything, but I'll tell you about it when I collect the prints.'

'Leave it to me Mr Tolson, be with you as soon as humanly possible.'

'This is my number, ring me as soon as they're ready.'

I slipped him a swift fiver as thanks for the loan of the equipment and told him to rush the prints as much as possible - and he said that he would. A good day's work done.

I walked back into the flat somewhere around six thirty and was met as ever by Ellingham.

'I trust you have had a pleasant day sir?'

'Thank you Ellingham yes I suppose so, quite fun really if a little scary at times.'

'I'm sorry to hear that sir, may I enquire what has been the cause of the fear sir?'

'Miss, blasted, Jane Barrington-Ross, Ellingham; that's what or rather whom.'

'Ah, I see sir.'

'I doubt it; Ellingham, I doubt it. But let it pass, 'tis but grist to the mill.'

'As you wish sir; the kettle is on the point of boiling, perhaps a cup of tea would relieve the stress sir?'

'It will help Ellingham, but whilst you prepare I

think I'll help myself to a swift slug of whisky.'

'Very wise sir, might I enquire if you will be dining in tonight, sir?'

'No I'll away to the Boater about eight and eat there I think. Might pick up a bit more gossip about the stolen stole. I say that's rather good, *stolen stole*, don't you think?'

'Indeed most amusing sir.' And off he trotted to the kitchen to brew the jolly old cup that cheers. Or rather he started to, and then he turned, on the point of opening the door.

'Remiss of me sir I forgot to inform you that a telegram arrived for you; shortly after you left at lunchtime. I did not of course open it sir and it is at present beside your chair in the sitting room.'

'Oh no, now what?'

'I could not say sir, I did not open it as I said, but I did observe that it was handed in at Much Moreham Post Office sir.'

'Worse and worse, Ellingham.'

'Possibly so sir.'

Much Moreham is the village nearest to The Willows, my uncle's country seat you will remember. I seated myself in my chair and picked up the envelope, turning it in my hand unopened. It was still unopened when Ellingham entered with the tea.

'I suppose I had better open it, Ellingham?'

'It would certainly be difficult to ascertain its contents without doing so sir.'

'Right-ho here goes.' I tore the bally thing open with a flourish and there was as expected a telegram from Much Moreham. From the pen, if you can say that about a telegram, of my Aunt Evangeline.

'It's from Aunt Evie,' I informed the man, 'I'd better read it.'

'By far the best plan of action sir.' He was of course right and I settled down to do just that as Ellingham poured the tea. It read –

LISTEN YOU YOUNG WASTE OF GOD'S GOOD AIR.

YOUR UNCLE JOSH TELLS ME THAT YOU MADE SOME LAME EXCUSE OR OTHER FOR NOT WISHING TO ACCEPT MY VERY KIND INVITATION TO SPEND AN ENJOYABLE WEEKEND DOWN HERE AT THE WILLOWS. YOU WILL BE HERE, TIME AND DATE AS STATED. BRING NOT ONLY BEST BIB AND TUCKER BUT ALSO COUNTRY CLOTHING AS I ANTICIPATE A SUNDAY AFTERNOON RAMBLE.

I WISH YOU TO MAKE AN ESPECIALLY GOOD IMPRESSION UPON SOMEONE.

YOU WILL COMPLY WITH THIS AS REQUESTED, YOU MUDDLE HEADED GUMOZZLE, OR ASSASSINS WILL BE DISPATCHED.

LOVE AUNT EVANGELINE.

My aunt is never one for mincing words or indeed shortening them for telegrams. The art of reducing the amount expended on them by careful editing has completely passed her by. I dread to think of the cost of this one at tuppence per word.

'My aunt reinforces the requirement to go down for the weekend.'

'I suspected that could be the case sir.'

'She says she wishes me to make a good impression on someone, no doubt some poor unsuspecting potential employer of my services. Or,' and here I think I gave a shudder since I spilled a not inconsiderable amount of hot tea in the lap, requiring a change of clothes, and cooling of self. 'Or,' I said continuing my thoughts through the bedroom door, 'she has lined up some dreadful female as a lifetimes soul mate for me. Ye gads, Ellingham, what if that's it?'

'I fear only time will tell sir.' And of course he was right.

A couple of hours later, I poked my head through the kitchen door and said -

'I'm off to the Boater then Ellingham.'

'Very good sir, I wonder if I might bring your attention to the item in last evenings newspaper sir.'

'Last evening's paper – um, refresh my memory Ellingham.'

'Regarding the young gentleman of your acquaintance who has had an entanglement with the police, sir.'

'Spotty Bagshaw and the drunk in charge?'

'Indeed so sir.'

'Your point being Ellingham?'

'I was merely thinking sir, that whilst driving *to* your club would cause no problem. Using your motorcar as a means of return, should the police be in the midst of some sort of anti drinking and driving campaign, might not be the wisest of options.'

'Good lord, never thought of that, what ever would I do without you Ellingham?'

'You are most kind, one tries to give satisfaction sir.'

'And one gives it in lorry loads Ellingham. With your newly directed chain of thought I will walk to the Boater and get a taxi back.'

'Very wise sir.'

It was a pleasant evening, and even though I live just off the centre of town the walk to the Straw Boater, *Club for young gentlemen,* passes along tree lined streets and although the traffic noise often blots it out there is birdsong audible in the quieter moments. The trees were in full leaf and flowers of various types; I'm not all that up on flora and fauna and all that sort of thing, were in full bloom and their scent filled the gentle breeze. Life seemed good, or would be if only blessed aunts and ex-girlfriends would keep their noses out of it.

Halfway to the club who should I meet but the aforesaid Wilberforce (Spotty) Bagshaw. Why he's called spotty I've no idea, lost in the mists of time I dare say. I suppose at some time in his early life he must have had an over generous plague of spots, but peaches & cream complexion these days if you can say that about someone who looks quite so much like a sad bullfrog. I'm told that when at school he played *Toad of Toad Hall* in a musical production without the need for make-up, but that could be just hearsay. His eyes bulge a bit and he sort of closes them when he swallows, further accentuating the frogginess of his looks. But, as they say, you can't judge a book by its cover and Spotty is the salt of the earth. I first met him at the Boater. We both joined on the same day and had to go before the selection committee one after the other. A friendship sprang from that and many a happy day has been spent in his company.

'What ho Spotty old chap, how are you.'

'What ho to you with brass knobs on Josh, bit depressed if the truth be known; had a bit of a run in with the gendarmes.'

'Yes, hard to miss, made the local rag and all that; bet the dear old parents are none too pleased?'

'Father took it in his stride, but Mother has failed to see the funny side.'

'Is there a funny side?'

'Well no, not really. She's put me on foot till further notice; in fact I was rather hoping to cadge a lift back with you.'

'No, definitely on foot tonight as you see, but we might share a taxi back, what?'

'Won't really need a taxi, also restricted to orange juice or lemon cordial.'

'That's not good, seems a very strict sentence.'

'It was only my mother pleading my case that saved me from fourteen days. So I suppose she has the right to set the terms, yer know?'

'Yes, see yer point, how long is it likely to last?' I asked.

'My mother has a long memory; I can't say that I can look forward to any major change in circumstances in the foreseeable future Josh.'

'Oh well, look on the bright side old thing.'

'What bright side?' he moaned.

With that we changed the subject and chatted about this and that, and by the time we walked up the steps and through the wide-flung portals of the Boater we were both bucked up a good bit, and were in a frame of mind to enjoy ourselves.

Having signed in and agreed to share a table for dinner we went our separate ways: him to see a chap about some business deal or other, me in search of John Manson. He was not immediately visible to the naked eye since the club was back to its usual busy status. Enquiries at the desk confirmed that he was not among those insitu, so I left a request that he seek me out should he turn up and went off to find a drink. A chap I was at school with was sitting on a stool, one of those very high ones you often find lining the customers side of the bar intended no doubt to allow said customers to lean on the aforesaid bar. This is exactly what this chap was indeed doing and in a rather despondent way.

'What ho, Chas, looking a bit down in the dumps what?' I said.

'Hello Josh, not only down in them, but wallowing, fairly wallowing,' he replied.

One hates to see an old chum in this sort of state, so I offered the old shoulder if he needed to cry.

'Sorry to hear that, anything I can do to help?'

'If, by that, you mean poke your nose into my private business, no.'

'I say old chap, a bit uncalled for what, only trying to help an old school chum. But no wish to pry don't yer know?'

'You're right I shouldn't have snapped like that, sorry Josh. It's just that I've broken it off with Millie.'

'Millie, do I know her?'

'Doesn't matter Josh, she's last months flavour. I've a new love now,' he sighed, and took on the despondent look again.

I have to say I wasn't in the least surprised to hear this; Charles (Chas) Bestwick had fallen in love with almost every girl he had ever seen, seemingly as soon as he was out of short trousers. Whilst the rest of us were playing and talking football or cricket with perhaps the odd risqué joke, Chas was off getting the old passion in a big way with one of the girls. Not by any means one, come to think of it, almost all of the girls at St. Joseph's Girls School just along the road from our school. As a man I can't say that I'm a very good judge of what girls see in men, but if it's the sporty physique and the handsome good looks then I have to say Chas fits the bill and with some to spare. You might say Chas is what Spotty Bagshaw would become if a princess kissed him.

'If new love has come, why the solemn face?'

'She's too good for me and I'm just looking from afar, don't know her, can't tell her how I feel you see, afraid she will laugh in my face,' he groaned. This was a new experience for me, Chas unable to set things in motion with a girl. Could this be the real thing I asked myself.

'I see. What's her name, do I know this wondrous female?'

'I think her name is Jane, she has the hazelest of hazel eyes and the bounciest way of walking, and the sweetest smile, and the most amazingly white teeth, and.' I cut him short.

'The reddest of red hair?' I said.

'How do you know that?' he asked, his eyes

48

closing just a little.

'Inside information, I think I know the lady in question.'

'You lucky beggar. Here, I say, you wouldn't be a rival by any chance, because if you are I'll have to fight you to the death so to speak, what?'

'Fear not - I'm not in the running, I have a love of my own.'

'Good, glad to hear it, hate to have had to kill you and all that.'

'Quite understand, perhaps I could arrange for you to meet her?'

'I say that's awfully kind of you, could you, would you do that old chap?'

'Consider it as good as done,' I said and with that he bought me a whisky and soda.

I explained that I would be meeting his new, prospective love at some point next day to carry out the final stages of a secret assignment.

'You lucky blighter, could I tag along too?' he asked.

'No, but you could turn up in the middle of things and I could introduce you as an old and dear friend, and all that rot, then the rest is up to you.'

'I say that's a topping idea, and you'd do that for me?'

'My pleasure dear friend, my pleasure.'

'When's all this to happen?'

'Can't tell you just yet but probably late afternoon.'

'Oh, heck, I've a meeting with the board at three thirty tomorrow, got a new client on board, *Woofalot* dog food. Need a new slogan or eye catcher. So the afternoon

49

is rather off limits so to speak,' he said sinking back into the dumps again.

Chas is one of those poor fellows who has to eke out a living by the sweat of his own brow and all that, and is at present employed as a copy writer, if that's the right title, in an advertising agency where he's expected to say witty things about all manner of dodgy stuff to make joe public want to buy it; *Woofalot* being the latest I supposed.

'You must kerb this tendency to blow hot and cold old chap, I'll arrange to meet her at seven thirty for dinner. Problem solved pal of mine.'

'Josh Tolson, I've said it before and I don't mind saying it again, and they can put it on official record if they like, you top them all.'

'Have you ever said it before?' I asked.

'Well no probably not, but I've certainly meant to. So, when people call you a buffoon and a drip of the first water just refer them to me.'

'Do people call me a buffoon and a drip of the first water?' I asked.

'Oh, don't they? Oh well perhaps you're right.'

'Then buy me another whisky and soda to take into dinner with me.'

'Consider it done. You're dining here tonight, mind if I join you?'

'Yes I'm dining here, but I've arranged to dine with Spotty.'

'Spotty won't mind, we could make up a jolly threesome.'

I never did see John Manson that evening and so it was three happy chums over dinner, having a laugh and a joke together, much leg pulling and general banter and a good time was had by all, as the saying goes. So it was with a happy frame of mind that I entered the flat just a tad before midnight. Ellingham was, as ever, there to greet me.

'Good evening sir, I trust you had a pleasant meal.'

'Such was indeed the case, Ellingham; I dined with Spotty Bagshaw and Chas Bestwick amid much merriment.'

'I am pleased to hear it sir, I trust the two young gentlemen are in good health?'

'In good health yes, but each has their cross to bear.'

'As indeed we all do to some degree sir.'

'True. Spottys' mother has grounded him till further notice, and Chas is in love for the umpteenth time.'

'Neither fact is particularly surprising to me sir.'

'Nor, come to think of it to me, but I'll tell you something that will surprise you. Guess who Chas's new love is?' I asked with wry smile.

'I could not begin to imagine sir.'

'Hold on to your hat, Ellingham, Miss, wait for it, Jane Barrington-Ross.'

'You have indeed surprised me sir, though I can see the attraction sir. If I might say sir, should it reach the stage where they were to marry Mr Bestwick's life would be far from dull.

'Ain't that a fact, though as yet they haven't met, he loves from afar.'

'I see sir, perhaps you might be able to affect a meeting sir,' he said.

I got his meaning alright, putting Chas in the

51

running takes me out. I had already told him, as you know, that such is the case but I suppose he is a bit over protective of the young master at times.

'I have already told him that I will do so, his gratitude was without bounds.'

'I can imagine sir. Speaking of the young lady in question she was on the telephone at nine thirty-seven sir, I explained that you were at your club and I asked if she would like to leave a message. She asked me to ask you about your joint project. I took the liberty of informing her that I understood you had the matter in hand sir, I trust I did not overstep my duty?'

'No Ellingham, such is indeed the case, what did she say to that?'

'She said sir, and here I quote, "Oh, rightie-ho, toodle-pip," whereupon she rang off sir.'

'Bet that pleased her, the outcome is indeed nigh, I will be in a position to put you wise after lunch tomorrow.'

'I will look forward to it, sir. I have also taken the liberty of placing a restorative on your bedside table. If there is nothing further I will wish you goodnight sir?'

This restorative is his own concoction. Don't ask me what's in it, I don't know and indeed don't want to know, but take a slug of this foul stuff on retiring and any hangover that you might have had doesn't get a look in. Both Spotty and Chas, and a number of my other friends have on occasions found the need for it - they all agree to it's effectiveness. Spotty tells me that whilst at school he ran full pelt into one of the goal posts, and swears the result of drinking Ellingham's restorative has much the same initial feeling.

'Thank you nothing more Ellingham, so

goodnight to you, or perhaps, *toodle-pip*?'

'Indeed sir.' And so I went to bed, not forgetting to hold the old nose whilst taking the aforesaid elixir.

I rang Jane at nine thirty next morning and arranged our meeting for seven thirty at the hotel where we had lunched previously. I then rang Chas and told him to be there at about eight thirty. Considering that to be as far as I could take things at the moment I pottered around the flat reading this and that, having the odd gasper and generally getting under Ellingham's feet, until it was time to go to my photographic friend's establishment.

In the end I couldn't wait for him to ring and set off just before noon to get under *his* feet, so to speak. Just as I was opening the door to leave, the phone rang; I picked it up just as Ellingham appeared from the kitchen. I nodded to show that I had the task in hand and he gave an acknowledging nod and disappeared again. It turned out to be John Manson, he had turned up at the Boater and been told that I had requested him to contact me. Not quite the state of the case but no matter.

'It's John Manson here, is that you Josh?'

'None other, what can I do for you? I asked.

'Nothing, just ringing to keep you in the picture. I've suggested to my cousin that you would like to meet her, she has no objection.'

'Good man, does she perhaps remember me?'

'No I don't think so, I described you of course but it didn't ring any bells with her, sorry old chap. Oh, there is just one thing old chap that I had to suggest to make it seem more natural.'

'Yes.'

'I rather took the liberty of suggesting that - oh, I'd better explain. You see she's involved in this schools

53

for Africa thing ...' I cut him short.

'I know, it was in the paper.'

'Oh, you know, I see, well I rather suggested that you wished to see her to make a donation. Hope I didn't overstep the mark.'

'If a suitable donation will set up an introduction then you didn't overstep the mark as far as I'm concerned, a donation will be forthcoming.'

'There's just one other thing. She's going to be out of town for a few days so I can't set up anything definite just at the moment, but I'll keep you posted as soon as she returns.'

'That's fine, I'm going to be away in the country myself so I'll wait to hear from you.' And with that we rang off.

I poked my head around the kitchen door to tell Ellingham I would be back for lunch but out to dinner. Then tootled off to see aforesaid photographer.

'You're a bit handy with a camera, Mr Tolson sir,' he said, 'couldn't have done a better job myself; always difficult to get the focus just right on flowers.'

'I gave it my best, yer know.'

'Still waiting for the prints to dry, but they look the bee's knees, won't be long, a few minutes that's all, can't rush the drying.'

'I'm in your hands dear fellow, only perfection will fit the bill!'

'Exactly sir, and that's what I think you'll agree you've got.'

I nodded and did a bit of pottering about his shop whilst he went of into the back, to the darkroom I expect. Poking about in lenses and cameras and the like is nothing of a chore to me and a pleasant twenty minutes or so passed in this way, interrupted occasionally by people dropping in rolls of film or collecting prints and such. Eventually the time came for the viewing of my handy-work, and though I say it myself, they were pretty damned impressive. He'd done them on a sort of silk-finished paper, pretty big too. I think it's called ten-by-eight and the detail was stunning, the colour just as I remembered it.

'Colour printing is very time consuming sir, so they have set you back one pound two and six-pence, Mr Tolson sir.'

'You, my dear fellow have done me proud, please accept a fiver and I consider it money well spent.'

'Thank you sir, most kind.' He placed the prints in a large envelope and passed them across the counter to me.

3

I returned to the flat and Ellingham had prepared a salad lunch, what he calls a cold collation.

'Since the weather is a little on the warm side, I trust it will meet with your satisfaction sir?' he explained, making it a sort of half question.

'It certainly looks excellent, Ellingham, and I feel in the very mood to do it to death.'

'I am pleased to hear it sir, your journey proved fruitful sir?'

'I think I might say that, Ellingham, cast your eyes upon those beauties.' And I tossed him the envelope. He opened it and took out the photographs and you could tell that the man was impressed.

'Go on, what do you think?' I asked pointedly.

'I have no doubt that in terms of form and colour they do Lord Westcott's rose justice, if it is indeed his rose that you have captured on film sir?'

'None other, Ellingham, not bad eh?'

'As you say sir, not bad. There is however the original problem remaining, which if you remember sir, you did not require me to appraise you of.

'Oh get on with it Ellingham, don't spare yours truly, if there's a flaw let hear it now.'

'The problem with a photograph even a very good quality colour photograph is not only that the colours are not always true to life.'

'You do them an injustice Ellingham, the colour is

exactly as I remember it,' I put the fellow right.

'I am pleased to hear it sir, but in the case of a photograph of a rose, by it's very nature, being but paper, it lacks the one thing for which roses are renowned sir.'

'Which is?'

'A rose by any other name, sir.'

'Would still smell just as sweet, or whatever it is - lummy, no scent?'

'Exactly sir,' he said putting the photographs back in the envelope and heading back to his kitchen. Leaving me to ponder this new problem.

I'm sure you must have found as I have that there are normally not enough hours in the day to do all of the things that you have to do, or want to do. But today found me with a sizeable hole in the programme of events; this being so I decided to go for a stroll in the local park to mull over Ellingham's bombshell. Just as I was alongside the lake, though I suppose it's more of an oversized duck pond, a sad scene was unfolding itself before me. In the distance, over to my left, one of those nurse or nanny kind of people was frantically searching for something in the bushes or shrubbery alongside her pram. Clearly, I thought, she must have somehow lost the prams contents and was madly in search of same, when I spied on the ground crawling towards me her baby. Well not perhaps *her* baby you understand but the baby that was in her charge.

As I have said before, with me to decide is to act and I scooped up said baby with a shout.

'Look your baby is here,' I yelled and began to walk rapidly towards her. She glanced in my direction then she also began to walk rapidly, but strangely in the other direction.

'Hoy, HOY your baby's here,' I yelled at the top of my voice, which caused three things to happen almost simultaneously; the nurse began to run *away* from me, the babe in arms let out a fearful cry and from behind me there came a shout.

'Stop. Baby snatcher, stop him.' I looked around me for this baby snatcher, couldn't see him so carried on with my major task of reuniting nurse and baby. I broke into a run, the nurse ran faster, the baby cried harder, and the shouting became louder.

'Stop him, stop him, he's got my baby,' yelled the voice behind me. From the aforesaid bushes or shrubbery there appeared two burly gardener types who grasped me by the arms. In the distance I could see the nurse had found and was talking to a policeman who, even at one hundred and fifty yards away was clearly a touch overweight, but began to run most forcefully in my direction, proving to be a good deal nimbler than one might have expected. Hey, ho. This was going to be interesting. The policeman and the child's mother, at least I now assumed that it was she who had been shouting behind me, arrived upon the scene at more or less the same time, both of them a bit out of breath. The policeman was the first to regain composure and said -

'Right, what's all this then?' addressing me. But before I could speak the child's mother, for such she indeed turned out to be, broke in.

'Snatched my baby he did, in broad daylight.'

I have no doubt that in less stressful situations she would have been considered quite pretty, but a scowl spoiled her face. Her lips were puckered and she glared at me with piercing brown eyes.

'Did `e indeed?' said the copper, giving me the

look he no doubt saved for Saturday night drunks who have just been sick on his boots.

'Saw it with me own eyes, one minute little Oswald is crawling on the grass minding his own business, then next second this ruffian is grasping him up and running off with him towards his accomplice.' She nodded towards the nurse who had now stopped to observe the proceedings, at the same time snatching the baby away from me, and beginning to pacify him. One of the gardeners mumbled something about his daughter but nobody took any notice. The policeman was clearly a bit puzzled; it was after all the nurse who had first alerted him to the problem. Meantime the mother was continuing her speech for the prosecution.

'Well, aren't you going to arrest him officer, go on arrest him, he's a baby snatcher,' she said, her face calming a little as she realized that no harm had been done to the child.

'Yes officer you should arrest him,' said the older of the two gardeners and his mate nodded.

In the hullabaloo, I had been trying to put my side of things as you would expect but to little avail. My attempts to explain were being drowned out by the gardeners who were also adding their two-penn'oth. Enough is enough and I decided to put my case more strongly and yelled.

'Hoy. Just a minute.' The policeman nearly jumped out of his skin.

'Stop yelling like that, you'll get your turn down the station my lad.'

'Yer, that's where 'e should be,' said the gardeners with one voice.

'Yes lock him up and throw away the key,' said

59

the kid's mother.

This was not going at all well and I spoke more quietly to the constable.

'Constable there has been a simple but massive misunderstanding. If I could put before you the chain of events as they happened I'm sure you will agree there has been a laughable misunderstanding.'

'I find it hard to consider baby snatching as a laughable misunderstanding,' he said fiddling with his handcuffs.

I don't know if you've ever been in this sort of situation but if you have you would have been aware, as I was, that things were rapidly getting out of hand. What was needed was a masterstroke, and I was dashed if I could see what it could be. If only Ellingham had been there it would all have been ironed out in a moment. I tried desperately to think how he would have handled it. He normally works on the principle of "Who has most to gain?" and at that moment I seemed to be the only one.

'Please officer, let me tell you my side of it.' I said.

It then occurred to me that the one thing these upholders of the law like least about the job is the amount of paperwork involved.

'A simple explanation,' I continued, 'could well settle the matter without the need for official statements and the like.'

His face brightened at this and he looked as though my plea made good sense to him. But the rest of the assembled crew saw it differently.

'Lock him up,' said the mother, and I noticed that she was beginning to smile.

'Yer, lock 'im up, let 'im tell it in court,' said the

older gardener and Tweedle-dee nodded.

'I shall need you all to come down to the station to give your witness statements, to put it officially on record what has occurred,' said the policeman, pulling his own little masterstroke of diplomacy.

He had judged his witnesses well, for the mother, her face clouding again said -

'Perhaps we should hear what he has to say.' She turned around consulting the small crowd, which by this time had gathered.

'Can't do no 'arm,' said Tweedle-dee.

'Move along please.' The policeman addressed the crowd whilst considering what to do next.

'Lock him up,' said a voice at the back of the crowd who had only just arrived and clearly knew little of what had occurred.

'Move along please, before I arrest the lot of yer,' said the policeman beginning to lose his cool.

The crowd drifted off mumbling and muttering about the unfairness of it all, clearly sorry to miss the outcome of the event.

'Right my lad, tell me what happened and make it good,' he said, the veins on his nose standing out a deep blue.

So I started. 'I was walking along in a southwesterly direction,' I glanced at the copper and saw a nod of approval, 'when I saw by these bushes a nurse who was clearly looking for something. I assumed, wrongly as it turns out that she had lost the baby.'

'That was my daughter Phylis, like I said, she was trying to find me to give me me lunch what I had left at 'ome,' said the old gardener.

''S, right, she was,' said Tweedle-dee.

And things, as you can imagine, got considerably brighter from then onward. The outcome was I suppose, that this would become one of those things that in old age I will laugh about and bore friends and relatives ad nauseam. But it had me rattled at the time, I don't mind telling you. Still, looking on the bright side, its all part of life's rich pattern, what?

I thought that the thing had come to an end and I suppose it had. What happened next was nothing to do with the event, though perhaps the way I handled it had. I had decided to wander back to the lake and tell the ducks about the sorry situation. I find ducks very forgiving, unlikely to point the accusing finger, if you see what I mean. I was making the necessary consultation, mentally of course, one doesn't want to appear unstable to the world in general, when I became aware that another scene was being played out behind me. A toddler, perhaps two years old was running across the grass in my general direction, towards the lake. He ran unsteadily perhaps due to the tenderness of his years, or as likely as not due to the shoes he wore. They appeared to be about two sizes too big and constructed along the lines of hob-nailed boots. He was being pursued by a lady that I took to be his grandmother or perhaps an elderly aunt, waving a walking stick. She shouted for him to be stopped as she ran. I noted that she was rapidly catching him and would no doubt have caught him up before he encountered the lake. That together with the event a few minutes earlier decided me to sit, or rather stand, this one out. The kid ran towards me, and was collared just in time as I suspected that he would be.

'Why didn't you stop him? Didn't you hear me you imbecile?' she said and hit me a swift one on the shoulders with the walking stick.

The kid stuck his tongue out and used one of the hob nailed boots on my shin.

'Serves you right!' said the child's keeper and marched off, leaving me to do a one-legged war dance, which ended in the lake. The only saving grace, the lake at that point is only a few inches deep, with a wide concrete step. So although I have a pretty wet foot and trouser bottom, and suffered the indignity of squelching all the way home, no real harm was done, save a pretty sore shin. I made a mental note to steer clear of the blasted park in future.

As you might expect I had found no answer to the problem of the scentless rose photos when I met Jane for dinner that evening, and decided to leave showing them to her until after we had eaten, in the hope that one would present itself. It's always amazing that when you are hoping that the service, in this place or that, will assist in creating a delaying tactic the damned food is on the table almost before you've ordered it; and such was the case on this occasion. So dinner was over in double quick time and I had no alternative but to show her the photos.

'This is what you call having the matter in hand is it?' she snarled.

'I thought they were rather good myself.'

'Well I don't. I said steal a rose for Uncle Rothwell not just photograph it.'

'Hard to steal one without it being noticed when there's only two or three of them on the bush,' I said, thinking on my feet. Well bottom really I suppose, since I was sitting down at the time.

'Oh, you think they'd miss it I suppose. But it's

not good enough,' she said, snatching up the photographs just as Chas walked into the restaurant.

'It will not do, it will not do at all.' And she swept out leaving me standing at the table looking at her disappearing back.

'I say isn't she magnificent when she's angry?' Chas said as he sat himself at the table. 'No chance of an introduction this evening then?'

'That's a fact old pal of mine, not this evening I'm afraid, and possibly not for a day or two.' I said.

'Oh well,' he sighed, 'perhaps if you hadn't upset her?'

'Our joint venture didn't work out quite how we intended; anyway by the time you see her again you'll probably have found another new love,' I suggested.

'You make out as though I fall in love at the drop of a hat, and nobody could possibly replace her, nobody,' he said, and I let it pass.

We sat together over coffee and brandy, and thus I finished the evening with a different dinner partner than the one I started out with. Nothing to be done about it, of course.

I awoke next morning, if awoke is the right word to use after one of those nights when you toss and turn around, with the events of the previous day jumbling themselves up in your mind. And I was still mulling them over when Ellingham entered with my morning cup of tea.

'I trust you had a good nights sleep sir?'

'No, afraid I didn't.' I said.

'I am sorry to hear that, is something troubling you sir?'

'Many things, Ellingham, many things.' I took a sip of the proffered restorative and set about putting him in the picture. I told him first of the baby-snatching incident, not forgetting the second child related situation.

'A most amusing case of misunderstanding, sir,' he smiled, or as near a smile as he allows himself on these sort of occasions; that is, the corners of his eyes wrinkle a little and one side of his mouth twitches a bit.

'It was, I assure you, not altogether amusing at the time,' I pointed out. 'And I have lost much sleep mulling over what might have been the outcome.'

'I can indeed see that such could well be the case, baby-snatching is looked upon as a very serious matter sir.'

'Still, all was ironed out in the end and I suppose it passed the time. Though it does add credence to the old saying "Damned if you do damned if you don't, what?'

'As you say sir. There are times when all one can do is take a philosophical view of life's twists and turns sir. '

'Changing the subject, I had dinner last night with Jane; showed her the photographs, she was as you suggested less than pleased with them. Whilst not actually throwing them back in my face she let it be known that they were a very poor substitute for the real thing.'

'It is hard to see how Miss Barrington-Ross's original request could have been met in any case sir.'

'You know that and I know that Ellingham, but Miss J. Barrington-Ross sees not a problem.'

'Indeed so sir; I take it that you were in that case unable to effect a suitable introduction between the young lady and your friend sir?'

'That's the other thing Ellingham, she was just sweeping out in high umbrage; if, that's the term I mean?'

'Or perhaps, dudgeon sir?'

'As you say, high umbrage or dudgeon, just as he was making his entrance. The two of them passed as ships in the night.'

'The young gentleman in question must have been most disappointed.'

'Took it on the chin, actually. Must say I was most surprised.'

'So I would be disposed to imagine. Perhaps the young gentleman is already beginning to cool towards Miss Barrington-Ross sir?'

'Not so, still got it bad I'm afraid, have to admit I can't see what's to be done about it.'

'It is hard to see how anything can be done to get the two young people together before you return from Much Moreham sir.'

'I see it much the same myself, let time be the great healer, eh Ellingham?'

'Just so sir.' And out he went to see to the young masters breakfast.

It's strange the way things pan out I've always thought, for although I was not looking forward to visiting The Willows, for reasons already stated it turned out to have hidden benefits.

4

And so the great day dawned when we set off to the depths of Gloucestershire to visit my uncle and aunt. Ellingham loaded the car with all of the necessary clothes and equipment a young gentleman would need on a country visit, or at least he assured me he had, and I had no reason to doubt the man. We started just after lunch in weather that set the heart aglow, or should have done had I not had the feeling of dread of which I have already made mention. On occasions like this we are more like old friends than employer and employee. We were bowling along merrily passing the time in idle chitchat, as one does when time isn't a pressing concern, when a thought occurred to me.

'I say Ellingham?'

'Sir?'

'You did remember to pack the Quacking Duck?'

I've always thought that the best way to stay young is to do childish things from time to time, especially away from prying eyes. My own indulgence happens to be bath toys. I had got totally fed up with the plastic warships, I bet if you've got them you've found as I have; they all sink to the depths at the slightest wave in the bathwater, except of course the submarine which manages to stay afloat even under the weight of a wet flannel. And so my latest novelty is the aforementioned Quacking Duck. If you've not come across this one, I can highly recommend it. It sort of sits on the surface as any

67

rubber duck but then every so often, seemingly at random, it dips its beak in the water, tail up as ducks will, then returns to the float again making a loud quacking sound. As infectious as that laughing policeman thing one puts a penny in at the fair.

'I had anticipated that you would require it sir and it is packed away with the miniature flotilla sir.'

'You may discard the boats at your earliest Ellingham, I have tired of them, they are surplus to requirements. You may distribute them among the poor.'

'As you wish sir,'

I changed the subject.

'So what do you think to "Ramona" now, Ellingham? I asked.

'Do I assume correctly that you have given the vehicle that name sir?'

'Your assumption is without fault Ellingham, fits her rather well don't yer think?'

'It is perhaps a name a little too much on the lines of Jezebel but suitable enough, sir. From a passenger's point of view I have to say the ride is most comfortable sir. However, as I have not yet had the pleasure of driving the vehicle I can not offer more in the way of an opinion in that direction sir.'

'You'll have your chance Ellingham. When the love affair is cooling; you'll get your chance.'

'Thank you sir, I will look forward to it. In the mean time I would value your thoughts on the vehicle sir.'

A bit patronising I suppose, but the man was probably only trying to regain lost ground with regard to past problems so I let it go.

'It's hard to put into words, but I suppose it's as though they have tied up all the loose ends; it feels, I don't know, sort of clean if you know what I mean?'

'Indeed sir, you were perhaps thinking that the vehicle has come of age; become almost part of the driver's own body sir?'

'I say, that's rather good Ellingham. That's exactly it, complete and finished and like I said, clean, somehow.'

'I understand sir.'

'Talking of clean, or rather cleaning; that stuff, er, Kleeno, have you tried it yet?' I asked.

'The occasion has not as yet arisen when I have found the need of your kind gift sir.'

'Well try it when we get back. It's expensive stuff Ellingham, I'd hate to think of it going to waste,' I said.

'As you wish sir, perhaps I could deliberately burn a pan so as to be able to properly ascertain its cleaning properties, sir?'

'That's the spirit my man. Give it of your best.'

'I will attend to the matter the moment we return home sir.'

As you see all was sweetness and light when all of a sudden there was an almighty bang and "Ramona" lurched from side to side, across the road, this way and that, and we near as damn it ended our journey in the ditch. A front tyre had blown and we were miles from anywhere.

'Front tyres gone Ellingham,' I pointed out in case the matter had passed him by.

'So I had ascertained sir.'

'We're miles from anywhere.'

'As you say sir, the last village is some three miles back and the next one a similar distance ahead sir.' He no doubt pointed it out, in case the matter had slipped *my* attention.

'Suppose we'll have to change it?'

'That would indeed seem to be the case sir.'

'Could you do that Ellingham?'

'I have no first-hand experience of such matters sir, however there is, I believe, in the glove compartment, a bound document explaining the sequence of events on these, and similar occasions. I could if it would be helpful read the relevant section for you as you carry out the procedure sir,' he said making it quite clear that in this matter I was on my own.

If you've ever had occasion to find yourself in the middle of the country with a motorcar that's thrown a shoe, you will know that it is a tricky matter to put right. The first thing you need to do is to find the bally toolkit; this is of course located below all of the luggage you, or in this case your manservant, has carefully stowed away for the journey. Having eventually found it your problems begin. If you are aware of these things you won't need me to tell you that the sporty wheels on the Tolson Mk14 Super Sports are held on by one of those pretty chromium spinner things in the middle, which you need to bash the right way to make it undo, put the jack in a suitable place, and so on. Anyway to cut a long story to the bare bones it was the best part of an hour before we were again on our way. I had badly scuffed the toe of my right shoe, torn the knee of very nifty pair of trousers, somehow got grease on the shoulder of my favourite jacket and received several badly barked knuckles in the process. Ellingham had received a rather nasty paper cut from one of the pages of the owner's manual. Hah, serves him jolly well right what?

We pulled up outside The Willows a good bit

70

behind schedule as you might imagine. We always eat early when at The Willows, due to my uncle's digestive system needing a goodly length of time to deal with his last meal before retiring. My aunt herself was at the door; doing the face like thunder, arms folded, foot-tapping routine.

'You're late, and why, may I ask, have you arrived at my door looking like a down-and-out scarecrow?' she asked.

'Had a bit of a problem with the old jalopy Aunt, rather in need of a bath I think.' Though I'm sure the matter had not escaped her attention.

'Be gone foul beast,' she misquoted then spoke to Ellingham. 'I've put the young idiot in the green room again, above the tack room, though no doubt you remember. Dinner is in twenty-five minutes, have him washed and scrubbed, do not spare the scrubbing. I wish to see much raw flesh, and have him in presentable form by then Ellingham.'

'I will of course see to the matter Madam.'

'See that you do,' she said and waved us on our way.

As time was now a pressing feature, I assisted Ellingham to carry in the luggage, though following his singular lack of assistance with changing the wheel I did it not without the hint of a grudge. However by the time we were walking along the first floor passage of the west wing I had forgiven the chap.

'The green room again, eh Ellingham? Hardly the honoured guest what?'

'The room as I recall it, is pleasant enough, if a little on the small side sir.'

'Small, small you could hardly swing a cat around

71

in it, as the saying goes.'

'Perhaps your aunt did not envisage that to be an activity in which you would be indulging, sir,' he said as he opened the door to the green room, (clever, but not his own, I've heard it before somewhere but I let it go.)

'True, I say it seems a good deal greener than I remember it Ellingham.'

'Perhaps your aunt has seen fit to have it redecorated since your last visit sir.'

I could see what he meant. My last visit had ended up with a small fire, due to me accidentally setting flame to the bedclothes whilst trying to control a small blaze in the waste paper basket caused by a cigarette end which I was sure I had extinguished, and *it* was sure I hadn't. Whilst there had been no need to call the local brigade, there had been much smoke damage and I had left under a cloud, in more ways than one if you take my meaning.

'Again you speak the truth Ellingham, but this is not getting me a bath. Lay out some clothes suitable for dinner and I'll run my own bath.'

'I already have the matter in hand; I will call you in time to dress sir.'

I entered the dining room some twenty-three minutes later, the only outward sign of my on-road ordeal being the three rather painful knuckles. But I forgot about them completely when I saw who was among the gathered throng - none other than Miss Elizabeth Manson. You could have knocked me down with the proverbial feather.

'Ah, Joshua, there you are,' my aunt yelled across the room and she was right, there I indeed was, proving that not much slips past Aunt E.

'Come here dear nephew, there is someone I wish

you to meet.'

'Right ho,' I tootled, not missing the import of the *dear nephew* bit, hoping that this person she wished me to meet might be Miss Manson. And this indeed proved to be the case as she walked me over to the aforesaid young lady.

'Elizabeth, this is my favourite nephew, Joshua Tolson. Joshua, Miss Elizabeth Manson, Elizabeth is just back from doing good works in Africa,' my aunt explained. 'Well I'll leave you two young people to get to know each other; I've seated you together at the dinner table by the way.'

And she was gone, but not without giving me a withering look which said I wish you to make a good impression on this young lady and the wrath of an aunt will follow if such is not the case.

Since it was also my intention to make a good impression, I set about it.

'It's Josh, please call me Josh,' I said and held out the old hand.

'Then please call me Liz, all my friends call me Liz.' She grasped my hand in a purposeful handshake, then let it go again as I winced.

'Oh dear what have you done to your poor hand?' she asked taking it in both hands and gently inspecting it.

Before I could reply the dinner gong went and we made our way to our appointed seats. We were directly opposite my aunt, and it was clear that she intended to keep an eye on the proceedings. I had not at this point been introduced to my fellow house-guests, and my aunt proceeded to do this as we settled ourselves to wait for the first course.

'Everybody,' she said and tapped her water glass

with a fork, 'this is my nephew Joshua Tolson.'

They all said hello; I say all but in addition to Liz there were only three other guests.

'Joshua, Miss Manson you have already met of course. This,' and here she pointed to a crusty old cove with eyebrows that made him look as though he was peering under a thickset hedge, 'is Major Charles Chesterton, one of your uncle's oldest friends.'

'What yer aunt means is I'm his longest standing friendship, not that I am the oldest friend he's got, though come to think of it that's probably true as well. Anyway pleased to meet you young fella-me-lad, though I have to say I'm rather sorry you've turned up,' he said rubbing his nose with the ball of his thumb, a nose I noticed that was no stranger to a glass of port.

'Oh, why's that?' I asked. Amazed that I seemed to have got under his skin even before meeting him; strange as this usually takes at least half an hour.

'You've pinched me damned place that's why. I was sitting by Liz last night, I was about to ask her to marry me tonight don't yer know,' and here he winked at her and gave a little nod, 'yes you've scuppered all of that, yer young blighter; but pleased to meet yer. Don't stand on ceremony by the way, call me Major.'

'This is the Major's wife Mrs Dorothy Chesterton.' This time my aunt was indicating a thin scrawny woman sitting next to my uncle, a good deal younger than the major though the years had clearly not dealt her a good hand. Her eyes had those deep bags under them that make the eyes seem old and tired. Though I have to say, the eyes themselves still held a degree of sparkle, which suggested, *"Don't write me off, there's still life in the old bitch yet."*

74

'Pleased to meet you, I'm known as Dora, please it's Dora,' she said to get it clear.

'Rubbish,' said the major, 'call her Dotty, everyone calls her Dotty,' and he laughed.

The look on her face clearly sent the message that although people might indeed call her Dotty she preferred Dora. The third person was a strange looking chap in middle age, with more teeth than the size of his mouth could handle; when he grinned it was like he had lifted the lid of a grand piano. A couple of gaps in the upper set completed the illusion by looking like the black notes.

'This is Mr Danvers Tideswell,' said my aunt, and she smiled at the man sitting at the side of her, 'he is the friend of a cousin of mine, here for a few days rest and quiet.'

'Humph,' said Uncle Josh, and received a withering look from Aunt E.

'Ye*sh*, I'm afraid life ha*sh* got a little on top of me ju*sh*t lately and your aunt kindly invited me to *sh*tay for a while.'

'Humph,' said Uncle Josh, this time under his breath.

'*Sh*ince I am a keen amateur gardener, your aunt ha*sh* a*sh*ked me to help her remodel the formal *sh*ection, though I fear that your uncle is not altogether in favour of the *sh*cheme. They call me Dan by the way, plea*sh*ed to meet you.'

I've tried to write it as he said it. It tended to get a bit splashy, all those teeth getting in the way I suppose.

The food at my aunt's place is always down to earth good British fare, nothing fancy, just plain good eating. We started with a thick cream of chicken soup, and very tasty it was too, made all the more so by the

75

pleasant conversation I was having with Liz.

'You were about to tell me how you damaged your hand,' she said.

'Bit of a problem with the old jalopy, front tyre burst and we nearly ditched it,' I said.

'A bit scary that, I know, it happened to me a few days before I left Africa. But you said *we*, are you down here with someone?'

'Only Ellingham, my manservant.'

'Really, I didn't think such people still existed here in England; we have them in Africa of course. But if this Ellingham changed the wheel, how did you damage your hand?'

'The Ellingham's of this world are rather a dying breed, I'm lucky to have him. He's the salt of the earth and all that. But he draws the line at getting his hands dirty in the service of the master. Especially since he was not happy about the choice of colour scheme on the vehicle in question' I explained.

'I've just worked out who you are; Joshua Tolson, the car maker's son, that's right isn't it?' she asked.

'That's right, I saw you the other night at the Straw Boater club. Though we never actually met,' I said.

'Now I come to think of it I do remember seeing you there. My cousin John said something about you wanting to see me to make a donation to my Africa charity,' she smiled.

'I think that might be arranged, I've always had a soft spot for schools in Africa.' I thought a little white lie might not go amiss, but she's a canny girl this Liz Manson and spotted it a mile off.

'I bet you've never even heard of schools for Africa until you saw it in the newspaper, I assume you did see it in the newspaper.'

'You're right of course, but it does seem to be a good cause and one I feel I should be involved with.'

'I'm sure a donation from you would be most welcome, but the real money, the money that makes all the difference, comes from the large manufacturing companies,' she sighed. 'Sadly they are the hardest to make contact with.'

'Now there I know I can help.' I said.

'Oh, could you really? That would be a wonderful thing.'

'Yes I'm sure I can. Look it's a pleasant evening, after dinner why don't we stroll down by the river and discuss it?'

'Yes I'd like that very much,' and she smiled and I got soup all over my napkin.

I don't know the name of my aunt's cook, she or he being ensconced down in the bowels of the building, but I made a mental note to get Ellingham to find out, since, on leaving, I intended to reward said cook with camels and ivory and apes. Well perhaps a well aimed fiver anyway, for work well done. What had set this idea in my mind was a simply divine rhubarb tart; yes I know you think it's only a rhubarb tart, but you dear reader did not taste it. There seemed to be just a hint of ginger in it, anyway whatever it was made all the difference. Perhaps you might suggest that my table companion was causing me to see such things through rose coloured glasses; I have to admit that sitting chatting to Liz Manson, especially with the prospect of a walk by the river on the cards, could have had that effect on me but even so it was a quite remarkable rhubarb tart.

We chatted of this and that, all the time under the

watchful eye of Aunt E. Gradually she, my aunt that is, began to relax as it became clear that the young lady in question was responding in a positive way to my conversational leads, and I have to say I was rather glad that she was doing so myself.

'Your work in Africa,' I said, 'must be very rewarding, seeing all of those little faces smiling back at you?'

'Sadly, I don't get nearly enough chance to see the schools themselves, being mainly involved in fund raising and general organisation,' she replied.

'Must make it tough not actually being involved in the villages and seeing how all of your efforts are being put to use.'

'Oh, I do get to see the end results; about once a month I make a point of just picking a school at random and making a special visit.'

'Catch them on the hop, so to speak?' I suggested.

'No not really, I always make sure they know I'm on the way. In any case you can't keep a thing like that quiet in Africa, everyone would know even before you set off.'

'The jungle drums what?'

'Well yes something, like that,' she smiled, and the old ticker fluttered a bit.

My aunt signalled that dinner was over by rising and suggesting that the ladies' might like to retire to the withdrawing room.

'If you'll excuse me Mrs Tolson, Joshua has offered to show me the walk by the river.'

'Of course my dear, it's an excellent evening for it, go ahead, it's a most pleasant walk. I would suggest a change to sensible shoes though, as it can be a little muddy in places,' she beamed. 'Take good care of my guest Joshua,' and gave me a little nod of approval.

And so with sensible shoes in place, and the rare blessings of Aunt E. we set out down the driveway towards the bridge.

'You were saying about the jungle drums,' I prompted.

'Yes, even without the modern aids of our age they always know the latest news, often, it seems, before it happens.'

'Must get a bit scary, with all those lions and tigers and crocodiles and stuff?'

'Oh, I'm perfectly safe, Mumbo, he's my chauffeur-cum-bodyguard, is always at my side.' she smiled.

I've never met this Mumbo chap, but I took an instant dislike to him, always at her side foresooth. I changed the subject.

'Are you over here for long?' I asked.

'I'm here for three months; I aim to raise thirty thousand pounds before I return to Africa.' She smiled and I had another ticker fluttering sensation.

'Thirty thousand smackers eh? Sounds a bit of a tall order to me.'

'I can't pretend it will be easy, but without it the work will just grind to a halt.'

'How many schools do you need, before it's finished I mean?'

'If it was just providing the schools, that would be comparatively easy. Getting people to give money to tangible things like the building doesn't really present a problem, it's the other things that we, I, have difficulty promoting.'

'Other things?' I asked.

'Chalk, paper and ink, not to mention the cost of training suitable teachers. That side of things is less tangible. People are less likely to feel good about buying twenty gallons of ink or one hundred and twenty chalk slates. But they are just as important as wood and corrugated iron.' This time her smile was deep and wistful, but the effect was even more powerful than any so far and I almost fell over a protruding stone at the edge of the drive. We both laughed, that easy laughter that comes when you know no offence will be taken. The beginning I suppose, of true friendship.

By this time we had reached the bridge. It's quite interesting as bridges go and I made another mental note to ask Ellingham what he knows about its history. You never know when that sort of insider knowledge might be useful, especially as I intended these river walks to become a permanent feature of my plans, being in a position to impress is one that a chap should always try to achieve, what?

'Here we have a choice, at this point we can either walk this side of the river with a view of Much Moreham, a charming village, replete with post office, two pubs, a church and all the usual fixtures and fittings, over the river to our right.'

And at that very moment the clock on the church in the distance rang half-past eight, to complete the scene.

'Or, and I always think this the nicer option, we could cross the bridge and follow the path the other side, with a view of The Willows to our left,' I said, feeling rather like one of those cheap travel guidebooks.

'Over the bridge sounds fine, it's nice just walking and talking anyway on a beautiful evening like this, don't you think Josh?'

More smiling, and heart fluttering and stuff.

'Oh, rather,' I said.

We crossed the bridge and began walking along the footpath; at this point the house is not yet visible due to overhanging willow trees. We had scarcely gone ten yards when Liz grabbed my hand and told me to shush. As I hadn't been talking at the time, still deciding how to start the next bit of conversation, I was a bit nonplussed.

'Eh, what is it?' I asked.

'Shush, Josh; look over there.'

I didn't say anything at this point, not I think, because she had asked me not to, but because she had stopped me and she still had hold of my hand, and I grasped hers a bit tighter in return.

'Look, over there,' she whispered and pointed at this long-legged bird thing, 'a grey heron in the water over by the other bank.'

'Oh, is that what it is?'

'Quiet, you'll frighten him away; look I think he's spotted a fish,' she said still whispering. 'See how he's holding his head on one side. Now look, he's looking down his beak, he'll strike at any moment.'

And be blowed, if the damn thing did just that and came up with a fair-sized fish. At that very moment there came the sound of an engine starting up at the house, and the heron if that's what it was, flew off with the fish in his mouth.

'Shame we didn't see him swallow it,' she said, still whispering.

'That's my car,' I said. 'I'd know the sound a mile off.'

And down the drive, being driven with a good

81

deal of flair and panache was the Mark 14 with Ellingham at the wheel. I raced back to the bridge, and I was just in time to stop the man in his tracks and ask him what the devil he thought he was doing?

'I took the liberty of telephoning the factory whilst you were having your bath sir, to request another wheel. They have just been on the telephone in return to tell me that a replacement wheel is already on its way to Much Moreham railway station, and likely to arrive shortly; I trust I have not exceeded my duties by taking your car to collect it sir?' he said.

'Bit late to be delivering wheels what?'

'It has been despatched on the evening slow train sir. If you wish me to leave its collection until morning sir, I will telephone the station and ask them to safe keep it until then.'

'No no, carry on Ellingham.'

'Thank you sir.' He gave us both a little bow, or as near as you can come to a bow in the driving seat of "Ramona".

'Please could I have my hand back?' asked Liz. It was at this point that I realised that I was still holding her hand and that she had had no choice but to follow me full pelt back to the bridge.

'I say most awfully sorry. I thought my man had taken it into his head to go for a merry jaunt whilst the young master was otherwise engaged,' I said.

'Are you otherwise engaged?' she asked.

'At this moment yes, with a very charming young lady.'

'Oh, do I know her?'

'Ah, oh, no, I see what you mean. No, no one in the offing on the marriage stakes. Single, definitely single.   I meant I was out of the old homestead entertaining you.' And I rather think I blushed.

'I know silly, I was just pulling your leg.' There followed more of the smiling and heart fluttering stuff. As I said earlier in this piece: what a girl.

Next morning started with overcast sky.   It constantly looked like rain but never actually got there. The effect was that it was going to be one of those days that turn hot and sticky without the benefit of the sun to blame it on. It wasn't helped in any way by my mood following what had happened when we ended our walk back at the house the night before. Aunt E. had met us virtually at the bally doorstep again to inform us that she had a merry jape organised for this morning.

'Oh good, you're back,' she had said. 'Elizabeth, I have arranged to take you over to meet the Farrington-Brown's in the morning; they are very interested in your schools' charity. The Farrington-Browns' were out in Africa for many years and will no doubt be very sympathetic with your aims, my dear.'

'That's very kind of you Mrs Tolson, thank you for taking the trouble to think of me.'

'Not at all, the Farrington-Browns' are old friends. My husband would have loved to come with us but he has a long-standing engagement in Gloucester to take care of. So you young man,' and here she looked at me, 'will be taking his place.'

'Oh I say, Aunt E., that's a bit stiff, they are unlikely to welcome me with open arms,' I said.

'Yes, the least said about the last time you were their guest the better. You will not, under any circumstances, make mention of it; the incident is still very fresh in dear Gwendolyn's mind.'

'Understood.'

'To put you in the picture my dear,' she said to Liz, 'and to save you inadvertently saying something out of place, this is what happened.'

And here she gave what can only be called a very jaundiced, one sided description of the events. But one knows better than interrupt or correct an aunt in full flow, though one bally well wanted too like the dickens.

'We had been invited to the Farrington-Brown's because they wished to show us their drawing room; they had just had it redecorated and refurnished in the regency style, by one of the top London designers. It was, I have to say, not to my particular taste for a room intended to be relaxed in, however be that as it may, they had invited this young man as well, an almost fatal flaw in any gathering it might be pointed out; however we arrived as requested and Gwendolyn, Mrs Farrington-Brown, took us through to the room in question. After the necessary inspection of its many and varied qualities we were invited to sit and chat, during which coffee was served. At this point I should tell you that the Farrington-Browns' have two corgis, two rather highly-strung corgis. Joshua here somehow managed to so sufficiently antagonise one of them as to get it to bite him on the ankle, whereupon he promptly kicked over the small coffee table, dispatching coffee and biscuits and assorted chinaware over a wide area, which caused the other corgi, the least stable of the pair, to bite the maid. The poor girl in shock fell against an antique glass-fronted china cabinet, rendering it and it's contents beyond repair. Luckily the poor girl, though much alarmed, was unharmed save for a few minor scratches. One would have considered this to be sufficient

84

catastrophe for a single occasion, but not so. The disaster goes on; George, Mr Farrington-Brown, was not with us in the room at the time, but hearing the commotion came rushing in to find out its cause; seeing the maid in great distress he made swiftly to assist her, stepping as he did so on a jagged piece of glass. Since he was at the time wearing only carpet slippers, this caused him an injury, which had him limping with a stick and a heavily bandaged foot for many weeks. Even this is not the end. Whilst hopping around clutching his injured foot he inadvertently fell against the large coffee table, upsetting it, breaking one of its legs and several of Gwendolyn's prized Crown Derbyshire plates. To prevent himself from falling he made a grab at Gwendolyn for support and knocked her spectacles to the floor in the process, then managed with his very next hop to render them also to an unusable condition. After making suitable apologies we left to allow these poor people to commence the unenviable task of rebuilding their home and lives,' said Aunt E., and she gave me a withering look.

'It must have been very upsetting for your friends,' said Liz, keeping a straight face with a great effort.

'It has taken many months to rebuild our friendship following the incident; so you young man,' and here she gave me yet another withering look, 'will be on your very best behaviour.'

'I say Aunt, in my defence...'

'There is no defence, if only there were a defence. Off with the both of you and be ready to leave by ten thirty in the morning.'

I gave it up.

5

As ten o'clock was being signalled by the great clock in the hall I sat in my room having a last gasper - my aunt frowns on smoking in public - and talking to Ellingham.

'You see the posish Ellingham, self under the usual cloud of an aunt's disapproval, going to a place which, by no fault of my own though I of course got the total blame, had on a previous occasion been rendered near uninhabitable, and I am to make a good impression. I'm open to anything you can suggest,' I said.

'The young lady, Miss Manson, seems to interest you sir?' he said thoughtfully.

''Tis so Ellingham, the old heart yearns a good bit, what.'

'Then if I might suggest a solution which may meet with your approval?'

'Suggest away dear fellow, the riper the better.'

'Since your aunt wishes you to redress yourself with the Farrington-Browns, and at the same time Mrs Farrington-Brown must be a little apprehensive at you again being a house-guest, even though as you rightly point out you were blameless to the unfortunate incident on the previous occasion...'

'Put a sock in it old chap, come to the nitty-gritty, get to the crux, I'm leaving for the bally place in twenty-five minutes,' I said.

'I'm sorry sir, I was merely about to point out that if you were to excuse yourself as soon as Miss Manson has concluded her charitable business with Mrs

Farrington-Brown and invite the young lady to take a stroll in the garden it might be seen as most suitable on all fronts sir.'

'So let's get this straight, I take myself out of Mrs Farrington-Brown's hair, gain a scout badge in aunt's approval for impressing Liz, and spend time alone with the lady in question?' I said.

'That is indeed the gist, nub or crux, of the plan sir.'

'And I have to say it's a corker. Well done Ellingham, I will have no cause to give you anything but the most glowing reference when I marry Miss Manson and have to let you go to pastures new, though you will be greatly missed,' I said and I meant it.

'I had no idea that you had already proposed to the young lady sir,' and he squinted a little.

'Oh lor' no not yet, don't want to frighten her off what, but when it comes to a suitable time the question will be popped, don't yer know.'

'I see sir. As you suggest, to reach your ultimate aim Miss Manson would need to reach a favourable state of mind towards you sir,' he said.

'Working on it like the dickens, I think she rather likes me.'

'I am sure that must be most gratifying for you sir.'

'It is and that's a fact.' And I left him musing on the fact to go down to the hall so as not to gain further disapproval of Aunt E. by being late.

As I descended the stairs I was aware that there were already people there; a conversation was going on between Aunt E. and the man Danvers Tideswell.

'I think that's a capital idea, and you've already

spoken to him on the telephone?' my aunt was saying.

'Ye*sh* indeed and he will be mo*sh*t honoured to give hi*sh* advi*sh*e. I took the liberty of inviting him today, *sh*inshe I will be leaving on Tue*sh*day nex*sh*t and I am mo*sh*t intere*sh*ted in what he ha*sh* to *sh*ay. He arrive*sh* on the one thirty train,' the man said, showing more teeth that a pride of lions.

'That is a little inconvenient, I will be using the car to go over to the Farrington-Browns',' said my aunt.

'I'm *sh*ure a tax*sh*i would *sh*uffic*sh*.'

Seeing a chance to ingratiate myself I said, 'If it would help Aunt, what if Ellingham were to collect this person from the station in my car?'

'Goodness me, that's the most sensible thing you've said since you arrived,' my aunt said and almost smiled. And at this point Liz arrived on the scene looking fresh as a daisy in spring.

'Mr Tideswell, Dan, pray go and find this man Ellingham and give him the details. Our car has just arrived at the door and we need to be on our way.'

'Ye*sh*, and thank you *sh*o much,' he said and he started to climb the stairs.

We all good-morninged and were soon off to the Farrington-Browns.

Uncle Josh had bought the car, one of my fathers earliest models in the early twenties, and although it is conspicuously out of date it is immaculate. Liz started the conversation soon after we settled ourselves for what could be a long journey, Beddoes, my aunt and uncle's chauffeur not exactly being renowned as a speed merchant.

'What a delightful car Mrs Tolson, I love it, what is it?' she asked.

'Oh it's just a car to me, Josh can tell you more about it, but don't bore the poor girl, I suppose she only asked out of politeness.'

'No I'm really very interested, we have lots of old cars out in Africa but the heat and dust makes it hard to keep them looking like this.' She turned to me. 'Tell me about it please.'

As I've already said motorcars and me don't mix mechanically but that doesn't mean I can't talk about them, the history and such, and this one especially.

'I can't pretend to understand the finer points of the mechanical things, but I can tell you that it was originally built as a prototype. My father saw what he thought was a niche in the market for a large car at a reasonable price; it turned out to be a much smaller niche than he had anticipated and only twenty six of these were built. Stop me if I'm boring you,' I smiled at Liz.

'Well you're boring me,' said my aunt, 'but Miss Manson is hanging on your every word, so carry on.'

'Yes please, I'm fascinated.'

There's nothing like an attentive audience to improve the telling of a story and we were still discussing motoring in general as we turned into the Farrington-Brown's driveway. By now the sun had burst through the clouds and it looked like things were turning up a bit, in more ways than one.

It was the china-cabinet-busting maid that opened the door to us; clearly she had not been informed that I was to be among the gathering as she froze for a moment when her eyes fell upon me. Recovering her composure she said -

'Good morning, Mrs Farrington-Brown is expecting you.' She closed the door behind us then continued, 'if you would follow me please.'

She took us from the hall through the room that I remembered as the disaster area, even though it had, by now, been extensively restored, out through a pair of double doors, French windows I suppose you'd call them, and on to a sort of paved sun terrace, where Mrs Farrington-Brown was seated on a rather nice three-seater oak bench. Two matching benches made up a set, and were arranged in a sort of horseshoe shape to allow group conversation. In the centre of the terrace was a table with its own six chairs. Mrs Farrington-Brown got up as we arrived on the scene.

'Your guests, Madam.'

'Thank you Millie, that will be all.'

'Yes Madam,' and she disappeared back through the French windows.

'Evangeline, so nice to see you again, this must be Miss Manson; I've heard so much about you my dear and your work in Africa. Please sit down everybody.' Here she looked at me, 'Josh, glad you could come. I have decided that it would be less constraining if we were to eat out of doors.' The remark was not lost on me; give a dog a bad name what?

'Mrs Farrington-Brown, it's so good of you to show interest in my schools, what would you like to know?' It was Liz who spoke.

'I'm very interested in everything, please tell me all,' said Mrs F-B.

Liz is a good ambassador for her own project and I dare say that had I not heard it before I would have been equally as captivated as my aunt and Mrs Farrington-Brown. But since I had I drifted off into a little reverie, if that's the word I mean, thinking what life might be like married to this wonderful woman. Liz I mean of course, not Mrs Farrington-Brown. And a pretty picture of domestic harmony I created I don't mind telling you. It would mean living in Africa and facing on a daily basis lions, tigers, crocodiles and all kinds of other fierce beasties, but with Liz, well need I say more? I was dragged back from my musing, perhaps that's the word I meant, I'm not sure, by the fact that the maid was addressing me.

'Do listen to the girl Joshua,' my aunt was saying.

'Ah, er what, yes sorry I was deep in thought,' I said.

'There is always a first time for everything,' Aunt E. said none too quietly then to the maid. 'Well get on with it girl.'

'Yes Ma'am. You are wanted on the telephone sir.'

'Me, oh, right, who is it did they say?'

'The gentleman said his name was Elvington sir.'

'Who is this man Joshua?' snapped my aunt.

'Never heard of him, don't know him from Adam.' I said and I spoke the truth.

'Well don't just sit there, go and see what he wants.'

'Yes Aunt.' And I followed Millie back through the reconstructed war zone and into the hall where the instrument in question was sitting beside a large vase of flowers, on a small table just inside the front door.

'Hello, Joshua Tolson, speaking.' I said.

'Ellingham here sir,' said the voice at the other end.

'Ah, the maid said you were a Mr. Elvington, but it's you Ellingham?'

91

'Indeed that is the case sir.'

'Mistaken identity, what?'

'Perhaps the line is not as clear as it might be sir?'

And he was right, it wasn't. You know how it is sometimes, when you think the person at the other end has said one thing when in fact they have said something completely different?

'What's the matter Ellingham, why the call?'

'I thought you would be interested in the turn of events here at The Willows sir.'

'Well inform me.'

'Shortly after you had left your room to keep your appointment with your aunt sir, Mr Tideswell came to ask me to collect a new guest from the railway station sir.'

'Yes that's right, I suggested the idea as a way of ingratiating myself with Aunt E,' I said.

'I suspected such to be the case sir, and was most willing to carry out the request.'

'Good, so what's the problem?'

'The gentleman in question is here to give professional advice on the remodelling of the formal part of the garden, the rose section to be precise sir.'

'Yes, yes get on with it.'

'The person is Mr Walter Thomas, sir.'

'Walter who?' I asked. A crackle on the line had made me miss the chap's surname.

'I fear you did not hear me correctly sir; the gentleman's name is Walter Thomas, sir.

'Name seems familiar Ellingham; do I know him?'

'Perhaps it has slipped your mind sir; Mr Walter Thomas is the rose grower you visited recently.'

I must have given one of those visible starts that

people are always talking about, because I somehow managed to knock over the vase of flowers, barely saving it from ruin on the floor. By the time I had righted it, Ellingham was saying -

'Hello sir, are you still there?'

'Yes back with you, I thought I heard you say that this new guest was W. Thomas the rose grower?'

'That is correct sir.'

'What - you are serious Ellingham?'

'Never more so sir.'

'He'll recognise me, what the hell shall I do?'

'I think that stout denial will fit the bill, and perhaps parting your hair differently sir.' And here I could have sworn I heard a chuckle at the other end but it was probably the bad line.

'But the car, Ellingham, he must have recognised the car.'

'That would no doubt have been the case, however I took steps to change it as soon as I realised the name of the gentleman I was to collect sir.'

'But if he thinks he recognises me isn't he sure to mention that the fellow at the rose garden had a red car; if my aunt hears that she's sure to suspect me, she always suspects me.'

'In conversation with the gentleman as we returned from the station I happened to mention that I had just picked up the car having replaced a bright red one which you had had on trial for the previous day; and which you had not been at all happy with sir.'

'Good thinking Ellingham.'

'Thank you sir, so since the only thing to connect you to the person at his rose garden is that you look somewhat similar, stout denial should be sufficient.'

93

'The car Ellingham, you say you changed it; how, where, and more importantly for what?'

'I fear I will have to go now sir, the gentleman has asked me to take him a whisky and soda sir. I will of course appraise you in full of the situation when we next meet.' And the blighter rang off.

Leaving the telephone I crossed the hall and was about to open the door to the disaster room when it was opened from the other side by Millie. She was carrying a silver tray which thankfully was empty and hanging at her side. On seeing me almost face to face with her, she promptly managed two things simultaneously; she gave out a high pitched little squeal and dropped the tray on the floor with a silver-tray-dropping-on-the-floor kind of noise. After a moments hesitation we both dived to rescue it and in our impetuosity, as I've heard Ellingham call it, we hit heads.

'I say I'm awfully sorry Millie; I made you jump,' I said as we both rubbed our respective heads.

'You did give me a bit.. of.. a.. start... sir,' she tailed off slowly, and blowed if she wasn't looking somewhat intently at the jolly old trouser area; a thing one doesn't expect maids to do. I looked down and dashed if I didn't have an embarrassing wet patch all down the front of the old bags what? I hadn't been aware of it before, but it was hard to escape it now. Realising that the vase of flowers was to blame for the girl's attention, I explained the situation.

'I wonder if you would be kind enough to put a drop more water in the flowers by the telephone. I inadvertently upset them, hence the wet patch I'm afraid.'

'Yes, sir; certainly. Would you like me to fetch a cloth to dry... so that you can dry your trousers sir?' she

94

asked shyly.

'Thank you no, they will no doubt dry in the sun, it's only a drop of water.'

'Very good sir; lunch is served on the terrace sir.' She gave a little curtsey and skipped off nervously toward what I suppose was the kitchen.

I arrived back at the sun terrace and thought I had better explain my wet patch.

'I'm sorry Mrs. Farrington-Brown, I accidentally tipped over a vase of flowers by the telephone but Millie is going to sort it out for me.'

Mrs. Farrington-Brown caught her breath in an alarmed way and gazed at me open mouthed. But it was my aunt who spoke.

'There was a squeal and a sound like an express train colliding with a dinner gong a few moments ago,' my aunt said, 'what was that, pray?'

'I'm afraid I startled Millie and she dropped a tray.'

'Thank goodness that is all the devastation we have to worry about,' said Mrs. F-B with a nervous little laugh, relaxing once more.

'Oh I dare say there is still time for more,' my aunt whispered to Liz.

And I don't mind telling you I thought it was a bit thick what?

The food was very good; a bit more adventurous than my aunt's, and very enjoyable. I managed the whole meal without disgracing myself further and by the time it was over, Liz had bagged a cheque for five hundred smackers. A fair old dollop toward the target, you could tell that she was over the moon. I suggested that a turn around the excellent gardens at the F-B place, whilst my aunt and Mrs. Farrington-Brown chewed the fat, as females of a certain age do.

'That seems an excellent idea,' said my aunt, 'if Miss Manson is agreeable?'

'Yes, I miss the beautiful gardens. I had quite forgotten how beautiful England is at this time of year, so yes Josh, I would love to stroll with you.'

'Oh jolly good, shall we?'

'Lead the way, kind knight,' said Liz with a little nod. And my aunt gave a self-satisfied smile, and the old heart gave the usual leap.

We strolled down the path that followed the side of the house, the house on our left the formal garden to our right. As I said I'm not much up on flowers and trees and things, but I know a good-looking garden when I see one. And this was one of the best. Liz, of course, knew every flower by name. So to hide my ignorance I set the conversation moving in a different direction.

'Mrs. Farrington-Brown was very generous,' I said.

'Yes it was nice of your aunt to introduce me to these kind people.'

'You'll soon reach your total if everyone drops you five hundred smackers.'

'It is certainly a very important step towards my goal.'

'I bet you don't get anywhere near that amount out of Aunt E.,' I chuckled.

'Oh, but I have, your aunt has been very generous. I can't tell you the amount as I'm sure you'll understand, but it was, is, considerable.'

'Well I'm dashed,' I said, 'Aunt E. the benefactor, this is new ground.'

'You seem to be in awe of your aunt?'

'Too true, from a little child I have had to take it on the chin, so to speak, from a gaggle of aunts, by far the worst being my Aunt Evangeline. Pure horror comic stuff. Rumour has it that she eats babies alive, can smash granite with a mere glance, dances in full witches costume at midsummer's eve and sleeps on broken glass.'

'She seems charming, warm and very much the perfect host,' she said.

'Pure window dressing, reserved for people who are not *me.*'

She laughed and put her hand in mine again.

'You are funny,' she said.

And I was at a loss to know how to go on from there. However we had by this time come into a sort of walled garden full of vegetable kind of things, which all seemed to have large terracotta labels at the ends of the rows so even I could be as wise as the next man. An old fellow and a younger one who had their backs to us were deep in conversation pointing here and there as though discussing, I suppose, the state of play on the pea and runner bean front. I took them to be the gardeners. Typical gardeners as gardeners go; hearing us they turned and the older one gave a little jump on seeing us.

'Good afternoon sir, madam,' he doffed his battered hat. We both returned the greeting. I had the feeling I'd seen the cove before somewhere, but I couldn't remember where.

'I hope you don't mind us looking at this part of the garden?' I asked.

'No sir, please, help yourself,' the older gardener mumbled, but even so the voice was one I was sure I'd heard before. It was of no great consequence, just one of

97

those annoying, niggling little things that get under your skin. You know the sort of thing; you're telling a story to a person, about another person, if you see what I mean, but the person's name, the second persons' name that is, just won't come. You know it begins with an "R". Rodgers or Rumbould or some such, but it just stays on the tip of your tongue and spoils the whole day. Then at three o'clock in the morning you wake with a start and you know in that instance – Jefferson, that's it; Jefferson. Well it was like that. Except of course the great revelation would wait it's time, probably, as I said, until three o'clock in the morning. Oh well that's life.

We wandered off looking at onions and leeks and broad beans and the like, and a handsome show they made I must say; a credit to these two fellows and no mistake. The Farrington-Browns must eat very well if this display was anything to go by. Eventually we came back to the two gardeners; two trouser seats told us they were deep in weeding or some such activity. In politeness as we passed I said -

'Thank you, excellent, they are a credit to you.'

'Thank you sir,' said the old gardener, raising his hat again, and it was revelation time. I had him; I knew who he was.

'I'm so sorry I didn't recognise you at first; it's Mr Farrington-Brown isn't it?' I said loudly, very pleased with myself.

'Oh my god, keep yer voice down, don't want the good lady to hear,' he said. 'She doesn't like me to be enjoying myself in the garden; thinks it's beneath me don't yer know. She thinks I'm away in Gloucester on business so not a word eh? '

'She won't hear it from me,' I said.

98

'Of course your secret is safe with us,' said Liz.

'Very grateful. I find it very relaxing down here. Can smoke me pipe yer see, not allowed to in the house; have to stay in the walled bit with the veg you understand, so as not to be seen. Just telling Chivers here me guilty secret,' and at this point he indicated the other fellow. 'He's new here, first day today. That's so Chivers?'

'Aye sir, right enough,' he replied and he looked directly at me as he said it.

'Excellent chap, lucky to get him. Worked for one of the big parks departments, until yesterday. Anyway mums the word what?'

Now I looked more closely at the fellow there was something about him that suggested I had seen him before as well. In a flash it came to me; worked in the parks until recently, lummy, Tweedle-dee. I thought I'd better nip him in the bud before he had time to drop yours truly deeply in the mire, so I said -

'I think we have spoken in the park on at least one occasion, Chivers?'

'I feel sure we 'ave sir. Thank you sir,' he said and he gave me a look that said, I remember you, you are the baby-snatcher, and I may not be saying anything right now but it might be brought up and used in evidence against you, should the need arise.

It was Mr. F-B's turn to speak again,

'You must be the young lady from the African schools thing?' he said, addressing Liz of course.

'Yes that's right, Elizabeth Manson, but please call me Liz,' and she held out her hand. Mr. F-B wiped his hand down his trousers, looked at it and offered it to Liz.

'Bit earthy I'm afraid but it's honest dirt, and it'll

wash off what? And it's George by the way.' She took it and said -

'Pleased to meet you, George.'

'My pleasure Liz; I assume the better half has made you a suitable contribution to your little, well I guess not so little, enterprise?' he asked.

'Your wife has been most generous.'

'Five hundred pounds, that's my guess, old skinflint,' he sniffed.

'It was five hundred pounds, for which I'm most grateful.'

'Worked all my life in Africa you understand, made a very nice little nest egg out of investments there. In short, not to put too finer point on it, we're rolling in the damned stuff. Absolutely stuffed to the back teeth with loot, much more than I can ever use in my lifetime. I'll do you a deal young lady, sorry Liz; you keep my guilty secret safe and I'll double it, another five hundred pounds, how's that?'

'It's most generous of you, but there is no need to buy my silence or Josh's for that matter I'm sure. We have already given our word,' she said.

'Of course, of course, don't mean to give offence, just checking you see. Can't be too careful what? But I want to give back a bit in thanks for a very comfortable life. No cheque book on me at the moment; can't come back to the house with you. Still in Gloucester you understand. If you've a card on you I'll forward my extra bit in due course,' he said and he smiled. 'Oh by the way,' he continued, 'should we meet again, don't let on we've met before in front of the little woman, yer get my drift?'

Chivers was looking a bit down in the mouth

seeing more than three year's wages given away, just like that.

'You are very kind, George,' and she produced a neat little card from her shoulder bag. We said our farewells and promised to be on our guard and meandered back to the house.

'Well Miss Manson, sorry Liz, what do you think to my garden?' asked Mrs F-B.

'I love them, you must be very proud of them,' she said.

Tea was on the table, the drink that is, not the meal and I poured one for Liz and helped myself to a cup.

'Did you go into the walled kitchen garden to see my vegetables?' Mrs Farrington-Brown asked me. I hesitated for a moment before I said -

'Yes, yes, very impressive.'

'Then no doubt you saw my husband down there, pretending to be a gardener?' and she looked at me with a wry smile. And for the second time on these premises I spilled the contents of my cup, this time tea, all down the leg of my latest best grey flannels, augmenting the flower-water stain already in evidence.

'No doubt he told you that I thought he was away in Gloucester on business, though why that should be the case on a Saturday I've no idea. Oh, don't worry I've known for sometime that that is where he goes. He smokes his smelly old pipe there, and I have to give credit where credit is due, he really does produce the most tasty of vegetables for the kitchen. No doubt he has sworn you to secrecy; I told Evangeline he would so no need to admit or deny that you saw him.'

'It is good for a man to have one guilty secret from his wife,' said my aunt, 'it stops him from needing

101

others,' and the women laughed.

'Yes, he's sure I don't know about it and I intend to keep it that way. The fear of discovery is doing him good; stopping him fading away, if you see what I mean. I have no doubt that he has given you an additional sum to secure your silence. Again there is no need to confirm or deny this. If you should see my husband again at any time I wish to maintain the status quo, I will therefore ask you to go along with his little charade. Liz if you would be so kind as to return the cheque I gave you a few minutes ago I will gladly replace it with this one.'

Liz, extracted the original cheque from her bag, reached over the table and the two bits of paper were exchanged.

'A thousand pounds, Mrs Farrington-Brown are you absolutely sure?'

'I would have made it double that if I had only seen my husband's face when he knew you had recognised him.' And the three of them laughed like drains. Women – hah.

I suppose that that is all there is that's worth telling about the visit to the Farrington-Browns', except that just as we were about to leave, Mr Farrington-Brown turned up at the front door; clean and neat and tidy as though he had just returned from Gloucester on business. He met us with a little wink as he said hello and was sorry to have missed us.

'Important business meeting, but I know Gwendolyn will have looked after you, Miss Manson.' He spoke to Liz.

'Thank you yes; and she has most generously given me a cheque for my African schools' charity.

'Good, good, pleased to hear it, must look after

the little ones.'

'These two young people have taken a turn around the garden and are most impressed by what they saw, weren't you?' said Aunt E.

And she looked at me with a mischievous twinkle in her eye; how she loves to put me on the spot. As you might expect, George F-B almost jumped out of his skin for the second time that day.

'Oh don't worry,' I said, 'the secrets of your growing techniques are safe with us,' and I gave him a conspiratorial wink.

'Ha ha, no secrets in my garden young man, just plain hard work, not a secret in sight,' he said visibly relaxing.

If only he knew how truly he spoke.

As you can imagine I was a gibbering wreck on the way back to The Willows. I was not looking forward in the least to the first meeting with this rose-grower chappie. I have to say it rather put the kibosh on any major conversation, on my part, in the car. But my aunt was at her best, telling Liz the sort of things that only girls find of interest. And so I was left to brood on this latest turn in my affairs, which of course always seems to make matters worse.

The first person I wanted to see on my return to my aunt's abode was of course Ellingham, to get the low down on the car and this Walter Thomas bod. But fate doesn't work like that does it? The first person, or rather two people I did meet were Danvers what's his name, and Walter the rose grower. They were just strolling around the end of the house as the car rolled up.

'Mi*sh*esh Tol*sh*on; thi*sh* i*sh* Mi*sh*ter Thoma*sh* the ro*sh*e ex*sh*pert.'

No points for guessing who had spoken.

'Mr Thomas, pleased to meet you. So good of you to give up your valuable time to advise me on the redevelopment of the garden,' said my aunt.

'My pleasure Mrs. Tolson, I only hope I will be able to improve on what is, I have to say, a very remarkable garden already,' he said.

Clearly a man who knows his stuff, when it came to impressing ladies of my aunt's ilk, for she beamed at him.

'Thank you, I will arrange for you to stay in the clock room, and you will of course dine with us this evening. But it's remiss of me, I haven't introduced my other guests. This is Miss Manson, she is here for a few days. She runs a Schools for Africa charity and I am introducing her to a few of my friends, in the hope that they might help.'

'Miss Manson, Walter Thomas, pleased to meet you, and make it Walter if you would.' And he took her hand and gave a little bow, like you only see on the stage these days.

'In that case Walter, I'm Elizabeth; but everyone calls me Liz,' and he gave another little stage bow.

'And this, is my nephew Joshua Tolson,' she said with an apology in her voice as one might excuse a cake that hasn't risen properly or a bad mannered mongrel dog. Damned annoying but nothing to be done what?

'Mr Tolson, hello,' he said looking me in the eye.

'Hello, I'm Josh, pleased to meet you, I'm sure my aunt will make you most welcome, it's only nephews who fall beneath her plough,' and I laughed a merry laugh.

'Take no notice of the young gumozzle, he needs a firm hand to keep him in line, ha-ha.' She smiled at

104

him, whilst at the same time giving me a look that said don't get too cocky young man; a thing that only aunts can do. She continued -

'Please excuse us, we all need to freshen up after our journey; we will no doubt meet again over dinner. I will be most interested to hear your preliminary thoughts.'

'Thank you, yes I look forward to it.'

Safely ensconced back in the green room a few moments later, I had that chance to talk to Ellingham.

'I met Walter thingummy at the front door and exchanged pleasantries; I don't think he recognised me.'

'Thomas, sir, the gentleman's surname is Thomas. It is most gratifying that he seems not to know you; if I might suggest a way that will keep the chances of recognition slight sir?'

'You may by all means Ellingham.'

'Well sir, I think that if you were to seek out the gentleman's company rather than shying away from him, he might be less inclined to think you have something to hide or fear sir.'

'You mean I wouldn't be hob-knobbing with him if I were the bloke he suspects I might be, is that it Ellingham?'

'Precisely sir.'

'You think it will work?'

'It will cast a doubt upon his doubts, if you take my meaning sir.'

'Won't get much chance to do it, he'll probably be away on tomorrow evening's train,' I said.

'Perhaps if you were to include Miss Manson in the exercise it might seem more natural.'

'You mean explain all to her?'

'Not necessarily sir, just ask her along and happen

105

to meet the gentleman. He might even be inclined to make a donation sir.'

'You've done it again Ellingham, another pippin straight off the tree. I don't know how you do it.'

'Thank you sir, one tries to give value sir.'

'And gives it by the lorry load, I say by the lorry load.' And I meant it.

'If you are ready sir, I will run you a bath?'

'Yes, that's fine; and whilst you do it I think I'll sit for a while and have a smoke; I was adding it up as I climbed the stairs, it's over five hours since my last cigarette. The human frame is not intended for such ordeals Ellingham.'

'How true that is sir.'

You've perhaps noticed that one of the things I was intent on having out with Ellingham had completely slipped my mind. As you can imagine as well as musing upon the fair Miss Manson my mind wandered on to the events of the day, and when it finally dawned on me that I hadn't tackled the blighter about the car I was about to close the bathroom door.

'Oh, yes, tell me about the car Ellingham, but shout it through the door there's a good chap.'

'I fear that may not be wise sir; raised voices may well be heard in the clock room, and I understand Mr Thomas is already in residence sir.'

This clock room of which there has already been mention is a room identical to the green room but immediately above. It's called the clock room because the workings of the stable yard clock are high up in one corner. As a child I nearly always drew the clock room as my abode when visiting my aunt and uncle; in those days the damned thing still worked and although the ticking

106

was gentle and soothing enough, it was intended to strike the hours. At some point in the past the ensuing chimes had been disabled; but with every hour, at the point when it should have chimed it gave out a loud click, awakening me at regular intervals. As you can imagine the news that this rose grower was in residence there made me wish the clock could somehow miraculously spring back to life.

'I take your point Ellingham, just tell me what colour it is and leave the rest of the sordid details until I'm bathed and dressed,' I said, fearing the worst.

'The vehicle had to be procured at very short notice sir, as I am sure you will understand, and the available vehicles left me with little choice in the matter of colour sir; the vehicle is however, pleasingly finished in two different shades of grey sir.'

'Pleasing to you no doubt Ellingham,' I said and I hope it hurt his feelings.

I always find a soak in a nice warm bath can soothe away not only the physical strains of the day but often the mental ones as well. And this was the case now; a few minutes spent in the company of the aforesaid quacking duck was enough to raise the most flagging of spirits, so when I next spoke to the blackguard, I had become resigned to a grey car for the foreseeable future at least.

'I commend your quick thinking Ellingham, but how on earth did you manage to change the car so quickly?' I asked.

'On realising whom it was I was being requested to collect from the railway station I recognised the possibility of your discovery would be greatly increased if you were to be noted driving a vehicle so, to put it bluntly sir, immediately recognisable...'

107

I cut the fellow short.

'This is old news Ellingham, cut to the chase, what,' I pointed out.

'I was merely setting the scene as I saw it at the time sir, however it occurred to me that whilst assisting you with the changing of the wheel...'

I cut him short again.

'As I recall you simply read the instructions from the bally book Ellingham.'

'As you say sir I was the messenger so to speak, however, they also serve who only stand and wait sir, because I did happen to notice that at the back of the publication your father has seen fit to provide a list of the agents providing sales and service to Tolson cars sir. Noting that there is one in the town of Cheltenham I rang the factory and spoke to Mr Fothergill, you may remember him as the service manager?'

'Yes, Fothergill, nice chap, continue.'

'I found it necessary to perpetrate a little white lie on your behalf, sir; I told Mr Fothergill that you were a little nervous of continuing to use the car after the mishap with the front wheel and could he arrange for the Cheltenham agency to replace the car temporarily, whilst they made the necessary safety checks.'

'Brilliant Ellingham, you are forgiven for telling little white lies, well this one anyway,' I said.

'Thank you sir, I am pleased to say that Mr Fothergill rang me back within a few minutes with the news that all had been arranged and I could pick up a replacement car at eleven fifteen, which whilst very close timing should have allowed me to pick up Mr Thomas at the appointed time. Although in fact I was a little delayed, so was the train, with the combined result that Mr Thomas did not need to wait.

'Fine so far Ellingham, but I see a flaw in your scheme,' I said.

'I trust not sir, what is your concern if I might make so bold as to ask sir?'

'Firstly my aunt saw us arrive in a red car and suddenly it is,' and here I would have said to him with a reproachful eye, 'grey, Ellingham, GREY.'

'To deal firstly with the colour of the car sir there was only one sports two seater in the local agents stock, the other twelve vehicles being various saloon versions in black sir; with regard to your aunt, I think if you were to inform your aunt as early as possible that I have changed your vehicle and why sir.'

'Tell her the same white lie; is that what you mean Ellingham?'

'If you wish to put it in those terms sir.'

'This rose grower fellow; if he should remember the likeness of myself and his bogus photographer, mentions that his chap drove a red car, and then my aunt puts two and two together and comes up with her usual five... sort that one if you can Ellingham.' And I rather think I gave a little nod.

'The eventuality had not slipped my notice sir, and as yet I can see no other answer than the one I gave earlier sir; stout denial, sir.'

'I can't deny that I had a red car, especially if he asks me in front of my aunt.'

'Very true sir. Then perhaps a little subterfuge; if you were to state, should the gentleman ask, that strangely you also had a red car but that the vehicle was only collected on the morning of your visit to The Willows, sir, on approval for the period of your visit; but again the mishap with the tyre had occasioned the change sir. It is far from agreeable to me to have to suggest a solution which is untruthful sir. However I see no alternative at the moment sir.'

'Nor I Ellingham, nor I. Only time will tell what?'

'As you say sir, time will tell. If a better scheme occurs to me before the need to use this one I will of course keep you informed,' he said as I opened the bathroom door.

'Do that Ellingham,' I said and I set about another gasper before dressing for dinner.

Ellingham had suggested seek him out, Walter Thomas that is, as the best way to allay his suspicions if you recall; and at the pre-dinner gathering that's exactly what I did. He was there talking to "Piano Dan" and I went over to them.

'Good evening to you both.' I said and they good-eveninged back. So I continued. 'I hope you don't mind me butting in but I'm dying to know what Mr Thomas thinks to my aunt's gardens; I have to say that I have always found them most charming.'

'On first looking around the gardens, you may remember, I complimented your aunt on their quality; now having taken a more careful look I can see why she has certain reservations,' he said.

'*Sh*e *sh*owed me *sh*ome bushe*sh* that cau*sh*ed her con*sh*ern, *sh*everal day*sh* ago. La*sh*t *Sh*aturday to be pre*shish*e, and thi*sh* i*sh* why,' and here he gave me a little conspiratorial wink, 'I called in Mi*sh*ter Thoma*sh*.' You would wonder why Dan didn't rephrase it in some way, if only to reduce the chances of personal dehydration.

110

'In the morning,' said W.T., 'I will set about making a plan of recovery, and make a water colour sketch of how I see the gardens, for your aunt's approval.'

And I have to say he had begun to look at me more closely as he said this last bit, he continued -

'Forgive me I'm sure I've met you somewhere before?'

'We met at the front door a couple of hours ago,' I quipped.

'I was of course thinking of before that occasion,' he said looking closer still.

'Well yes quite possibly, I get around a bit don't yer know.'

'Your face and voice seem familiar; I remember thinking so when your aunt introduced us this afternoon.'

'Everyone always seems to say that about me; I suppose I must have one of those faces that people think they remember what?' I smiled, though I didn't like the way this was progressing in the least.

'Have you ever been to my nursery?'

'Shouldn't think so, I live in a town flat, no garden you see. Ellingham, that's my man-servant, has a small window-box outside the kitchen window, herbs and things I think, but that's all,' I said.

'I pride myself that I never forget a face. It pays in business if you can greet a customer with their name; it gives a personal touch you see.'

'As I said I'm sure I won't have been a customer.'

'Funny, you ring a bell with the rose nursery in some way or other, no matter it'll come to me, you see if it doesn't.'

Thankfully at this point Liz walked in and I hiked her over.

111

'Hi Liz; Mr Thomas was just telling me about his plans for Aunt E's gardens.'

We all helloed, and Liz started us off again.

'Have you sorted it out already? How clever of you Mr Thomas,' and she beamed at him. And W.T. forgot about me in an instant.

'Well I'm still looking of course but certain ideas are already formulating themselves; but I must put my thoughts before Mrs Tolson for her approval before divulging them generally, I'm sure you understand?'

Pompous ass, it's only a few bally roses not the plans to a new battleship or something, but he was speaking again.

'Enough about roses Miss Manson, tell me about Africa. What is it you do there exactly?'

But at this point the dinner gong sounded and we took our places.

My aunt had rearranged things so as to be able to have Mr Thomas sitting next to her and this put me with Danvers Tideswell on one side and Liz on the other. The Major sat the other side of her again much to his satisfaction. But I guessed he would be a good deal lighter in the pocket by the time she had finished her Schools for Africa bid so I let him monopolise her for the duration of the meal, much to Dorothy's chagrin.

So my conversation was mainly with splashing Dan.

'I'm mo*sh*t grateful to your aunt, thi*sh* few day*sh* here ha*sh sh*et me up no end. I wa*sh* down in the dump*sh* you *sh*ee, per*sh*onal matter*sh* which need not con*sh*ern you, but thi*sh* ha*sh* been a great re*sh*torative.'

'I'm glad, and I'm sure my aunt will be pleased

112

that she has helped, but you speak as though you will be leaving us?' I said.

'Ye*sh* indeed that i*sh sh*o, I have revi*sh*ed my plan*sh*. I will be leaving with Mr Thoma*sh* on the twelve o'clock train on Monday. And I have to *sh*ay that I am mo*sh*t grateful to you al*sh*o Mr Tol*sh*on.'

'Oh, right, grateful to me erm, why would that be?' I asked. After all I'd never met the chap before dinner the previous night.

'Well both you and your man-*sh*ervant of cour*sh*e.'

'Oh, collecting Mr Thomas from the railway station, think nothing of it. One likes to do a fellow house guest a good turn if one can what?'

'That al*sh*o of cour*sh*e, but I wa*sh* meaning the other thing, the thing you don't want your aunt to find out about. Your *sh*ecret i*sh* *sh*afe with me Mi*sh*ter Tol*sh*on,' and he tapped the side of his nose.

'Oh, right ho, thank you,' I said, and he went on talking of various things. I just said yes and no as I thought was appropriate but as you can guess I was wondering like mad what the heck he thought was the secret I didn't want my aunt to know. As I'm sure you can guess I have many things that I would rather my aunt didn't find out about, but nothing that Danvers Tideswell was privy to as far as I knew. But mysteries have a way of solving themselves, and so long as my aunt didn't find out about whatever it was I didn't want her to find out about, then all should be well; and alright by me, if you see what I mean.

Halfway through dinner everyone jumped, causing food, cutlery and in one case a dining chair to go flying. Even though I had been expecting it to happen I was startled by the sudden violence of it; the afternoon had been hot and sultry and as often happens, the evening fell foul to a thunderstorm heralded by a blinding flash of lightening and what seemed to be instantly followed by a room-shaking crash of thunder. This caused everyone at once to be saying "I knew it would thunder" – "There'd be a storm" – "This was on the way", or some such thing though of course no one had mentioned it beforehand. The rain came down in torrents causing those nearest the doors out onto the garden to rush to close them.

I had intended, as you can imagine, to invite Liz to stroll in the gardens, or some such thing, after dinner but this new turn of events looked rather as though it had put the kybosh on that for the evening. I was drastically trying to come up with an acceptable alternative when I became aware that Dan was again speaking.

'I have already men*sh*ioned how grateful I am for your aunt'*sh* kindne*sh*, and would of cour*sh*e like to be able to repay her in *sh*ome way, to offer payment to the dear lady would I feel *sh*ure only give offen*sh*e. I would therefore much value any *sh*ugge*sh*tion you might be able to make to repay her in a way *sh*e would find acc*sh*eptable,' he said, his face had a deep and pensive frown, making him look rather like a grand piano with worry lines on its forehead.

'I'm sure my aunt would be pleased enough to know that the peace and quiet of The Willow has had the necessary effect, but I understand that we all like to return the kindnesses that are extended to us and I will of course give it some thought.'

'I have already made her more than aware how grateful I am for my re*sh*tora*sh*ion to health, yet even a*sh* we *sh*peak I believe an an*sh*wer to my problem ha*sh*

114

occurred to me.' And he now resembled a grand piano in a thoughtful frame of mind.

'That's good; it often happens doesn't it? Put a problem into words and you're half way to solving it, what?' I said.

'That i*sh* of cour*sh*e *sh*o, I wonder would you mind if I gave you an outline of what I propo*sh*e, you might be able to *sh*ugge*sh*t if it would be *sh*uitable?'

'By all means my dear chap; give me the low-down and I'll pass it about the old brain a bit, what?'

'Again I am indebted to you for your kindne*sh*.' He smiled (enough said), 'I think perhap*sh* your aunt will be *sh*ugge*sh*ting that the ladie*sh* withdraw at any moment, perhap*sh* we could *sh*peak then?'

'Yes we'll do that,' I said and I rather think I gave him my impression of a grand piano.

As this chap Tideswell thought, Aunt E. did indeed break up the party shortly afterwards and we, the men that is, were left with the after dinner drinks.

'To continue with our conver*sh*ation of a few minute*sh* ago,' it was Dan speaking again of course, 'a thought ha*sh* occurred to me; your aunt i*sh* kindly helping Mi*sh*s Man*sh*on with her charity work, and I wondered if a dona*sh*ion from me offering my thank*sh* for her kindne*sh* to me, would fit the bill?'

I could see his point, and since it would help Liz I saw only one flaw in the scheme.

'I think that's a splendid idea, but if I might make a suggestion?'

'Ye*sh* of course, plea*sh*e do,'

'Give your cheque to Liz, and simply thank my aunt for making it possible for you to contribute to such a worthy cause. I think in that way whatever amount you decide on can't possibly be linked as your valuation of your stay,' I said.

'*Sh*plendid, *sh*plendid, I am again deeply indebted to you. Your aunt could not po*sh*ibly take offence if the donation is made in that way, yet at the *sh*ame time ac*sh*ept it as a *sh*ign of my gratitude. *Sh*plendid,' he said again, just to rub it in I suppose.

6

Sunday morning opened with Ellingham throwing back the curtains to display a warm sunny day; thankfully the window of the green room looked away from the rising, or rather risen, sun and only gets it second-hand so to speak, lessening the shock of it all.

'A fine morning, if I might make the observation sir?'

'Rain seems to be over, is it Ellingham?'

'Such is indeed the case, the blighting clouds have gone away, and left a new enchanting day sir.'

'I say that's rather good. Your own Ellingham?'

'Yes sir, it seemed to just spring to the lips sir.'

'Well jot it down somewhere, it's too good to lose.'

'You are most kind, however if I might change the subject sir, breakfast is laid and everyone is on the move, so to speak sir.'

If you've been following these jottings in any great detail, you'll probably remember that in her telegram Aunt E. had requested that I not only bring the necessary formal clothing but also outdoor stuff for her walk on the estate. The thought of a stroll in the country with Liz seemed just what the doctor ordered if you get my meaning.

'Is Liz, Miss Manson, up and doing Ellingham?'

'Indeed so sir. I happened upon the young lady and your aunt in the dining room a few moments ago as

117

they served themselves from the buffet breakfast sir. I would not have taken the liberty of awakening you in the normal way sir, as you know, however your aunt requested that I should inform you that she expects you as soon as possible sir.'

'I bet she didn't say exactly that, what?'

'You are most perceptive sir, your aunt was indeed somewhat more forthright in her request; I have merely translated the meaning of her remarks sir.'

'I assume that I am to make myself available for church eh?'

'It is your aunt's intention to attend the morning service. She has I understand been in communication with the Reverend Bowman and requested him to make reference to the young lady's charitable work in Africa sir.'

'You have to say, although Aunt E. might be by far and away the nastiest piece of work since Jack the Ripper, she never misses a trick to get what she want, eh Ellingham?'

'I have always found Mrs Tolson to be strict but fair sir, but as you say she always tends to pursue her goals with a high degree of vigour sir.'

'You intimate that the Rev. Bowman is still in harness in Much Moreham Ellingham?'

'That is correct sir.'

'The chap must be a hundred and forty if he's a day.'

'The gentleman is, as you suggest sir, long past the first flush of youth, and indeed also retirement, but he sees himself as still having worth in the community sir.'

I have no doubt that he was a very worthy chap in his prime, but time has left him forgetful to put it as

118

charitably as possible. The last time I was down at The Willows the chap gave, so I am reliably informed, the same sermon two Sundays on the trot.

'I can't say I'm looking forward to his sermon Ellingham. They can be a bit lengthy, what?'

'If I might make a suggestion sir?'

'Suggest away Ellingham.'

He quickly outlined a plan to get me out of the church whenever I wished. I'm certainly going to miss him.

'Better run me a bath then Ellingham,' I said as I began to haul myself from the comfort of the old sack.

'It is already close to the appointed level, if you care to listen sir, you will no doubt be able to hear the sound sir.'

And the chap was right, the welcoming sound of a well-run bath was indeed in the offing, and he nipped off to attend to the water.

'Right ho, lay me some clothes out; lay out also clothes for the afternoon stroll Ellingham then you may take the rest of the day off. I'll see to myself,' I said.

'You are most kind sir, however I have been asked by Mrs Tolson to assist with the preparation and serving of a picnic tea by the river sir. It is I understand her intention to finish the walk on the long lawn by the edge of the river sir.'

As Ellingham is more than aware, I positively hate picnics. Eating out of doors is for the animals of the field and birds of the air, not civilised human beings.

'Ye gads' – sandwiches and wasps, cold tea and flies, squatted on the grass. The whole being revolts Ellingham.'

'I well understand your feelings but your aunt

119

seems to wish it sir.'

'Hey-ho, little to be done then?' I sighed.

'I fear not sir.'

'You haven't a scheme to extract me from that I suppose Ellingham?'

'I regret not sir.'

'Then take off as much of the day as picnic arrangements will allow, but use the time wisely, thinking how to extract me from the blighted affair.'

'I will indeed give it thought sir.'

I shut the bathroom door, and lowered the body into the inviting liquid. Even if it was to be only a short love affair with the warm and soothing, not forgetting the dear old Q-ing Duck, one can still enjoy it what?

The church service at Much Moreham begins at ten thirty and ends whenever the Rev. R. Bowman rambles to the end of his sermon, and allows the singing of the final hymn. I have it on good authority that there is within the congregation a section who take in with them Red Cross food parcels just in case. The Willows troupe, being among the local bigwigs so to speak, are positioned close to the front. To allow myself to carry out Ellingham's little plan I positioned myself at the end of a pew by the side aisle. Apart from a few words over breakfast I had not, much to my chagrin, been able to talk to Liz. She had been commandeered by the major, and since I didn't want to upset her chances of a hefty donation I left them to it. He had managed to get himself next to her in church whilst I sat next to Dorothy.

'My husband seems much taken with Miss Manson,' she said. 'He talks of little else in fact.'

Very hard to know what to say to something like

that, without upsetting the dear lady.

'I think the major is very interested in the schools thing.'

'Perhaps you're right,' she said.

And before we could talk further the vicar entered and we all stood. We were at the wire, so to speak.

By the time the aforesaid vicar began his sermon, the church was already hot and sticky and beginning to attain that strange country type aroma; a mixture of farmyard whiffs and lavender cherished Sunday best clothes that always seems to attend a country church on these occasions. You will perhaps remember me, when telling you about my photographer chappy, commenting upon the milk of human kindness. Well that was the subject of the Rev. R. Bowman's sermon. It was however covered in somewhat greater depth than I had done. So that twenty minutes into it, as there was little indication that it was anything but just getting into its stride for the long gallop, I decided to put Ellingham's plan into action. Being hot and sticky as I have intimated, there were as I'm sure you can imagine a number of flies of varying species flitting about. Following the plan to the letter I made a sort of gasp, followed by a cough, clasped the handkerchief to my mouth as though I had swallowed one of god's little creatures, and made my escape to fresh air with a series of choking sounds.

It has come to my notice over the years, and perhaps you have noticed it too, the problem with any workable plan of action is that it doesn't take long for it to attain a certain degree of acceptance. It can quickly become the fashion, so to speak. This was indeed the case in point. Even before I had got halfway through the first gasper I was joined by a farmer-type fellow, suffering an

121

equal coughing fit. He gave me a wink and settled himself on one of those graves that look rather as though the coffin has been built of stone and left on the surface, and lit his pipe. Having got himself comfortable and got his pipe going to his satisfaction he nodded towards me.

'Luvly day for it,' he said.

'Swallowed a fly,' I said in a gasping sort of voice.

'Oh aye, only just beat me to it though,' he winked.

'You swallowed one as well eh?'

'Oh aye, swallowed a fly, oh yes, ha, ha. Real convenient, them flies, ha, ha.'

I took it that he must also be swinging the lead.

'I didn't really swallow a fly, just an excuse to get a smoke I suppose,' I confessed.

We were joined, before we could converse further, by a thin sad faced chap who, if he wasn't actually the local undertaker, could certainly have been his stuntman. He had also exited the church mid coughing fit.

'Didn't take you long to cotton on young fella,' he said.

Whilst I was pondering the meaning of this statement, farmer and undertaker were chuckling away merrily. And yet another pair of the Rev. B's male congregation had joined the happy band, each handkerchief to mouth.

'Can't be many ruddy flies left in there now,' remarked the farmer amid suppressed laughter.

It was all a bit beyond me I don't mind admitting. Could Ellingham have suggested his plan to the whole village? But then things took a more sinister turn, and I decided that I had better return to my seat, when a pack of playing cards appeared.

'Rummy or penny-glance?' asked one of the new comers'. As they all made their way behind a building I took to be a small mortuary, in one corner of the churchyard.

I hate to be uncharitable to anyone, especially my trusty manservant as I'm sure you will have guessed by now, but I couldn't help thinking a few black thoughts of the man. After all had I been unwise enough to get myself entangled with the card school, and my aunt, or even worse Liz had found out, my stock in both cases would have equalled the Wall Street crash. But Josh Tolson can improvise with the best of them; on my way back in I found a tap and wet my eyes remembering that the eyes have a tendency to pump water like a village fountain when you've swallowed a winged beastie, I also found a small glass, filled it from the aforesaid tap, and made my way back to the pew, wiping the jolly old eyes and sipping the water. I settled myself back in my place beneath the jaundiced eye of Aunt E.

The proceedings finally dragged to a close and we all filed out past the Rev. Bowman and thanked him for the service. When he got to me he looked me in the eye and said -

'Ah, Mr Tolson, I must apologise for the insect problem within the church. It seems to be getting worse week by week. Strangely it only seems to affect the male members of the congregation, I remember remarking upon it to your Mr Ellingham.'

'You told Ellingham of this?'

'Oh, but yes, the young gentleman was polite enough to make himself known to me and wish me good evening. Friday it must have been, I believe he said he was on this way to collect something from the railway station.'

'That's right he was, but you told him about flies?' I said, completely at a loss to see why.

'We commented upon the warmth of the evening, and I just happened to say that the church had been heavily infested with the pests of late.'

That must have been what put the idea into Ellingham's mind, I thought, a bit like my aunt I suppose; never misses a trick. And I had been on the point of forgiving the blighter. After all, how was he to know he was suggesting a plan already in use by all and sundry. But then I could hardly believe my ears when this man of the cloth dropped a real bombshell.

'I happened to tell him, for he seemed to me to have a young and agile mind and possibly might see why a strange thing was occurring. Although the church has always had a problem with insects in the warm weather, there had, again of late, been a spate of the male members of the congregation accidentally swallowing them. He was at a loss to see why, as I am myself. However, I regret we are holding up these good people. Good day to you Mr Tolson, and God be with you.'

'Er, yes, thank you vicar, good day,' I said.

Why would Ellingham have apparently tried to drop me deeply in the soup, for what reason? The mind was in turmoil, I don't mind admitting. As I stood mulling this latest development over in the old cranium so to speak, my aunt caught up with me and we waited for Liz who was talking to the vicar.

'What was that ridiculous coughing routine, you young gaffoon?' she asked.

'I swallowed one of those beastly flies, Aunt.'

124

'I should have warned you about this, but it did not occur to me until after the service had started. It seems to have become the vogue for the lower elements of the community to leave in droves pretending to have swallowed a fly.'

'But Aunt I did swallow a fly; beastly thing seemed to be the size of a small mongrel and went down fighting and kicking all the way.'

'I will give you the benefit of doubt, since you were the first to leave, and were probably unaware of the general situation. And because you did in fact return, and not go off playing cards or some such similar activity, as I strongly suspect that is what this is all about. But let me warn you of this. If, young man, I find out that this was just a silly prank to get outside to smoke one of those foul cigarettes of yours, you may expect the very forces of darkness to befall you, is that understood?'

'It is understood, but you do me an injustice Aunt; fly-swallowing-coughing-routine, totally genuine,' I said. Fingers crossed behind my back, what?

'Mm,' she said. And said it in that tone of voice which meant she really wanted to say, "Oh, yer?"

You know what they say, *it never rains, but what it pours.* Before I had even begun to get over the fear of Aunt E. getting wind of the truth about the fly episode, something else reared its ugly head. We were strolling our way back to The Willows, in twos and threes, and I happened, not entirely by chance, to be grouped with the rose grower and Dan Tideswell, doing as Ellingham had suggested, you remember. Dan had stopped, bending down to tie a shoelace. We had walked on a few paces before we noticed, but then stopped to wait for him.

'I've got you yer know,' said the rose grower in a

125

half whisper and looking me straight in the eye. 'I know who you are, you're the bogus photographer,' he said tapping the side of his nose.

It's not physically possible to jump a mile, but I bet I made a passable attempt at it. By this time Dan had finished tying his lace and was back with us again. No use denying it, the man was adamant. As I'm sure you can imagine my mind was doing mental loop-the-loops and I took little part in the conversation that followed. Eventually the conversation between this rose man and Dan faltered, and the former turned to me.

'I wonder if I might have a word or two in private, say in the rose garden, about what your aunt would think to a thought that has occurred to me?' the rose grower said in a very pointed sort of way.

How could I possibly refuse when put like that, though as you can imagine I was far from looking forward to the interview and said -

'Oh, yes of course, if I can be of help. My pleasure.'

'The plan*sh* for the garden *sh*till developing then?' asked Dan.

'Yes you could say that, and I think Mr Tolson here could have something interesting to add. I think I could say that, don't you Mr Tolson?'

'If you think so,' I said.

'Oh, but I do, I am in fact sure of it. In fact if you would care to do it now it could save time.'

We were just walking up the drive, and were only a few hundred yards or so from the appointed place. Better get it over with, I suppose.

'Yes I agree, no time like the present,' I said. Though as you can probably imagine, it was really the last thing I wanted.

Dan wished us good day, said he would see us both at lunch, and we were on our own.

'Just what the hell do you think you were doing taking photographs of my roses, or more especially the rose I created for Lord Westcott, without my express permission?' he said now that we were away from prying eyes and ears.

'I'm not sure where to start,' I stumbled.

'I'll bet you don't know where to start, however the beginning and the truth is normally considered adequate.'

'It's rather complicated and involves a certain person, whose name I would not like to divulge,' I said.

'I bet I could give you a list of likely people. Ah, magazine editors and the like?'

'I doubt if the person in question would be on your list, Mr Thomas.'

'Look, I intend to get to the bottom of this, my reputation could hang upon it.'

'I'm sure I've done nothing to cast aspersions, if that's the right word, on your good name, but I can only tell you so much without compromising a young lady.'

'Young lady eh, curiouser and curiouser. I wonder who she might be when she's at home?'

Damn, the word has just slipped out; see what I mean about Jane, blasted, Barrington-Ross. I knew she'd drop me in a pickle over this, but I always was a sucker for the easy life. Much simpler to just say yes than stand the old ground, what?

'Yes it is a young lady, and she would not thank me for involving her name in what is really only a bit of a harmless prank,' I said.

127

He looked at me with a look that could have stripped wallpaper.

'If I tell you what I think, and then you can tell me where I err?' he suggested.

'If you wish to do it that way, be my guest.'

'The only motive I can think of for your conduct is purely monetary. I think someone offered you some huge incentive to get the drop on the official presentation. How's that for starters?' And he stuck his chin out defiantly.

'Missed the mark by a mile old chap. Not a penny changed hands to my advantage, in fact I ended a good deal out of pocket,' I said, 'and anyway the person who wanted the photographs is the very last person you would think of.'

'I can't think of anyone who would want photographs of a rose who didn't expect to make a financial gain from them. Come come, young man you're trying to pull the wool over my eyes.'

'If you were to think hard, I'm sure you would find that there is a person who is positively itching to see the blasted thing,' I said.

You're having me on Mr Tolson, and I can't think why you should be doing so. I was most annoyed at the time, and I'm still very hot under the collar about the episode. I was on the point of involving the police, I don't mind telling you, though no doubt they would feel they have bigger fish to fry. So the matter is one which still rankles deeply with me and I am still considering all my options.'

'Please don't be too worried by the event. I assure you that no harm was intended, and in any case the photographs, even though I say it myself are of excellent quality, did not fit the bill with the person concerned.'

'Well I can't think who, but if you assure me that what you did will in no way affect the outcome of the presentation I will say no more for the present. I would not after all wish to cause any unpleasantness under your aunt's roof. Though I have to say I am still rather suspicious of your motives. I've got my eye on you young man, and don't you forget it.'

'Other than a harmless prank which has somehow backfired, I am I assure you, whiter than white.'

'Are you in some way sworn to secrecy with regard to the matter, Mr Tolson?'

'Something like that, yes.'

'I must admit, it's a damned mystery to me, why you should want to do me harm in one direction whilst at the same time doing me a great service in another,' he said.

I was at a total loss to follow what the chap was on about.

'Oh, I'm sorry, I didn't quite catch that,' I said.

'Mr Tideswell has already made me aware that there are certain matters which you are at great pains to ensure your aunt does not find out about, and with regard to that, I have to say that though I am greatly in your debt my lips are sealed only as long as it does not adversely affect me. Do I make myself clear, Mr Tolson?'

Damned if he did, he was talking in riddles, and not the only one. Dan had intimated something similar if you remember, beyond me to understand, so I suppose I just nodded. We headed back to the house in silence to go our respective ways to get ready for lunch.

Arriving back in the green room, I wasted no time in making my feelings felt.

129

'I've a bone to pick with you Ellingham,' I said as I entered.

'Indeed sir, have I in some way failed to give satisfaction?'

'I don't know, but certain things suggest that that could be the case,' I said, and I gave him my version of the wallpaper-stripping look.

'I am sorry to hear that sir. If you were to point out your worries with regard to my conduct, I might possibly be able to suggest a solution which might allay your fears, sir.'

'You mean, say why?' I said unsure whether I had grasped his meaning.

'Just so, sir.'

'Okay, then. Why did you suggest that ridiculous fly-swallowing routine, knowing full well that it was already being used by practically the entire male population of Much Moreham?'

'I had become aware of the situation on meeting the vicar...'

I stopped the man in his tracks.

'All of this is already known to me Ellingham, and I have to say it is what incriminates you. Knowing that my aunt must also be very aware of these goings-on you continued to suggest this as a means of escaping the sermon. I find it hard to think other than the worst of you Ellingham.'

'It seemed to me on putting forward the course of action that one of two things might occur, both of which I was sure you would be more than capable of carrying off sir. Either you would be the first person to effect their escape, in which case you could claim innocence from the remainder of the perpetrators. Or, if someone else had already made their escape, you would wait a suitable length of time before following, or perhaps abandon the idea, especially if you saw that it was somewhat common practice.'

'There is of course a third possibility.'

'Indeed, sir?'

'Indeed Ellingham, the possibility of dropping myself deeply in the mire with Aunt Evangeline if she were to suspect, as such was nearly the case, that I was swinging the lead. There is an even deeper, and more sinister quality to the massed fly-swallower's of Much Moreham; were you aware that the gathering degenerates into a card school, of which incidentally my aunt suspects?' And I looked the wallpaper-stripping look again.

'The Rev. Bowman did not inform me that there was a card game involved sir; perhaps he was not aware that such is the case. But with regard to the other matter, I discounted the possibility of you being found out. I was sure your ready intellect would be more than a match should the occasion arise sir.'

Shear buttering up of course but I let it go for the moment.

'Well thankfully, such was indeed the case. On recognising what was going to happen I went back into the church, rubbing the eyes and sipping water, the prompt action of which allowed me to get the drop on my aunt. Though she was, and still is, deeply suspicious.'

'As I suspected sir, you were more than a match for the situation.'

'Perhaps it has escaped your memory Ellingham, but I wish to continue to gain ground with Miss Manson; had I got myself entangled with the aforesaid card school and been found out, it could only have had an extremely handicapping effect what?'

'I regret you are indeed correct, not, as I said, being aware of the ulterior motive of the escape, that possible eventuality had not occurred to me. Please accept my apologies sir.'

I spent much of the country ramble in the company of Liz, and I have to say that I think my stock in that direction was just about as far from the Wall Street crash situation as it could get. Before we started there was what amounted to a pep talk from Aunt E.

'It is a lovely afternoon, ideal in fact to enjoy the beauties of The Willows estate. I plan to take you through two of the farms that, although they are now rented out to tenant farmers, are still Willows land. I have not planned, and do not wish, that this turn into a route march. Please,' and here she looked at me, 'take your time to enjoy what there is around you; stop for a moment, as you will to marvel at the wonders of nature. We will be covering about four and a half miles of fairly easy walking. Starting off through the wood you see on the side of the hill in front of you, this is likely to be a little muddy still, following last nights rain; I see you are all wearing suitable footwear. Jenkins, one of the farm hands, has, I understand placed little wooden markers along my proposed route, so if you get separated simply follow the markers, any questions?'

'I*sh* there anything you feel we should e*sh*pe*sh*ially look out for that i*sh* of out*sh*tanding intere*sh*t or beauty?' asked Dan.

'There is one particularly picturesque view of The Willows, I have seen it many times, of course, but it still

132

inspires me to reflect how lucky I am to be privileged to have the status in life to call it my home. You will not miss it I assure you. You will find me waiting for you at that point, should you have fallen behind.'

'Aunt,' I said.

'Yes Josh.'

'Have you included the wild flower dell over the other side of the hill? I would go there as a boy; I'd like to show it to Liz.'

'I haven't but the path is clear enough to find. Show Liz by all means, in fact I think it's a good suggestion. We will all detour the short way to see it. I will inform the staff to expect us at the picnic about forty minutes later.'

We had chatted cheerfully of this and that, and on the odd occasions that I happened to meet my aunt's eye, stock seemed to be gaining ground in that direction also. And when we had reached the viewpoint of which my aunt had mentioned you could see what she meant; at some point in time the trees had been thinned leaving just enough of a clearing to allow a view of the Willows from a sort of small cliff or escarpment. The effect created by the mid afternoon sun was stunning.

'It's beautiful, so romantic,' said Liz, and she grasped my hand.

All I could do was nod, the moment was one to remember. A stunning view, a stunning girl, I am seldom lost for words, ask anyone at the Boater, but I just stood there, emotionally intoxicated I suppose Ellingham would have said.

Why is it that time has the capacity, I think that's what I mean, to drastically reduce the size of things we remember from childhood? The wild flower dell of which

I spoke is a case in point; in my minds eye I remember it as a deep gorge covering about an acre and a half. When we stood looking at it, it seemed about the size of a large dinner plate but Liz, never having seen it before was bowled over so it had the desired effect. Things just seemed to be all sweetness and light, so to speak; the walk was proving to be a good stepping stone in our relationship and I had made up my mind to ask the question to which there is only one satisfactory answer, before too long. But just when things seemed to be at their rosiest, it was time for the dreaded picnic.

Why women love eating in the great outdoors eludes me. They all seem to positively dote upon it; it holds for them perhaps something of a spiritual quality, a getting back to nature maybe. It holds too much nature for my liking as I have already stated. I can't pick up a bit of pork pie or a ham sandwich without subjecting it to the closest scrutiny to ensure nothing of nature is already consuming it; quite spoils the party if you know what I mean.

'You're not eating much,' Liz smiled.

'Not all that hungry I suppose,' I replied.

'I'm positively starving after that walk,' she said scooping something revolting from her teacup with a spoon.

'Not much for eating out of doors.'

'Not much choice in Africa. You get into the shade of course but almost every meal is taken out in the fresh air.'

'Really?' I made it sound like a question, though it was really more of a revelation.

'Oh yes, we take evening meals indoors. It tends to drop suddenly chilly in the evenings, but daytime eating

134

is normally done outside.'

This new state of affairs needed thinking about. Not my cup of tea as you know, but one has to be prepared to make sacrifices in the name of love what?'

'Josh?'

'Yes.'

'Why do you keep looking at me like a pet dog expecting a pat?'

'Eh, er, um, do I?'

'Yes, a sort of adoring simper and your mouth sometimes drops open.'

'I'll stop doing it if you'll agree to stop smiling at me in that amazing way of yours,' I said.

'Am I the cause?'

'Can't think of another.'

'Do you really want me to stop smiling at you? I like you, you're ever so nice, and you make me laugh.'

And at that point she leaned her head on my shoulder, and something squidgy squirted out of the sandwich I had been holding all down my shirtfront.

'Oh, I say, do you really mean it, I mean do I make you laugh?'

'I wouldn't say it if I didn't.'

As you can imagine I damned near popped the question there and then in front of everyone.

At the end of the long lawn, down by the river there stands a magnificent old willow tree, one of about thirty or so scattered along the river and around the grounds; no doubt the reason for the name of the place. Beneath it at some time in the distant past someone had built one of those seats that go around the trunk. Don't ask me what they're called I just don't know. But when the picnic was almost over, the weather gods decided that

135

we were desperately in need of another jolly good downpour. To a man we all made for that circular seat, deciding to risk the possibility of a lightning strike hitting the tree since there seemed to be no thunder in the air. By careful and indeed skilful positioning in the mad dash I ended up with Liz on one side of me, but alas, Aunt E. on the other. This, as I'm sure you will appreciate had a tendency to somewhat limit the topics of conversation, and so popping the question was er, out of the question if you see what I mean.

'The major seems very interested in your charity work?' I said as an opener.

'Yes, he's a real old charmer. Reminds me of Mumbo, always sort of flirting with his eyes.'

Mumbo again! I was taking a real dislike to the chap. If Ellingham would have to go when we got married, you could rest assured Mumbo's days were also numbered and no mistake.

'Is the major likely to be supportive of your schools, do you think?'

'He already has. I can't give you the details of course, but he has been very generous. At this rate it might be possible for me to return to my work much sooner than I had anticipated.'

'Oh, er, that is good news,' I said, 'not that I want you to go you understand, I'm just pleased for you.'

At this point, Aunt E. gave me a jab in the ribs with her elbow that had me rubbing the bruise for days. So she had marriage in sight for me. Well let her eat cake, I was there before her by a long chalk, and I'll pop the question in my own good time.

'I would love you to come out to see my work, I find it a very satisfying job, especially since my father was the person who set it all in motion.'

I said I'd like that and perhaps it might be arranged, and more was said along these lines, my aunt swelling with approval all the time.

As quickly as it started the rain stopped and we all trooped back to the house leaving the staff to clear up the debris. My aunt led us all into the drawing room and ordered tea. Mr Thomas had not been with us on the walk, a thing that, as you can imagine, I was quite happy about, and the reason for this was now quite clear for all to see. Sitting in the middle of the room, on a battered old easel probably borrowed from the playroom, sat a watercolour painting depicting the rose garden as he envisaged it, and as neat a piece of work as anything I've seen.

'This, as you can see Mrs Tolson is my suggestion for the redesign of the rose garden. If you care to look over on the table you will see a birds-eye view of the same thing,' he said.

'Why Mr Thomas, I had no idea you were an accomplished artist too?' my aunt said.

'Thank you Mrs Tolson. I get a degree of enjoyment in painting but I normally only have the time to use it to help people get a feel for how I see their finished garden, in my mind's eye, so to speak.'

'Yes indeed, may I ask if I might be allowed to keep it? I would love to see it framed, and hanging in the dining room.'

'Yes dear lady, it is yours of course. The idea is in my head and needs no memory jogger.'

All was sweetness and light, as you will no doubt have noticed. But into each life a little rain must fall, as Ellingham had earlier pointed out, and at this point in walked Uncle Josh, who had also been missing from the walk. You might remember that he was far from happy with the idea of Dan upsetting his beloved gardens, but add to this the new intruder and dear old Uncle Josh blew a fuse.

'Evangeline, I have made my wishes known on a number of occasions, I do not wish the rose garden to be altered. When I, we, bought the house it was if you remember the feature that we both fell in love with. I will not, I repeat, will NOT, see it destroyed. And just who invited this chap, whoever he is, to poke his nose into our affairs?'

'Please don't shout dear, I invited Mr Thomas, who incidentally is a rose grower of some note, at the suggestion of Mr Tideswell,' replied my aunt, for once on the back-foot.

The rose man had been standing in front of the painting open mouthed at the goings-on, but found his voice at this point.

'I was invited here by Mr Tidewell it's true, but I understand that he made it at the suggestion of your nephew here,' he said, pointing at me as though the room were full of nephews and the situation was in need of clarification.

Yet another carpet was subjected to the Tolson tea embalming ceremony, as I added another couple of inches or so to the Tolson jump-the-mile record attempt.

I have to say that I have always considered that my uncle sees me in a favourable light; he's not the practical type either and so he understands me well enough.

'Is this true?' asked my uncle, looking at me as if I had stabbed him in the back.

Before I could recover from the shock of what had been said, Dan chipped in.

'If I might put the record *sh*traight I did indeed *sh*uggest Mi*sh*ter Thoma*sh* to Mi*sh*i*sh* Tol*sh*on. But although the original *sh*uge*sh*tion came perhap*sh* from your nephew, it was actually relayed to me by hi*sh* man*sh*ervant Mi*sh*ter Ellingham.'

More tea – the same carpet this time. It's often the way, dependent upon point of view, that what one person sees as a stab in the back, another sees as a kind gesture. And so it was now. The sudden revelation affected three people each with their own particular reaction to it. Whilst my uncle was looking at me as though I had just put an indelible blot on the families good name, my aunt was smiling upon me, the little nod of approval she gave said I was still gaining in stock all the time for bringing this blasted man to her attention I was once again thinking less generous thoughts of this blighter Ellingham.

'I can only say that I acted in what I thought was for the best,' I said, putting a brave face on my confusion. 'I thought that if the rose garden, which I have to say I love as deeply as you uncle, has to be remodelled who better to do it than someone as eminent in the rose world as Mr Thomas, whom I have been acquainted with on a previous occasion.' Not bad for stand-up thinking what?

'Humph. Can't see why it has to be remodelled, nothing wrong with it,' said Uncle J.

'I have to differ Mr Tolson, many of the bushes are showing signs of disease and the only remedy is to replace them, and that is not a simple task,' said W. Thomas.

'Take one out, shove in another one, simple I'd

say, no need to remodel anything.'

'I would not advise simply replacing a new rose bush where an old one has been; it is unlikely to do well, especially if there is the suggestion of disease.

'Is that right? Are you telling me that to do well a new rose needs fresh soil? If so is there a way to keep the garden original?' asked Uncle Josh.

'The only real way to do that is to remove all of the old soil, to a depth of perhaps two feet, and replace it with new. At a rough estimate about two-hundred and fifty tons.'

'Is it really that bad? It's not as pretty as when we first moved in, but I thought a good prune would sort it out?'

'You are not as pretty as when we first moved in my darling,' my aunt said, 'and I doubt if a good prune would sort *you* out.'

'I'm afraid that the existing roses are on a downward slope. They will become less productive each year, and the disease will increase. Now is the time to do something, and this is my suggestion,' and he turned to the watercolour.

'Well let's see what you've got to show for yourself then, damn it,' said Uncle J. turning to the rose grower's painting.

'You wriggled out of that one nicely, young fella.' It was the major who spoke.

'My uncle's not too happy about it. Between you and me, I knew nothing about the damned chap coming here,' I said. 'In fact I would have preferred for several reasons that he hadn't.'

'I wonder why they thought it was you who had suggested him, then?'

140

'I'm blowed if I know, I'm the last person to suggest the man for reasons I can't go into.'

'Looks like that chap of yours, Hetherington or whatever his name is, is in it somewhere I shouldn't wonder, eh.'

'The name's Ellingham, and he has a good bit of explaining to do, I can tell you.'

I hunted the blasted man high and low but he seemed to be erased from the face of the earth, or at least the bit of it that was within my sphere. I had several things I wanted to question him about, all of which seemed to be instances of him not exactly working in my best interest. But they would all have to wait until it was time to hit the bed linen. But that was not how it was to turn out.

In the meantime, dinner was taken at the usual time, and I again had the pleasure of sitting with Liz. After dinner we walked to the village. The evening showed no sign of the earlier downpour, and with all the walking and talking it was pleasant but thirsty work. And so we gave our custom to the "Goose & Gander" on the main road. It's one of those country pubs that also let a room or two to passing trade. It smells a bit of spilt beer and *St. Bruno* but is the gathering place for the whole community. Rich and poor alike rub shoulders and it's first names all round. The landlord has a laugh like thunder in a barrel, if you know what I mean, and that's not where the resemblance ends. He is big and round and jolly; John Rowlands by name, Rolly is his more normal title.

'Good evening, Mr Tolson isn't it, good evening miss, what will it be?'

'Good evening, nothing wrong with the old

141

memory then Rolly,' I said, and I turned to Liz. 'What do you fancy?'

'Oh, something cool and long – er – I know, I'll have a pint of bitter shandy,' she said.

First time I'd ever heard of a lady drinking pints of anything. But I have to say the idea seemed sound and I ordered one for myself as well.

'Let's go out and sit in the garden,' said Liz.

'Oh, yes okay.'

The garden is to the rear of the pub and reached down a passageway that desperately needed a coat of paint, but then always has, past several doors, one of them carrying the legend, *private*, another *cellar*, and finally out into the fresh air of a summer evening. Four tables with benches were strewn around a largish lawn, cottage garden flowers bordered the grass and the gentle breeze wafted their scent upon the scene. Bees buzzed from flower to flower in that lazy yet industrious way that bees will, completing an idyllic scene. Although we were on our own, one of the tables held three empty glasses proving others, now thankfully littering some other scene, had had a similar idea.

7

As it turned out we were not to be alone in the garden. Toby, the landlord's Jack Russell had followed us out and came to say hello as we sat down. He quickly accepted that a pat on the head and a tickled chin was the extent of what was available and went off merrily sniffing at this and that, hither and yon as dogs will.

'So, how's the total coming along?' I asked, trying to judge how long Liz would be over here.

'I've still a long way to go yet, but I'm fairly confident that I'll reach my target.'

'That's really great. When I get back home I'll put you in touch with my father's business associates, see what that will bring.'

'Thanks, but look, enough about me, tell me about Joshua Tolson.'

'Me or my uncle?'

'You, silly, tell me about you, what do you do for a living, that sort of thing?'

Why do girls have this constant urge to expect a chap to earn a living? Anyway before I could frame an adequate reply things took a turn in an unexpected direction.

Toby, right from being a pup had developed a liking for spilt beer, he sees it I suppose as his way of earning his upkeep by saving Rolly the job of mopping the floor too often. As you can probably imagine in a busy little pub like the Goose, there is always an adequate supply of the stuff, so he would seldom feel redundant and is always in a mellow frame of mind. A goodish amount of the stuff had been spilled on the table with the empty glasses, and it didn't take long for Toby to locate it, seeing this as a further opportunity to carry out his life's work he had jumped up on the form and then the table. The beer had also caught the attention of the local wasp community, and they too were busy at the edges clearing up. A distinct clash of personalities ensued; Toby is one of those philosophical drinkers, taking the world as he finds it, happy to share a drop or two of spilt beer with whoever comes along. The wasps on the other hand were of the breed that, having taken a drop of the landlord's best on-board, were ready and willing to fight the world and all comers. This being the case they let Toby have it with both barrels. The first sting had him yelp with surprise, and I suppose that was what alerted us to the scene in the first place. The second and third decided him to exit forthwith, and clearly a dog of action, he didn't hang about giving it further consideration. Remembering me, no doubt as a friend in what was clearly becoming a distinctly unfriendly world, he made a bee line, or I suppose in this case a wasp line, to yours truly, jumping on my lap and as near as damn it having the remaining two thirds of my drink to deal with as well. I would have had no problem being used as a safe place in his life's adversities had the wasps stayed put, but the fight was on them and they intended to deal with this aggressor as they saw fit. It seemed that they now also saw me as the enemy's ally, I only seem to remember three or maybe four wasps dealing with the spilt beer, but now every wasp in Gloucestershire saw me as public enemy number one. At this point in the events, three things were happening in juxtaposition. Liz had leapt up and was making for another table, and I have to say love teetered on a knife-edge for a while; the wasps began to press home their attack and I received three stings within a few seconds. Toby recognising that I was not quite the safe haven that he had at first envisaged, dropped to the ground, ran through the legs of the table and was last seen heading for the pub passageway at a great rate of knots. But it turned out to be Liz to the rescue after all. She had by this time poured the remaining contents of her glass over the other table, the effect was magical. The third and fourth attack squadron did a nifty turn nor-nor-east and headed for the liquid feast, causing squadrons one and two to abandon the attack and go off in close pursuit.

After that everything is a complete blank as they say, until just after midnight. I awoke aware that I was in a strange bed, a hospital bed. It appears that after the wasps had left off, I became a bit disorientated, though how they could tell this I don't know. Liz spotted it, jungle training I suppose and had the landlord phone the local hospital. All of this of course I learned later, but the thing that awakened me was someone taking my pulse. In every account of this sort of thing I've ever read, the awakening process is done by a pretty young nurse. No such luck in my case. My nurse was fifty if she was a day, the weight of two pretty young nurses rolled into one, and a face that could sink Helen of Troy's thousand ships in harbour. Her face I suppose was not ugly, but her expression was, and her first words to me were just as ugly.

'Oh, you're awake are you?'
One can't deny these things, so I said.
'Why am I here? What happened?'

'Multiple wasp stings, you passed out. You're very lucky the young lady with you acted as quickly as she did. But it means you're cluttering up my ward, for which I had other plans.'

'Sorry, I had no intention of being stung. It sort of just happened what?' I said and became aware of a dull thudding, alternating with someone clashing cymbals in the old grey matter that made me feel like a well wrung out flannel.

'Were you aware you are allergic to wasp stings? Because if so you were most unwise to allow yourself to be stung, and to allow yourself to be stung five times was sheer madness.'

It might seem strange to her in her professional capacity, but I think it's unwise and indeed madness to allow myself to be stung by wasps even once, allergic reaction or not. But since her attitude was such that she could have understudied for one of that German chappie's henchmen, Hitler, is it? I merely said I wasn't aware.

'Um, well the swelling on your arm seems to be cooler now and your pulse is almost back to normal. I expect we will be releasing you after the doctor has seen you in the morning. In the mean time get some sleep.'

'I'm thirsty and I need the lavatory,' I said.

'The lavatory is at the end of the ward, please wash your hands afterwards, and there is water on the table at the side of you.' She turned and was gone.

Have you ever had a really good skin-full; the sort where you just know you'll pass out. Well that's how I felt on the way to the aforementioned facility. My head was buzzing and the jolly old vision was twisting this way and that. Not only that but this damned nurse had not been strictly honest with me. She had failed to tell me that

146

whilst asleep, they had swapped the old legs around.

I must have slept pretty well because I was awakened by a different nurse, not perhaps beautiful or even pretty, but cheerful. Clearly a nurse at the start of a shift, an altogether more amiable nurse.

'Wakey-wakey – Doctor will be here to see you in five minutes. Feeling better now Mr Tolson?'

'Yes thank you nurse, sorry to be all this bother what?'

'Come on sit up, have a drink of water, and tell me what happened,' she said.

I recounted all that I could remember.

'Well the young lady that was with you may possibly have saved your life. How did she know what to do?'

'I don't know for sure, but she lives out in Africa. She runs a sort of schools charity thing out there, I suppose she's seen it all before what?'

'Oh, is that the young lady who was in all the newspapers recently, Liz Manson?' she asked and a puzzled far away look came into her eyes.

'Yes, do you know her?'

'I'm not sure, her face seems familiar, but the name is wrong. The girl I knew was Phylis Hargreaves and she's definitely never been to Africa, that I'm sure of.'

'No, definitely Liz Manson, know her cousin.'

'Oh well, just a likeness I suppose.'

'Did your paper have a picture?'

'Yes, didn't yours?'

'No, damned cheap rag, I'll buy a different one in future, see if I don't.'

The doctor came, asked me how I felt and advised me to rest for a couple of days, but said I could go home if someone could collect me.

'If my chap brings the car here, will I be okay to drive?' I asked.

'I'd leave it until tomorrow. Twenty-four hours would be my advice. You'll probably still feel a bit woozy after the stuff we've given you, so no, don't drive.' He smiled and was off on his rounds. The nurse had been sort of hovering in the background, attending to the other patients. She now reappeared and told me to get up and dress as she pulled a screen around the bed.

'Will you be all right or would you like me to help you?' she asked.

'I'm fine, thanks, you couldn't do me a favour though could you?'

'I'll do my best, what is it?'

'Would you phone The Willows, I'm staying there you see, to ask them to arrange collection?'

'I would do so willingly but there's no need. A Mr Ellingham telephoned a half hour or so ago, asking about you. I told him I expected you to be able to leave after the doctor had seen you.'

'Good old Ellingham.'

'He said he was your "gentleman" or something, what did he mean?'

'Manservant I suppose. He likes to think of himself as "a gentleman's gentleman." More refined, he thinks. For me he can call himself what he likes, I just don't know what I'd do without the blighter.'

'So is that a sort of butler then?' she asked.

'Well, yes, but much more. Butler, housekeeper, secretary, even head chef, Ellingham does the lot. He looks after me in every way.'

'I see,' she said, and sort of giggled, pulled the

148

screen the rest of the way and was gone.

By the time I had washed, dressed and collected my things and put them in the brown paper bag that I assumed was for that purpose, the nurse was back again.

'Your gentleman is waiting for you at the front desk. Will you be all right with the stairs, or would you like the lift?'

'I'll try the stairs, I still feel a bit shakey, but I think I'll manage thanks.'

'I'll come with you then to give you a hand. Though I won't do all the other things you might expect of Mr Ellingham.' she said and giggled again.

And this time I had it, I saw what she was hinting at.

'Oh, I say, nothing improper, just the jolly old domestic chores what?'

'Sorry sir, I was just pulling your leg.' She smiled a sweet innocent smile.

Ellingham was indeed at the front desk, his black hair slicked down and parted in the middle, looking the picture of health. Why does that always get up your nose so, when you're under the weather yourself?

'Good morning sir, I was most alarmed to hear of your misfortune, I trust you are feeling a little better sir?'

'Not exactly fighting fit, but a little better thank you Ellingham,' I said, and continued, 'and thank you nurse I'll be fine now.'

'And thank you sir,' and she giggled and gave a little curtsy. Damned cheek.

'Your nurse seems very cheerful, if a little above herself sir.'

'Yes she's cheeky but nice, I wouldn't mind spending a few days under her, what.' An innocent

149

enough remark I had thought.

'Indeed sir?' And the blighter allowed an eyebrow to flicker, just that bit.

'Looking after me medically I meant.'

'Just as you say sir.'

By this time we were at the car and I put my brown paper bag in that bit behind the seats on a two-seater.

'Strange thing though Ellingham.'

'Indeed sir? – do you feel able to drive sir?'

'Doctor said better not. Yes Ellingham that nurse thought she knew Liz, Miss Manson.'

'Not impossible sir, they are after all of much the same age.'

'That's so Ellingham, that's so, but she thought she knew her as Phylis something or other. Harmison I think she said. Saw her picture in the paper.'

'Most interesting sir. I took the liberty of placing a travel blanket on your seat sir, thinking you might feel the cold. I fear the morning chill is still in the air.'

'You think of everything Ellingham, how ever will I manage without you?'

'You are most kind sir.'

And we were off, though I did think the chap let the clutch in a bit too fiercely, gave me quite a jolt. I knew of course that I had much to ask, no, confront the blighter with, but in my lowered state I couldn't for the life of me think what, so I knew it would have to wait until I was back in the land of the living, as the saying goes.

A bit under a quarter of an hour we were back under the roof of The Willows. It was Monday morning now of course, and the house had taken on its weekday identity. Uncle Josh made most of his pile from the

Tolson Cars shares he owns. But even in these difficult times he is rather good at playing the market, and is heavily involved with many other shares. For this purpose he was seated in one of the comfy chairs in the library looking at the financial pages of several newspapers. I knew better that to interrupt him when his nose is in the paper, and so I moved on trying to judge where my aunt would be, and equally, trying to avoid her. In my still groggy state I eventually found a nice quiet place, on a wooden two-seat bench in a known suntrap by some sort of flowering bushes, seated myself, and prepared to die. I was just nodding off when I was discovered by my aunt.

'Ah, there you are Joshua. You don't look at all well. Would you not feel better in bed?'

'I do feel a bit under the weather, but I was enjoying letting the sun and the peace and heavenly scents of your lovely gardens drift over me,' I said, knowing that this would be the right stuff to give an aunt.

'You know, sometimes I underestimate you Joshua. I treat you harshly and quite wrongly, see only in you the infernal pest that you undoubtedly are. For instance I had no idea that you had been instrumental in introducing me to Mr Thomas. His expertise and knowledge on the subject of roses has even managed to win your uncle over. I am most grateful to you, and in due course an aunt's thanks will see no bounds.' And she smiled a smile I have rarely received from Aunt E.

I didn't of course say that I had no idea that I had introduced the rose grower to her, but it did make me remember one of the things I needed to talk to the blasted Ellingham about.

'Dearest Aunt, I know that you always have my best interests at heart, like introducing me to Miss

151

Manson, a young lady whom I have to say I much admire.'

'I can see that you like her. She is most charming and she would make a wonderful life-partner for you. Her serious good sense would more than offset your often frivolous nature.'

And here she smiled again and patted my good arm, then continued -

'Since your poor mother died, leaving you without the advantage of a mother's good sense, I have seen it as my duty to make your life hell, in your interest of course. It would please me greatly to see you married to such a young lady. How would you see those prospects?' she asked and smiled again, making about a decades worth of smiles in less than two minutes.

'I intend, dearest Aunt, to ask the young lady the sixty-four thousand dollar question as soon as I feel the time is ripe,' I replied.

'You are aware that she is preparing to leave at this very moment?'

'I didn't know that, but we have already made arrangements to keep in touch.'

'Splendid, I will go and tell her that I have found you. I know she was looking for you, to say goodbye,' and she added a fourth smile to the bunch.

There was no way I was feeling up to the long slog home just yet. The few miles from the hospital had taken its toll. I intended to cadge another day or so under my aunt's roof if she felt she could put up with me the extra bit. As it happened the person who found me first was not Liz, but Ellingham. I had just drifted off into a fitful doze in which I saw wasps as big as crows all hovering for the attack, so I wasn't too displeased when

Ellingham introduced himself with a cough.

'Excuse me sir.'

'Ellingham?'

'I was wondering sir, perhaps it would be wise to leave returning home until you feel more yourself sir?'

'You judge correctly, I had come to that conclusion myself. I intend to ask my aunt, when next I see her, if I might extend my stay'

'Very wise sir. Changing the subject, Miss Manson is intending to leave on the eleven o'clock train this morning sir, would you, oh I was about to say, would you like me to tell her you are here, but I have just seen the young lady walking in this direction sir.

'Yes, my aunt has informed her of my whereabouts,' I said, 'so make yourself scarce for a few minutes, there's a good chap. But don't do a disappearing act, I have much to say to you.'

'Certainly sir.' He nodded and went off towards the river.

I bucked myself up as much as I thought fit, remembering that nothing interests a woman more than someone to nurse. And with this in mind was putting on the brave soldier face, if you know what I mean, by the time she arrived at my bench.

'Oh, Josh, you don't look at all well,' she said perching on the bench and turning toward me. 'I had intended being at the door when you arrived back but I have to be away in the next few minutes and needed to pack. But I couldn't leave without saying goodbye,' she said.

'Thanks for saving my life by the way, it happens to be something I'm rather fond of. Do you really have to leave? Is it really so important? I was hoping you might see fit to look after the wounded soldier for another day or so, or even just sit here and hold my hand. Yes, that would do nicely.'

'Nothing would make me happier that sitting in the sun holding your hand, but yes it is very important. I start a tour of meetings talking about my little charity this evening in Stratford upon Avon. So I must be on my way.'

'If I'm up to it by then, is it all right if I get Ellingham to run me over to see you knock 'em in the aisles, as the saying goes?'

'Oh, that would be lovely, yes if you're better, please come. But only if you really do feel up to it, promise?'

'Yes, I promise, but how are you getting to the station?'

'I was rather hoping your aunt would make the car available to me.'

'No need, I will get Ellingham to run you there. He's down there at the side of the river, I'll give him a yell.'

'Can I leave that to you to arrange? There are still a few things I need to pack,' she said, feeling in her handbag. 'This is a list of the places I'm going to be giving talks, so if you can't make the Stratford one perhaps one of the others?' And she bent across to me put a hand gently on my neck and kissed my cheek.

'Oh. Thanks. Yes. I'll do that.

Clearly she believed in the old theatrical saying always leave 'em wanting more, for with that she turned and headed for the house. I turned to watch her go and halfway she turned and gave a little wave. I waved back in a suitably enfeebled way, then turned to signal to

Ellingham that I wished him to present himself on parade, to find that he was already half way back; the man must have about eight or ten more senses than the rest of us.

'You wished to speak to me further sir?'

'Indeed so Ellingham. Firstly, I wish you to run Miss Manson to the railway station, she leaves on the eleven o'clock train,' I said.

'Certainly, sir; however I will need to be about that without too much delay. I fear that that time is already rapidly approaching sir.'

'Before you go, secondly: it has come to my attention that it was you who put the idea of inviting this rose chappie into the mind of Danvers Tideswell, is that not so Ellingham?' And I turned a withering eye upon him, or as near a withering eye as I could manage in my weakened condition.

'That was indeed the case sir. I thought it a wise move in the circumstances.'

'Oh you did eh? Would you like to enlighten me, as to what circumstances could possibly arise that would make you consider it a wise move to drop me deeply into the cream of chicken and mushroom?'

'My motives were as the driven snow, sir. But since it would need a rather lengthy explanation I fear it will have to wait if I am to give Miss Manson a hand with her not inconsiderable luggage sir.' And with a polite little bow the blighter made his escape, leaving me open-mouthed.

I must have closed my eyes again and drifted into a doze, this time with fewer wasps, but with me clearly making preparations for someone's murder. Well, ritual execution is more the phrase I suppose, Ellingham's I should think. It was obviously one of those mornings when I was not intended to get the rest the doctor had prescribed, for I was again awakened, it was Liz again.

'I'm off, see you soon I hope.' She kissed me this time gently on the lips, and was gone. You remember me telling you about the old ticker missing a beat and all that when she smiled, I've rather stopped mentioning it of late not wishing to bore you, but take it from me it has been a regular thing. Well now the blasted thing needed a damned starting handle to get it back in it's stride, don't you know.

Having closed my eyes again, for however many times it was now, the next people on the *let's keep Tolson awake* roster were the two gardening gurus' Tideswell and Thomas.

'*Sh*orry to di*sh*terb you Jo*sh*ua, but we will be leaving in about an hour or *sh*o. We could not of cour*sh*e, leave without *sh*aying goodbye, and thanking you again for your kindne*sh*.' You've no doubt guessed who spoke.

'Yes. Thank you, though I still can't quite see the answer to that other matter we spoke about, but rest assured I've not forgotten it,' said W.T.

'How are you both getting to the station? Can't offer to let my chap drive you there, I've only a two-seater, and he's driving Liz anyway.'

'Mr Tideswell has hired a car and he has kindly offered to run me back to the nursery. I would normally have come in my own car but it's unwell at the moment.'

'Ye*sh*, I intend to *sh*pend an hour or *sh*o won*ch*e we get there, looking at Walter'*sh* ro*sh*e*sh*,'

'Well goodbye to you both, have a safe journey.' I didn't add, you'll no doubt notice, go and leave me in peace. But since this was exactly what they did, I again closed my eyes and let nature's sweet restorer drift over

156

me.

I must have slept for quite a while, because I was awakened by Ellingham with a tray of tea.

'I have taken the liberty of bringing you some tea sir.'

'Thanks Ellingham, did Miss Manson get her train okay?'

'With a little time to spare sir, she wished me to convey her thanks sir.'

'Oh right ho, a charming young lady, don't you think Ellingham?'

'It is, I'm sure, not for me to comment on such matters sir, though I have to say she is a young lady with a pleasant personality and outlook, if I might make so bold sir.'

'You may Ellingham. I've arranged to have you run me to Stratford this evening if I'm feeling better, to attend one of her fund raising meetings,' I said.

'So I understood from the young lady on our way to the station. She did however charge me with ensuring you were fully fit before allowing you to undertake the journey sir.'

'I'm feeling better all the time.'

'I am most pleased to hear it sir.'

'However, touching on the other matter regarding the aforesaid rose grower; you were about to inform me of your motives in getting him invited here.'

'Your tea is getting cold sir.'

'Don't change the bally subject Ellingham. Cut to the crux, your thinking if you don't mind, and it had better be good,' I said, turning the watery eyes upon him again.

'Well sir, on the day of our arrival once you were suitably re-attired for dinner I made it my duty to pay my respects to your aunt's domestic staff. During the pleasantries that ensued, I ascertained certain facts from Mr Harcourt, your aunt's butler, you may remember?'

'Indeed I do, the only thing that amazes me is that he is still butling, or butlering or whatever the word is. He was old when I was a boy, can't be much younger than the Rev. Bowman. Old butlers never die they just hand in their silver tray, what?'

'Very droll sir. Mr Harcourt is perhaps not as old as you envisage, he is I believe on the verge of his sixty second birthday. When we are young, everyone over the age of thirty seems on the final slope to the coffin, sir. I think that he, Mr Harcourt, is one of those people who has always looked much older than his actual years sir.'

'Could be, but why have I not seen him around the place? There seems only to be that young chap,' I asked.

'Thornton, the young man is named Thornton sir, and the reason you have not seen Mr Harcourt is that he was on our arrival about to leave to visit his grandfather who it seems is dangerously ill.'

'Harcourt has a grandfather?'

'So it appears sir. One hundred and four, according to Mr Harcourt sir.'

'We digress, Ellingham, how does this fit in with the rose grower?'

'It is common practice when arriving at an establishment, for the staff to inform each other of the current situation within the two households sir.'

'Dish the dirt so to speak?'

'I would perhaps not have put it in those terms, but ensuring that the respective staff of both parties are aware that there are certain situation to be avoided sir.'

158

'Understood. Continue.'

'Mr Harcourt informed me of the other house guests together with a brief history of each, that I might be in the know so to speak sir, and thus be able to inform you of any situations of which to be aware. It was during his appraisal of Mr Tideswell that he informed me that he, Mr Tideswell, was looking into rearranging the rose garden, a task that Mr Harcourt thought was a little beyond him. Mr Tideswell that is of course sir.'

My head was beginning to spin again so I thought I had better clarify things.

'Harcourt thought that rearranging the rose garden was a task beyond the ability of Mr Tideswell, is that it Ellingham?'

'You have grasped the situation perfectly sir. If I might continue?'

'Continue away.'

'Thank you sir. It seemed to me that sooner or later either your aunt or Mr Tideswell would seek professional advice. Their obvious choice for so prestigious a garden as your aunt's would almost certainly be Mr Thomas. His name is highly regarded in horticultural circles and likely to be fresh in their minds due to the newspaper story sir.'

'Was it in the papers? I must have missed it.'

'Indeed so sir, perhaps I failed to mark it for your attention sir.'

'No matter.'

'I considered it prudent if it were to seem that the suggestion came from you sir, on two counts. If Mr Thomas were to turn up he would undoubtedly think he knew you, and the fact that you had recommended him would put him off the scent. Secondly I was desirous to improve your standing with your aunt, but if you were to suggest it directly to her she would no doubt have ridiculed the idea. I suggested to Mr Tideswell that you would prefer it, that your aunt was unaware of your suggestion, but that if it came from him, a person for whom according to Mr Harcourt she has a great regard, it would most probably be welcomed sir,'

'So to sum up, if this Thomas chappie is invited to do the re-hash, it's less suspicious on my part if I'm the one who seems to have suggested him?'

'Correct sir.'

'I have to say it has backfired a bit Ellingham. He has recognised me and was none too pleased about it.'

'Such eventuality was always a possibility sir, that being my reason for it being your suggestion. He would hardly be in a position to be too outspoken if the result of him being outspoken were for him to be removed from the household, and a worthwhile contract sir.'

'But my aunt would be more likely to remove *me* from the household.'

'Very true sir, but Mr Thomas would not be aware of that.'

'You've done it again haven't you? Sweetness and light where'er one looks. Dan Tideswell taken out of a hole, Aunt E. gets her garden with Uncle Josh's approval, Thomas gets a hefty contract, I increase my stock with said aunt and she introduces me to the one girl I want in my life. No losers, and you do it all without a thought for yourself. Ellingham I take my hat off to you.'

'Thank you sir.'

'But wait, there is a loser in all this?'

'Surely not sir?'

'Indeed so Ellingham, and it's *me*.'

'You sir, I fail to see how you could consider yourself at a loss sir.'

'Ramona, Ellingham, what about Ramona?'

'Your car sir?'

'My car Ellingham, what about my car?'

'I will make contact with the local agent as soon as possible, to seek its return, now that the situation has resolved itself sir.'

'Do that Ellingham, and without delay.'

'I will give it my urgent attention sir, but as I said earlier, your tea is getting cold, would you like me to pour you a fresh cup sir?'

'The car Ellingham, the car.'

'Yes sir.'

By late afternoon I felt a little better and began a gentle stroll around the place. The only guests left at my aunt's home by then were the Major and his wife, I found them in the sitting room with the French-doors open on to the long lawn.

'You've gone and let her escape, you young idiot,' the major said as I entered through the aforesaid French windows.

'Let her escape, whom?' I said

'Liz you young fool, who else? You do know she's gone?'

'Oh, yes, we've made arrangements to meet as soon as I'm back in fettle.'

'Pleased to hear it, can't let a choice young lady like that escape your clutches. The pair of you rather hit it off wouldn't you say?'

'Take no notice of my husband Mr Tolson, he has always rather fancied himself as cupid. Tell him to mind his own business,' said Dora.

161

'You do fancy her though, don't you? Must use the three-pronged attack; woo her, send her flowers, tell her of your undying love, don't you know?'

'Leave the young man alone Harold. He must do these things in his own time, when, and how, he sees fit,' she said.

'Nonsense, get at it man. She feels the same, said as much just before dinner last night, before you got yourself stung to ribbons.'

'She said she had feelings for me?' I asked.

'Don't tease the poor fellow so, he is still unwell and this is most unfair.'

'Unfair be buggered. Oh, pardon old girl, I mean it's the truth, that can't be unfair.'

'You think then, if I were to pop the question, even with so short an acquaintance she would be inclined to say yes?' I said. I needed it confirmed, don't you know.

'My guess is that she thinks the same as you; and you, it's easy to see, are as mad as a march-hare about her. Deny it if you can?'

'Stop putting Mr Tolson, Joshua, on the spot you wicked old man.'

'I do care for her, I think she is the sort of girl I could spend my life with, and to tell you the truth I have already intimated to my aunt that I intent to ask her to marry me. Liz of course, not my aunt.'

'There you are, told yer so, told yer so. You could see the look in his eye, and hers. A match made in heaven if ever there was one. Yes, yes, yes, told yer so Dotty old girl. Didn't I?' he said, and if he hadn't been sitting down at the time he would have strutted and danced about the place with pleasure.

162

'They do make a splendid couple, I must admit. And without wishing to be too premature I hope she will have the good sense to accept your proposal, and should that be the case I hope you will be very happy together,' Dora said and squeezed my hand.

'Well said Dotty, well said old girl. But don't wait for some other bounder to snap her up, I bet she's got 'em queuing up to propose. So get about it my boy, attack. Faint heart never won the fair lady as they say. Do it now, well as now as you can, if you get my meaning.'

'I don't intend it to be too long.' And I spoke the truth.

I've made no bones about my feelings in the direction of Liz, but to have it confirmed that my feelings were returned, if not directly from the horse's mouth then from the mouth of a horse that had had it from the horse's mouth, if you follow me, well it bucked me up no end, and that's a fact.

A search for Ellingham showed that not only was he nowhere around but the dreaded grey monstrosity was also missing. I could make no other conclusion than that he had taken the car to get Ramona back, and not wishing to awaken me had taken my last instruction and acted upon it. A look at the trusty old wristwatch showed that it was now fast approaching five thirty and that meant that going to Stratford to see Liz was fast becoming a non-starter. It was a further half an hour before the door of the green room, where I had gone to think on life, was opened by Ellingham, after a discrete knock. I'm sure the same thing must have happened to you, just as life looks to be all sweetness and light. God in his heaven and all that, then something else happens to put a hefty spanner in the

163

works.

'Replaced the car Ellingham?'

'Yes sir.'

'Ramona is back in the fold, then what?'

'I regret that that is not the case sir.'

'You've not got her back?'

'I am afraid not sir.'

'How come, it can't take this long to check the thing over?'

'You are indeed correct sir, the car was checked and approved the next morning.'

'So in that case where is the problem?'

'The vehicle was placed for safe keeping in the dealer's showroom, where it caught the attention of a potential purchaser sir. The dealer contacted the factory as to how to proceed, and was informed that he could sell the car sir.'

'WHAT, "Ramona", gone to another?'

'I hate to be the bearer of ill tidings sir, but such is indeed the case.'

'Then I'm left with the one you changed her for?'

'No indeed sir, in the meantime the factory had replaced the sale with a similar new model, and that has been vouched into your safe keeping in the normal way sir.'

'Ramona II what?'

'That is perhaps the best way to look at the situation sir.'

'Lead on, lets go and take a look at her.'

'If you were to look out of the window, it should be possible to see the vehicle, I took the liberty of parking it in the stable yard sir.'

'Good thinking Elling... It's BLUE Ellingham

BLUE.'

'Yes sir, the exact same model, but as you rightly point out finished in the Oxford and Cambridge blues' sir, a striking combination, don't you think sir?'

'But I ordered red Ellingham.'

'And the factory supplied that as requested, but that was of course before you found need to return it sir,'

'*You* found need to return it Ellingham,'

'Indeed so sir, but in your best interest at the time I'm sure you will recall sir.'

'I had little choice in the matter as I recall Ellingham.'

'I had to act swiftly to avert a situation that might have caused you some embarrassment sir.'

'You were instrumental in causing the situation in the first place Ellingham.'

'In that respect, I also acted in your best interest, in improving your standing with your aunt sir.'

'Granted, that is so. My standing has rarely been higher, and that in it's turn has made my aunt happy. All in all a happy outcome and me in a favoured position to plight the old troth to Liz, Miss Manson.'

'As you say sir.'

'But blue, Ellingham, blue.'

'Indeed sir.'

It was of course by now much too late to even consider the trip to Stratford, and in any case this latest set back had left me feeling unwell again. So consulting the list that Liz had left me, I decided to make it to the next meeting on Tuesday night in Buxton.

'I intend to visit Miss Manson tomorrow evening in Buxton, the next of her evening talks. I think it best if you were to return home by train in the morning. You can arrange me an overnight accommodation in Buxton, and I will return home on Wednesday. To this end I will require you to make up an overnight bag, the rest of the luggage you may take with you,' I said making my intentions quite clear I think you would agree.

'As you wish sir, I will begin attending to the matter forthwith. A thought has occurred to me sir, and if I might appraise you of it, it is one which might effect a meeting of your two young friends sir.'

'Chas Bestwick and Jane B-R, you mean?'

'Indeed sir.'

'Spill the beans then Ellingham.'

'Well sir, Mr Bestwick is I understand involved in an agency specialising in advertising. If you were to employ his services as a favour to Miss Manson, he would have to carry out your instructions with regard to how he went about the task sir.'

'So where does Jane come in?'

'I seem to remember that Miss Barrington-Ross is very keen on amateur theatricals sir. If Mr Bestwick were to request Miss Barrington-Ross to organise an evening of amateur entertainment in aid of Miss Manson's schools charity, she would be highly likely to accept, especially if Mr Bestwick were to make her aware that you were financing the operation and had suggested her for the position sir.'

'They would have to work very closely together, Ellingham.'

'Precisely sir.'

'Love could blossom?'

'Exactly sir, even if the outcome is less than anticipated at least you will have fulfilled your promise to introduce the young gentleman to Miss Barrington-Ross

166

sir.'

'The rest is up to him, what?'

'As you so rightly say sir, the rest is up to him.' And he said it with the gentle dip of the head that suggested that he was rather pleased with himself.

'I'll phone him first thing in the morning, I've got his office number somewhere in my diary.'

'Very wise sir, the sooner these things are set in motion the better. After all Miss Manson may not be in the country for very much longer sir.'

'Why do you say that Ellingham? Have you some inside knowledge that the rest of us are not privy to?'

'No sir, I was merely thinking sir, the young lady seems to be being most successful in her fund raising, and if I might make so bold sir, time is also running out if you wish to ask the young lady to be your wife.'

'That has not escaped me, I intend to take care of it as soon as the time is ripe.'

'Of course sir, I did not wish to appear impertinent, I was merely making an observation sir.'

'No offence taken Ellingham, now get about organising that overnight bag, and thanks for the thoughts on the Chas and Jane matter.'

'My pleasure sir, I trust it will prove satisfactory sir.' It might well seem to you dear reader that I have let him off too lightly, accepted the new vehicle also too easily, that I have failed to see the underlying fact that Ellingham had achieved his dastardly plan of getting rid of "Ramona" because he disliked the colour of her clothes. Well let me tell you, he has underestimated his enemy in this. I made it my intention first thing on Tuesday morning to ring our Mr Fothergill and get the matter rectified. No use being the boss's son if you don't pull rank, once in a

167

while, what?

There had been some overnight rain, so the morning started with that gentle haziness which suggested that as soon as the sun has had its breakfast and its first gasper of the day, spat on its hands and got down to work proper, it would turn into a real scorcher. By the time I had dropped Ellingham at the station, with instructions to expect me about mid afternoon Wednesday, it was already warming up. As I sat in the library back at The Willows, having switched the phone in the hall on to extension, the sun was streaming through the windows. After three attempts at ringing old Fothergill at the factory, I gave up for the time being and rang Chas. The phone buzzed at the other end and the connection was made.

'Sell-it-all advertising agency, how can I help you?' asked a female voice that I took to be very young.

'Could I speak to Mr Charles Bestwick please?'

'Who shall I say is calling?'

'Tell him it's Josh Tolson, please.'

'One moment please.'

There then followed the usual clicks and half heard voices, and eventually Chas came on the line.

'Hello you old eyesore, hope this is important – struggling with a buy-line for a new client. So make it a bit snappy,' he said.

It seemed he was always struggling with a buy-line for some client or other, so I hoped my news would put a spark into his dreary life.

'I am the bearer of glad tidings. I've come up with a way that not only introduces you to Miss Barrington-Ross, but also has you needing to work closely together.' And I outlined the scheme.

'I say thank Ellingham from me will you, it's brilliant,' he said.

'Why must it be Ellingham's doing? What if I was to tell you that the scheme was all my own work, eh, what would you say to that?'

When the laughter at the other end had subsided and he was again able to speak, I can't say I liked his tone.

'Josh, though I love you as a brother, better in fact than my own brother, who is as you know a stinker of the first water, you have to admit that when the brains of this world were being dispatched yours ended up marked return to sender.' And he started to laugh again. 'Use your loaf old chap, it needs real thinking power to come up with a diamond studded idea like this.'

'It was Ellingham's idea I admit it, but I think you are being rather hard on your truly, especially since I have not as yet given you her telephone number,' I said, and I bet that took the smile off his face.

'Take no notice of me old pal of mine, just my little joke, now about that number?'

'Firstly, do we have a deal? Will you take me as a client?' I asked.

'Take it as signed on the dotted line, m' dear chap. I'll put it to the big cheese as soon as you ring off, I see no problems.'

'Good, then this is the necessary low-down.'

I gave him the plan and detail and told him to get things on the move, and he agreed to give it top priority.

'You know, the agency could do itself a bit of good by being the promoter in the deal,' he said.

And I suppose he could be right, and with a cheery goodbye he rang off. You know how you sometimes find yourself sitting staring into the future with a self-satisfied grin? Well this was one of those times.

I tried for a fourth time to get through to Mr Fothergill, and this time, after being transferred to about five different departments, which is usually the case in this sort of thing, I managed to catch him.

'Mr Tolson sir, what can I do for you?' he asked.

'I had, you are perhaps aware, a mishap with the car you had provided, which ended with it being placed in the hands of one of your dealers for repair. With me so far?'

'Indeed, your Mr Ellingham asked me to provide you with a replacement vehicle, preferably in a different colour. Which of course I did. Is there a problem sir?'

'Well yes, it has since transpired that my car has been sold, and I am left with the same model but in blue which is not to my taste.'

'Oh dear, that does present me with a bit of a problem sir. The colour scheme of your original car has proved so popular, that your father has demanded a change in colour scheduling, as he requires every available car to be finished in red, to meet the demand. I can't see you being allotted a red one in the foreseeable future sir.'

'Mr Fothergill, this is your little joke, right?'

'Deadly in earnest sir, I will of course ask your father to see if he will make an exception in your case, but I really don't hold too many hopes in that direction sir.'

'No, no, don't bother him. I can't really demand the colour I like, I'll just have to make do with this ghastly blue thing. Thanks anyway.'

'As soon as a red model comes available I'll let your Mr Ellingham know sir.'

'No, tell me direct please Mr Fothergill.'

170

'I'll do that sir.'

As I rang off, still thinking about the car, a new idea had come into my head, "brains returned to sender" indeed.

It was time to do the rounds of farewell; you will remember that I had promised myself that I would reward my aunt's cook for her excellent output. I have not dwelt again upon these, my thinking being food should be enjoyed but is only a minor part of life's pleasures, though take it from me, the standard had not fallen and had often reached even greater heights. As anticipated earlier, apes, ivories and camels proved a bit thin on the ground in that part of Gloucestershire so I made my thanks known to her with a crisp new fiver for which she thanked me most profusely. I gave her another one to split between the rest of my aunt's staff, and this she promised to do.

I found my uncle salted away in his study; as I said earlier I would normally not disturb him, especially before about eleven o'clock. As up to that time he is checking his investments in the national newspapers. But since it was now approaching eleven thirty I was pretty confident that he would be engrossed in his other passion, one that I happen to share, philately and numismatics: stamp and coin collecting if you strip away its posh pretensions. I have a pretty nice collection, with some rather rare examples. It has been quoted more than once in these jottings that there is among my circle of friends the notion that your author is something of a wool brain, and even then unlikely to have enough of the stuff to complete a pair of babies bootees. Well let me tell you, when it comes to stamps and coins of the world I can hold my own with all-comers, though I suppose I shouldn't

171

really say it myself. As anticipated Uncle Josh was indeed pouring over his latest acquisitions.

'Morning Uncle Josh, all well with the world?' I asked.

'Still got the same ailments that I told you about on the phone, glad to say the old eye's stopped weeping, thank goodness. Poked it on the top of a cane if you remember, damned stupid things canes. Solved the problem though, put one of those little pill bottles you get from the doctor on the top of each one. Never throw anything away m'boy, that's my advice. I'd got dozens of the little blighters salted away. Gout's not so troublesome now we are getting a bit of warm weather, same with the old leg. Shoulder's giving me a bit of gyp now, if I lift my arm like this – ouch!'

'Perhaps you shouldn't lift your arm like that, then uncle?' I suggested.

'Quite so, m'boy. How's the collection coming along by the way? We ought to go into business between us buying and selling. Lots of folk with the same interests, what do you think?' he asked.

Well at least he had diverted from his ailments, so that had to be a positive move.

'Still keep adding a few odd bits, you know. As to setting up a venture, it could be just the sort of thing I might be rather good at, don't yer know.'

'My thoughts entirely, we should seriously look into it without delay.'

'Can't be today I'm afraid; going to one of Liz's meetings this evening then straight home from there. But I'll think on the idea and keep in touch.'

'Going to one of Liz's meetings? Your aunt is right then, you have got it bad eh?'

172

'I'm not altogether sure I like my affairs mulled over by all and sundry, present company excepted of course, but it seems a bit like being looked at from all sides. The major was badgering me yesterday about not letting the grass grow and all that.'

'Take no notice of us, we just think she's right for you, that's all it is.'

We then got onto collectors shoptalk, which unless you are into the subject, is probably meaningless twaddle to you, so I won't go into it. A bit like golfers when they start talking about birdies and nine irons and one over par, that sort of thing. Eventually I bade my uncle farewell and asked if he knew where I might come across the Major and Dora, but he was unable to help.

I tracked them down eventually. Not together but individually, Dora first; she was in the sitting room talking to my aunt, and it came as no surprise to me that Liz and myself were top items on the menu of things they should talk about. As I opened the door my aunt was speaking.

'— and they make a lovely couple. Ah there you are Josh, we were just talking about you. You look a good deal better than yesterday,' she said with a loving smile. Loving smiles were becoming a regular feature and a bit unnerving I can tell you.

'Yes you do,' agreed Dora.

'Yes I'm a lot better, almost back into peak form, still get a bit of a groggy head if I think too hard. And before you say it Aunt, I know it doesn't happen all that often.'

'Josh, my dear nephew, the thought never even entered my head.'

'I was just telling your aunt about the grilling my husband gave you yesterday, quite put you on the spot, the

173

mischievous old devil,' said Dora.

'Everything he said was perfectly true, and I intend to pursue the lady with a will. In fact I'm here to say farewell, I'm off to see her at one of her meetings.'

'Oh, that is good news,' said my aunt. Don't rush her, wait till the time is right.'

'Quite right, ignore my husband, take your time, but grasp the moment when it happens,' Dora agreed.

Not wishing to curtail in any way their collective enjoyment of discussing my life, I simply bade them farewell and asked them if they knew where I might find the man in question.

'He said he would be fishing down by the bridge,' Dora informed me.

'I'll catch him on the way out then. If for any reason I fail to find him, please wish him goodbye from me,' I said. And they said they would.

Ellingham had put the overnight bag in the back of the blue eyesore, and within minutes I was on my way with enough time to spare to find a nice country pub to take lunch. I found the dear old chap as suggested by the bridge, just packing away his fishing gear.

'Morning Major, any luck?'

'No, not a sniff, I think the blighters are further up river laughing at my efforts.'

'Oh well, they're not good to eat anyway. My uncle used to catch them years ago and force us all to eat them. Disgusting. Eventually even he gave up on them, personally I think that was the cause of his terrible digestion problems.'

'Don't want to eat the blasted things, just show 'em who's the boss, but it seems they already know.'

'Just stopped to wish you goodbye Major.'

174

'I heard your car, so I guessed you were on your way.'

'Yes off to see Liz at one of her charity talks, Buxton,' I said.

'I went to the place once, it rained,' he said as though that was the best that could be said for the famous old spa town.

'Ah, but you weren't going to see Liz at one of her charity talks.'

'True,' he said, 'I can see that that would make all the difference. What's a drop of rain in that case?'

'I'm getting lunch at a pub on the way, so I'd better be getting along.'

'Give her my love when you see her, and tell her – well you'll know what to tell her, but don't wait too long, some other bounder could beat you to it. Off you go then and god speed. By the way, I must be going a bit soft in the head but I could have bet money on your car being red, then I realised I was wrong it was grey, anyway I could have sworn it wasn't blue.'

'It was red Major, and indeed grey, but for reasons I've no time to go into now, I had to change it. If we ever happen to meet again I'll tell you the story, it should while away the hours no end. Goodbye to you Major, hope to meet you again soon.' And with that I hopped back into Beryl the blue peril and was on my way.

If you're travelling alone in your car, if you've got a car - and if my fathers sales figures are anything to go by you probably have - you will no doubt find yourself singing, or perhaps humming if that's your preference, to help pass the time. I was singing to myself, and had just finished counting down from twenty-seven men went to mow, when there hove into view a quaint old English village, with a quaint "Olde Englishe" pub, The George & Dragon, displaying a hand painted sign "LUNCHES". I pulled up alongside a very smart silver Rolls Royce, hopped out and made my way through the rather low doorway, into the public bar. George was standing at the bar, so presumably the dragon was somewhere at the back preparing the lunches.

'Good day sir, what can I get you?' he asked.

There must be some sort of script that these chaps have to learn; every pub landlord I've ever met, and I've met a few in my time, have always started with that same question.

'I'd like to order lunch first if that's all right?'

'A bit limited for choice today sir, I'm afraid. I can do you a cold chicken salad, roast beef and Yorkshire puddings with all the trimmings or my wife could do you a cheese sandwich.'

'I can highly recommend the roast beef,' said the well dressed chap at the corner of the bar that I took to be the owner of the aforementioned Rolls, 'I've just this minute eaten it and it was top draw.'

'I'll take your advice, and thank you,' I said to the chap and turned to the landlord, 'make that the roast beef please.'

'Certainly sir, it'll be about ten minutes. Can I get you a drink in the meantime?'

'It says above your door that you brew your own ale, if that includes a bitter I'll try a pint of that if I may.'

I glanced over to my friend in the corner, who raised his glass in approval.

'I certainly do sir, and as good as you'd find anywhere and better 'an most.' And with that he reached up above his head, took a gleaming glass, the sort with a handle, and pulled me a pint.

'Is that your car outside?' I asked my new friend.

'Yes and no. I've got it for the day, trying it out. It's not new but it's in good condition and the price seems right,' he replied.

'It certainly looks nice at the first glace, though I've always thought them a bit on the heavy side for my taste.'

'Yes, drinks petrol but a damned comfortable ride yer know, come miles in it.'

'Are you not a regular then?'

'No, just over from Cirencester, as I said, trying her out, half hooked I have to say, but can't just make the jump, if you know what I mean?'

'Ever thought of a Tolson?' I ventured. Thinking that one more sale could only improve my shares what?

'Not bad as mass produced junk goes, but I go for hand-built every time. I say have I just put my foot in it? Always doing that. Was that a Tolson you just drove up in?'

'It was and I rather like them. But you are entitled to your opinion,' I said.

'Convince me, show me over her whilst you wait for your lunch.'

'Call me when my lunch is ready, I'll be outside discussing motorcars,' I said to the landlord, and he nodded.

'I say, I like the combination of blues, go together really nicely,' he said.

'Hate to have to differ but I think it's awful,' I replied.

'So why did you choose it?'

I didn't want to go into the long, long story about aunts and roses and Ellingham and all that so I simply said-

'Well, I'm doing much the same as you, trying out a demonstrator and this was the only colour they could let me have. I wanted the two tone red,' I said which let's face it was near enough the truth.

'Well what do you think? Given that they can get you a red one, would you be taking it up?'

'Yes, I certainly would. I think it's a little marvel; it's got four gears, and synchronous meshing...'

The rest as you can imagine stretched my technical knowledge to the limit, and I was thankful when the landlord's head poked through the doorway.

'Your lunch is ready sir.'

'Enjoy your lunch,' said the chap getting into his Rolls, 'my friend here has agreed to settle my bill.' And with a shower of dust he was on his way, leaving me open mouthed. It was at this point that I first noticed that this landlord looked like an ex-boxer who did all-in wrestling as a hobby, and looked to be pretty good at it at that.

'I hope I've not just been made a fool of,' said the landlord, 'the local constable comes down very hard on tricksters.' And he looked at me in a strange way.

I think we all know who had just been made a fool of but I simply said -

'No, quite alright landlord, I'll pay.'

It was I'm sure a very acceptable meal but although I ate it, it was like eating the ashes from a fire grate. The thing had spoiled my appetite and no mistake, and when I had finished the landlord came over.

'Right sir, the gentleman's bill stands at two pints of bitter, lunch like yourself, a portion of my wife homemade apple pie with custard, and he finished off with a plate of cheese and biscuits. That added to your own drink and meal sir, comes to seventeen shillings and eight-pence.' And he handed me a slip if paper with it all added up.

'Seventeen and eight-pence, are you sure?'

'It's all down there, sir.'

How could I argue, there it was in black and white, and I had agreed to settle the bounder's account, and if I ever set eyes on him again, I vowed to settle his account for him once and for all, and no mistake. So I shelled out a pound note and paid the landlord, though I couldn't help thinking that both of them had taken me for a ride.

It's no use brooding on life's misfortunes; spilt milk and all that, life is too short, as the saying goes. And so I set off determined to put the sorry episode behind me. Now where was I? Oh yes.

'Twenty eight men went to mo-oo-ow, went to mo-ow a meadow.'

I arrived in Buxton in good time, found the hall, and guess who was the first person I saw. Well you couldn't could you, silly of me. Liz, looking as they say, like a million dollars, whatever that means. She saw me as I entered and clip clopped across to me on high heels.

'Josh, you made it, how do you feel now?' she asked, giving me a hug and a peck on the cheek.

'Back to mid-season form thanks. You look wonderful, but isn't it a bit over the top; might not give the right impression to the punters if you look too well off?'

'Oh I shan't do this talk like this I'll dress down,

I've just been to meet a group of local businessmen and needed to look my best.'

And as I've said *look her best* she did. I'd never seen her look better, but I wasn't sure I liked this approach, it seemed rather mercenary, but I suppose needs must as they say.

'Did you make a suitable impression?' I asked.

'Yes I got three more generous donations, I'm getting to my target quite nicely.

'Does that mean you will be returning to Africa earlier than expected?'

'No I can't, I've still got to carry out the meetings I've arranged, it just means that I will probably exceed my target. If tonight's meeting is as good as last night's I'll be more than pleased.'

'How many people are you expecting?' I asked

'You never know with these things, it might be fifty, it might be three hundred.'

'Seems a long way to come to talk to fifty people if that's all it is?'

'I'm getting rather good at this. When I've booked the hall in a particular place, I inform the local newspaper - they are always looking for items to interest their readers - and I ask them if they would be kind enough to set up a collection for people who are unable to attend. That brings in a nice bit, so even if the meeting itself is not so good I have this as a back up.' And she looked rather pleased with herself.

'Clever girl.' I said.

'Look, I've got about half an hour, come backstage, talk to me while I change.'

'Er, um, okay,' I said not quite sure what she had in mind.

'You are funny, surely you've seen a girl in her undies before?' she laughed.

I had of course, but somehow I – well you know.

If there's one thing you can say about Chas Bestwick, it's that he never lets the grass grow under his feet. As we arrived at the tiny room that they laughingly called the dressing room, a young man with a big nose wearing a motorcycle helmet, the young man that is, not the nose of course, came up to us and asked -

'Miss Manson?'

'That's me,' Liz answered.

'Telegram,' he said, handing it to her, 'sign here.' She did, quickly read it and said -

'Thank you, no reply.'

He turned and as quickly as he had entered our lives, he was gone from them.

'It's from someone signing himself Chas, asking me to ring him first thing in the morning, and saying that if you are here you will fill in the details.' Which, of course I did, whilst Liz disappeared behind a screen and began to change for the meeting.

'Let me get this straight, you have commissioned this Chas, what's his real name by the way? To set up a charity talent show for me?'

'Yes, but there are wheels within wheels. Chas, it's Charles Bestwick by the way and he's an old school chum; he's madly in love with Jane, though he has never actually met her.'

'Jane?' she asked.

It's a long story as you already know and though I spelt it out move by move, she of course, being a female, could not wait till the end to ask about anything she didn't understand; kept butting in, asking questions making me

181

lose the thread, well you know how it is, but eventually I finished the story and she seemed to have got the gist.

'Is he wanting me to ring him to discuss details, do you think?' she asked.

'I think that's a pretty safe bet, the sooner he knows where to fit into your schedule, the sooner he starts working with Jane,' I smiled.

'Aren't you clever, and nice of course, doing this for an old school pal. But this Jane though, I suppose she has no idea that she is being set up?'

'I think set up is the wrong word, well two words of course, but I prefer to see it as offering a chance of happiness when there is little likelihood of them meeting in any other way.'

'How do you know this Jane?'

'This Jane, is Jane Barrington-Ross, and I was engaged to her for a very short time. Lovely girl and I think she and Chas might just hit it off.'

'Ah, I see,' she said.

And you could see about a million and a half conclusions being jumped to in one fell swoop, if you know what I mean.

'I doubt it, but let it go, water under the bridge, in fact lots of water under many bridges,' I said.

The hall was about half full at the start of the talk, and a few stragglers came in as Liz was starting to speak. She spoke in a clear voice, explaining that these little African children were in need of help in many ways, and illustrated her various points with a series of coloured lantern slides. She spoke for about forty minutes, making her case in a straightforward unemotional way, then asked the assembly if there were any questions. I haven't told you that she had asked me to sit up on the stage with her

182

to give her moral support, and all that. Which of course being bound by the code of gentlemanly conduct I had done. And, be blowed if she didn't drop right me in it. Why do girls do that? At the end of the questions she said-

'I have not introduced my companion here on the stage, he is none other than Joshua Tolson, son of the motor manufacturer who has kindly come along to support my cause tonight,' and turned to me beckoning for me to stand and come forward.

I hadn't expected this, though I suppose I should have when she asked me on stage. Thinking on the old feet is something I think I'm rather good at; speak from the heart, say what you have to say, that was my recipe.

'Ladies and gentlemen, you have seen the plight of these young people explained to you by Miss Manson, and I think that you, like me, will have had your eyes and your hearts opened by her...' I was interrupted.

'Bet you've not opened your wallet though mate,' shouted an unknown voice from the back - much laughter.

I often wonder if it's the same voice, if someone dogs my movements so as to be able to make me look small on these occasions.

'On the contrary my good man, not only do I intend to give a sizable personal donation, but I also intend to canvas my father and his business associates to give very generous donations in the name of their respective companies.' And I rather think I nodded to suggest "beat that".

The wag from the back can of course always beat that, for he has little to lose.

'In that case she won't need our five bobs then, will she?'

183

Everyone laughed and started to leave the hall, with the result that the total collected in the tin by the door was a little over two pounds.

'Rather made a mess of that, didn't I?' I asked.

'It could have gone better, perhaps you shouldn't have mentioned your father's business associates, it seemed to make matters worse,' she said.

'I was rather goaded into it what?'

'Keeping your cool and just ignoring the heckler; works much better than rising to their bait.'

'Well perhaps if you'd mentioned that you wanted me to stand up and speak, perhaps I might have made a better job of it?'

'What would you have said then?'

You've perhaps noted that we seemed to be having our first argument. I have found in my life that arguing with women takes one of two directions; when in the wrong, they cry and, or sulk, or if right, bite with venom demanding the last word, no matter how long the exchange goes on. In either case I am always made to feel I'm the guilty party, whether I'm right or wrong. So this being the girl I intended to marry, I decided to pour oil on troubled waters, as the saying goes, and my next remark was intended to do just that.

'You're right. I shouldn't have bitten back, just carried on with what I had to say. Asked them to give what they could afford,' I said.

'Yes well, it's easy to come up with these things with hindsight. Oh, well there's still the newspaper appeal, that should have gone fairly well,' she said.

Not quite the calming reply I would have liked. Give and take, being the normally accepted state of play in these situations, but I let it go.

'Let me buy you dinner. Ellingham has booked me in at the Spa Hotel, and he rarely gets it wrong with the food that's on offer at these places.'

'Alright, I'll just collect my things.'

And a few minutes later we were walking into the aforesaid hotel. I explained that I was a resident and carried out the formalities. A table for dinner was already assigned to me, awaiting my arrival and was hastily laid with an extra setting. And we took our places. As we looked at the menu I said -

'What would you have expected from a gathering like tonight, how much I mean?'

'Hard to say, but this is a prosperous town. I suppose about fifty or sixty pounds.'

'Oh well, I'll write you a cheque for that and more here and now, by way of saying sorry for making a mess of it,' and I smiled.

'You can't buy me you know.'

I was taken aback, that was not my way of thinking of it.

'Nor do I want to, I just feel responsible for jiggering it all up.'

'Buy me dinner, run me to my boarding house, and we'll say no more.'

I had had it in my mind to pop the question that night, but that all seemed to have been put to one side by the evenings events.

'If that's what you want, I will of course do as you ask. But I still intend to make a worthwhile donation, and soon.'

'I almost think that Ellingham knew this would happen,' she said.

'Ellingham, knew what would happen?'

185

'When he suggested that I have you up on stage, that it would turn to dust.'

'Ellingham suggested that you had me up on stage?'

'There seems to be a strange echo in this hotel, have you noticed. Yes, Ellingham had a word with me on the way to the station.'

'Did he indeed?'

'He said that he was going to delay you from coming to the Stratford upon Avon meeting, feeling that you needed to be properly well. And I thought he was right.'

'He deliberately delayed me?'

'In your best interests, but he said he would make sure you were at the Buxton one.

'But you said, he'd said to get me on stage?'

'Yes he said you would be pleased to do it, but not to tell you that you were expected to speak as you always do the thing so much better if you do it impromptu.'

What was the blighter playing at? I couldn't make it out and no mistake. His every move seems to be intended to make things difficult for me, yet when tackled on the subject he can always maintain his actions are in my best interest. Except with regard to "Ramona" of course, but I had that in hand.

8

As I anticipated I arrived back at the old homestead around three thirty on the Wednesday afternoon. Although it was only a little over a week since I had first seen Liz, it seemed as though we had known each other for a lifetime. And by the end of our meal the previous night we were back on a good footing again. So much so that when we had said goodbye on Buxton station, she going off to her next meeting, (Manchester I think) she had again kissed me in a romantic way. It was then a Joshua Tolson with a happy heart that walked in through the ivory portals of home.

'Good afternoon sir, I trust you had a pleasant journey.'

'Yes. But what's all this white powder everywhere?'

'Police fingerprint powder sir, I fear you have been burgled in our absence sir.'

'Burgled?'

'Indeed sir. I first noticed that such was the case when returning home at roughly this hour yesterday, and called the local constabulary sir.'

'What have they taken Ellingham, the burglars of course not the constabulary?'

'I have taken the liberty of preparing a list of all of the items that I could think of to provide for the police sir. I have not done so as yet as there may be things you happen to notice that I have overlooked.'

'Tea, Ellingham, give me tea, I feel the need of restoration.'

'I had anticipated that such would be the case. The tea is at this moment brewing, and probably, indeed, ready to pour at this very instant sir.'

I think he must hear me on the stairs, or possibly at the garage putting the car away.

'Pour it and add a drop of the hard stuff, perhaps even two drops, then bring this list and let me peruse.'

And what a list it was: the burglar or burglars had taken only the most saleable things. Not just mine, Ellingham had not escaped their net.

'They must have been in the place for ages; they've taken their time and searched with a will. They've chosen well, easily saleable stuff,' I said.

'That was also the impression of the police inspector who is in charge of the case sir.'

'Do they know how he got in? I assume it must have been a he, but in these times of female emancipation who can tell. I've noticed no signs of a forced entry.'

'That was also noted by Inspector Jackman sir. He suggested that the burglar must have known that the flat would be unoccupied for a considerable time.'

'Inspector Jackman, you said? I know him, he's in charge of the fur stole case at the "Boater", I'm right?'

'You are indeed correct sir, he commented upon the fact that he thought he had spoken to you in that connection sir.'

'Rummy what, never spoken to a policeman, other than to ask the time of day so to speak, from one years end to another, then suddenly three times in a fortnight.'

'The inspector asked me to inform him by telephone as soon as you returned. He wishes to talk with you, as you would imagine sir. I will inform him now if that is convenient sir?' he asked.

'Yes go to it, let's get it over with.'

'Very good sir.'

He went off to make the dreaded call and I looked again at the list, realising that before this Jackman chap arrived he would expect me to have had a look myself to confirm that it covered everything. I looked around the room, noting several things that I had made my personal favourites were missing. One of them, a small gilt carriage-clock, not exceptionally valuable but pretty with a charming little tune on the hour, and extremely easy to sell I should think, also a pair of china figurines of girls dancing that don't leave much to the imagination, if you know what I mean. In the bedroom I noticed that the box on the dressing table, a rather nice piece in birds-eye maple had gone, complete with its contents; tie pins, cufflinks, the odd ring or two. All told I suppose about a hundred and fifty pounds worth or so. All of it seemed to have been listed in pretty close detail already by Ellingham. He had attached a second list with one of those curly wire paper clip things; items that were his own personal things that had gone missing. Although they were his personal items, I was sure he would have no objection to me quickly looking over them. Further proof, if such was needed, that the chap must have had run of the place for quite some time. His prized possession, his radio, had been taken, small as radios go, barely the size of a breadbin I suppose, it would still take some effort to remove it unseen. He returned from making the call with the tray of tea.

'They've taken your radio Ellingham?' I said.

'Indeed so sir.'

189

'I fear it may not have been covered on my insurance, I think that sort of thing needs to be itemised as a separate thing.'

'I was wise enough to insure it myself sir. The salesman at the radio dealers advised me that radios, particularly of the smaller variety, are a target should thieves break in, and so I took his advice sir.'

'Oh, well done Ellingham, one step ahead of the pack as usual.'

'You are most kind sir. I have just noticed that there is something that I need to add to my list sir.'

'Good lord, now what?'

'The burglar has also taken the present you so kindly gave me sir.'

'Present, not your birthday egg-timer with the little chicken on the top?'

'No sir, the thief must have completely missed the aesthetic value of the piece sir, I refer to the last present you were kind enough to give to me sir.'

'Refresh my memory, Ellingham.'

'The large economy sized cleaning agent sir.'

'Kleeno?'

'Indeed sir.'

'Well I'm blowed, why on earth would they have taken that?'

'Why, indeed sir.'

'Oh, I say, that means you won't be able to give it your stamp of – STAMPS – the collection!'

The shock made me jump but this time the teacup was still on the tray, however the milk jug was in my hand; enough said.

'Only the silver inkwell appears to be missing from your study sir, the collection chest is still firmly

190

locked.'

'He didn't force the front door Ellingham. A collection chest wouldn't worry him!'

'Very true sir; perhaps we should take a look.'

I was already on my way, milk soaked trousers and all. Outwardly the cupboard was as Ellingham had said, secure and apparently untouched. But internally totally bereft of stamps and coins, the whole collection was missing.

'Gone Ellingham!'

'As you say sir, gone.'

I slumped at my desk, too overcome to notice the missing inkwell.

'Fifteen years of work – gone. It's like a stab to the heart Ellingham,' I said and I held my head in my hands.

'I am very sorry sir, I know how much your collection means to you sir.'

'Thanks Ellingham. Will they catch this fiend, do you think?'

'I understand from the inspector that the thief is very clever. He has carried out a number of similar burglaries locally, but leaves no trace, or clue, that the police have as yet discovered, so I fear that the chances of regaining your collection is somewhat slim sir.'

'Oh, gosh!'

'As you say sir.'

'Oh my gosh.'

'Perhaps a refreshing cup of tea would reduce the impact of your loss sir. If you would care to change your trousers sir, I will pour you a fresh cup.'

Tea – nature's great healer and restorer, the answer to all life's ills, but somehow just at the moment it

191

didn't seem all that wonderful.

'I doubt if even tea can take away the ache in my heart; have you ever had a pet dog that died Ellingham?'

'No sir, thankfully that is one of life's misfortunes that I have not been subjected to. As a child I was not allowed to have a pet of any sort sir.'

'I'm sorry to hear that Ellingham, why was that?'

'My father was butler to one of the lesser royals sir, and a strict embargo of personal pets was enforced sir.'

'I didn't know your father had been a butler Ellingham.'

'Indeed sir, in fact still is, though somewhat higher in rank now sir. The gentleman's gentleman to the person in question sir.'

'Well I never, runs in the family what?'

'Indeed sir – the male line of my family have been in service to the nobility for at least five generations, and possibly longer sir.'

'I'm not the nobility Ellingham.'

'No sir, of late it has become necessary; or should I say new opportunities have opened to serve families of quality and the nouveau riche sir.'

'Well, they say you live and learn what?'

'One should never stop learning sir, and in fact I in my turn have to confess that I was unaware that you had suffered, as a child, the sad loss of a pet dog sir.'

'Oh, I haven't but I bet this is how it would feel, what?'

'Quite probably sir.' And as he turned to refresh my cup I thought I discerned the very slightest shake of his head, though I suppose my emotional state might have made me imagine it.

Inspector Jackman announced his presence by ringing the doorbell at a little after six in the evening. Ellingham opened the door and took his overcoat and showed him into the sitting room.

'Inspector Jackman sir.'

'Inspector, please sit down, can I offer you a cup of tea, or coffee perhaps?' I asked.

'A cup of tea would be most welcome sir, thank you.'

'Ellingham, if you'd be so kind.'

'I had anticipated the request sir, it will be available shortly,' he said, and turning, made his way to the kitchen.

'We meet again Inspector,' I said, a bit corny I suppose thinking back on it, but I couldn't think of anything better at the time.

'I'm sorry it has to be as a result of your own criminal loss sir.'

'Damned nuisance but what can one do?'

'It seems from talking to your manservant yesterday that every reasonable precaution was taken when you left, so it's hard to see how you could have lessened the chances.'

'Ellingham is most fastidious in his procedures for locking when we are out, and even more so if we are to be away for several days or more,' I confirmed.

'So I understood from Mr Ellingham sir.'

Ellingham arrived with the tea at this point and the usual short ritual of pouring, milking, sugaring and so forth took up the next minute or so.

'Don't go Mr Ellingham, I would like to talk to you both. Sometimes on these occasions, I've found that you might just jog each other's memory to something;

193

some small detail that would otherwise be overlooked,' the inspector said.

'Yes stay Ellingham, take a seat.'

'Thank you sir.'

'Inspector, let the interrogation begin.'

'Hardly an interrogation sir, I don't suspect either of you gentlemen. But I do think you could know more than you think. You see, this is forming a sort of pattern; yours is the tenth burglary in the area and including this one seven of them have involved members of the "Straw Boater" club sir.'

'Good lord, an insider job, is that what you call it?'

'An American term I believe sir, but it seems to fit the bill.'

'What about the theft at the "Boater" itself?'

'I have to consider that that is also connected sir.'

'Lummy, this is big Inspector.'

'As you say sir, big, and difficult, he leaves no trace. But mark my word sooner or later he will make a mistake, they always do. They get too clever you see, overconfident, that's when they trip up.'

'So ask away Inspector, let's nail the blighter.'

'Right sir, who was aware that you would be going away to Gloucester sir?'

'Not Gloucester exactly, to the little village of Much Moreham Inspector.'

'Just so sir, but did you tell anyone outside your family sir?'

'No, no-one.'

'That is not strictly true sir, if you recall you informed Mr Manson on the telephone that you would be away for a few days sir,' Ellingham pointed out.

'Well yes him, of course; but damn it he's a fellow "Boater".'

'Even so he was aware that you would be out of town,' said the inspector. 'Might I ask why you thought it necessary to inform the gentleman that you would be away?'

'Oh gosh, this is a bit personal, but if it helps; I rather fancy his cousin and he rang to tell me that she would be away for a few days and so he couldn't arrange anything in the way of a meeting until after she returned, and I told him no matter, that I would be away for a few days in the country myself. I think that sums it up Ellingham, would you agree?'

'Though I was not privy to the conversation, I understood at the time that that was the case sir.'

'So an innocent remark on the telephone?'

'Yes Inspector, other than that I can't think of anyone else who knew,' I said.

'What about you Mr. Ellingham, did you inform anyone?'

'Only the usual trades people; milkman, newsagent, baker, all of them above suspicion I would have thought.'

'If you could let me have a list of your tradesmen Mr Ellingham, and of your friends address Mr Tolson, I would be much obliged.'

'I say inspector, that's a bit thick what?'

'Normal practice, merely to eliminate them from my enquiries sir.'

'Oh yes I see.'

'Now I asked Mr Ellingham to prepare a list of things that are missing, have you done that for me?'

'Indeed Inspector, I also asked Mr Tolson to look

195

over it and add anything I might have overlooked.'

'Excellent, did you notice anything in addition to Mr Ellingham's list sir?'

'Yes, my treasured collection of stamps and coins is missing.' I had a catch in my voice.

'Now that could be just what we need. Specialized market you see, only of interest to another collector. I don't suppose you have a detailed note of your collection sir?'

'You jest inspector, I've over six thousand stamps, many of them run of the mill stuff, and about three hundred coins; I've quite a few that are rare as hen's teeth, I could tell you those off the top of my head, they are like old friends.'

'Make a list of them sir, if you'd be so kind. I can get it circulated around the specialist dealers.'

'My uncle who I was staying with is also a collector and knows many others. I could get him to pass it around, then if any of them are offered something from my collection he could get them to let you know.'

'Yes that's the sort of thing that could just crack the case. Where was your collection kept sir?'

'In a locked cupboard in my study, it has been opened and closed again without a trace Inspector.'

'You don't surprise me sir, we're dealing with a master burglar, no mistaking that.'

'But my stamps and coins could be his Hercules heel?'

'Achilles heel sir, from Greek mythology, currently meaning a small but fatal weakness sir.'

'Thank you Ellingham, I'm sure we are most enlightened by your knowledge, but the fact remains it could get things moving, eh Inspector?'

'Not impossible sir, I think that's all I need to ask now. Except perhaps this friend you spoke to on the phone, how long have you known him?'

'John Manson? Oh not all that long Inspector, but he's a fellow member, a "Boater", I think you can forget about him.'

'Mr Walters at your club suggested that there is a very stringent selection process for new members, is that correct sir?'

'Not half, they look into your background as though you were going to be entrusted with the crown jewels or something, you also need to be introduced by an existing member.'

'So all new members would have to go through that process?'

'Absolutely, inspector.'

'I see. If you could make me a list of the rarer items in your collection please sir and let me have it as soon as possible, then I can get it circulated.'

'Do you want me to alert my uncle so that his cronies can be on the lookout?'

'Yes the more people looking the better.'

'With respect Inspector, the more people involved the more likely this unknown person is to become aware of the police interest in these things and curtail his activities in that direction,' said Ellingham.

'Do you mean he might smell a rat?' I asked.

'Precisely sir.'

'I think that's a chance I'll have to take, it's the only lead I have. One thing occurs to me sir; three hundred coins would be a bit on the heavy side, would one person be able to carry all of them and the stamps?'

'And Ellingham's wireless, don't forget. No I'd

say you'd need two or three people or several trips, would you agree Ellingham?'

'I have to agree, sir, more than a one man job.'

'Yes I agree; thank you, and good evening then gentlemen.'

'Good evening Inspector, oh, Ellingham seems to think that I am unlikely to see my collection again, is that so?'

'I hate to have to say it, but Mr Ellingham is probably right, it all depends on how quickly we can apprehend this villain sir.'

'I'll set about that list this instant, you'll have it first thing in the morning.'

'Thank you sir.'

'I'll see you out Inspector,' Ellingham said, and as they went out of the door he said, 'about my radio inspector…'

At that point I went into the study to begin the task of making that list. It was some little time later that there came a polite tap on the door.

'Come in Ellingham.'

'Thank you sir, I have taken the liberty of preparing you a hot rum and peppermint, a thing I often do for myself at times of mental anguish, I find it helps the brain to concentrate upon the task in hand sir.'

'Helps get the job done what?'

'I certainly find it so sir.'

'Having one yourself?'

'I have allowed myself a small quantity, yes sir.'

'I have to say I'm struggling with this list, so I need all the help I can get.'

'Could I be of assistance sir? My knowledge of postage stamps and the monetary tokens of the world is limited, but I am well up on the various countries; geography was my favourite subject. I often earned some extra money by doing exams on the subject for the son of the minor royal, of whom I have already spoken; perhaps an alphabetical list of countries may prompt your memory sir?'

'Go and get your brain stimulator, and we'll make a start.'

'Certainly sir.'

He returned a few moments later, glass in hand, and we sat down to the task.

'Not wishing to be impertinent sir, might I ask the value of your most desirable items sir?'

'To what end Ellingham?'

'I was merely thinking sir that the rarer and more desirable items would be the easiest to catalogue and also for the police to trace sir.'

'I'd worked that out Ellingham.'

'If I might continue sir. If you use the value of your most desirable coin or stamp as a top marker, it will be easier to set a value band below that figure, to limit the number of entries to the list sir.'

'Slide that past me again Ellingham.'

'Let us say sir that the most searched after item you own has a market value of ten shillings, then we could discount anything valued less than say seven shillings and sixpence to create a focus list sir.'

'I see your point, but you are a bit out with ten shillings, fifty pounds more like.'

'Indeed sir, in that case perhaps a focus on everything over a value of forty pounds. We could lower the figure if necessary to encompass a greater number of entries if the list is too short sir.'

'I fear it would be very short, the next most valuable would be about twenty-five quid.'

'In that case shall we say anything valued at over ten pounds, sir?'

'Right, let's do it.'

Even so it was no easy task; we toiled away for several hours, but in the end we had created a list of about thirty coins and fifty or so stamps that would cause interest on the market.

9

Thursday morning there were showers and bright spells, about fifty-fifty. I had sent Ellingham to take the completed list to Inspector Jackman and had just finished speaking to Uncle Josh, putting him in the picture. He asked me to send him a copy of the list and I was in the middle of writing out the envelope when the doorbell rang. On opening this I beheld a rather wet and bedraggled Jane Barrington-Ross.

'Hello, muddle-head,' she said.

'Hello yourself, I trust you do not intend to enter my abode dripping water on my parquet flooring?'

But I was too late, she already had. I took her coat and hung it on the hallstand and invited her into the sitting room.

'I was about to make some coffee, would you like some?'

I wasn't about to make coffee at all but one has to preserve the niceties on these occasions what?

'Yes please, can you remember how I like it?'

'I can't, and I'm afraid you will get it the way it turns out, Ellingham normally does it, as you know.'

'Of course, the faithful Ellingham, where is he by the way? I say what have you done with that sweet little carriage clock, not on hard times Josh? Has your father finally seen through you and pulled the plug?'

'No indeed, I've been burgled. Ellingham is away taking a list of missing things to the local gendarmes,' I replied.

'Burgled? Much as I currently think you're lower than a snakes kneecap, I'm sorry to hear you've been burgled. Anything valuable missing?'

'They've taken Ellingham's wireless set and a quantity of easily saleable stuff like the clock, but the blighters have taken my collection.'

'Oh, nothing too bad then?'

'I happen to be very fond of my collection, and sitting with Ellingham last night trying to create a list of the most valuable ones, they happen to be worth a pretty penny.'

'Yes but they're only stamps aren't they?'

'And coins and as a matter of fact they might be the vital breakthrough in a series of burglaries in the area, the clue that solves the case,' I said, and stuck out the old chin what?

'Anyway, I've a bone to pick with you Joshua Tolson,' she said.

'What have I done now?'

'Chas, he's nice by the way, has told me that you got him involved with that gumboil of a girl Liz Manson and this charity concert or whatever?'

'Have a care dear girl, you are speaking of the woman I love.'

'Oh, dear god, she's awful; Chas and I went to meet her last night, at some godforsaken town in the Midlands. We didn't hit it off, she's just too full of herself, too goody-goody to be true.'

I was astounded.

'I intend to do this for her, there will be a charity concert. If you won't do it I'll get someone else.'

'Oh, I'll do it alright, it means working closely

with Chas and he's a real sweet strawberry.'

'I remember you saying that about me.'

'Yes well, this sweet strawberry has a means of support, he earns his keep by the sweat of his brow and the strength of his back.'

'He's an advertising copy writer, an under-advertising copy writer at that.'

'You know what I mean.'

'I have to say I thought you'd like him, that's why I asked him to ask you to help, if that makes sense.'

'I eventually got it out of him that you had suggested me, I consider that this almost compensates for that fiasco with Uncle Rothwell's rose.'

'I thought you two would hit it off together. He's resilient if that's the right word. What I mean is he'll be able to ride out the hard knocks and pitfalls that life with you, should he be daft enough to end up with a life with you, will undoubtedly drop in his path.'

'I'm not that bad, I intend to make him an excellent wife, if he asks me.'

'Has it got that far already?'

'No, I'm still in the little girl bowled over stage. I've seen only the good in him so far, but I don't see any bad, he makes me laugh, and if he asks me I'm tempted.'

'Take it from me, blighted female, there is no bad in Chas. He is, as you rightly state one of life's sweet strawberries, I've known him since he wore short trousers and cried for his mother at the school gate.'

'Oh the poor darling, did he really cry for his mother at the school gate?'

'If not him, someone did, and I rather think it was him.'

'I'm sure you must be thinking of someone else, it

wouldn't be Chas, he's so strong and masterful, you've got your facts mixed up as usual, like falling for this Manson woman. She'll leave you in the lurch, call it woman's intuition or whatever but be careful. Much as I have often hoped that hell would open up and swallow you, I still love you like a sister you er...'

'Muddle headed gumozzle?' I ventured.

'Yes that'll do, what's a gumozzle?'

'Sorry I'm not privy to that information, it's what my Aunt Evangeline calls me at times when I've infuriated her. Which if you remember my Aunt E. is about every twenty minutes, and I've never plucked up the courage to ask, though I think she may have read it somewhere.'

'Oh well, back to this concert. We've tied the object of your affection down to a fortnight tomorrow in Oxford, we think that a quick poster or two around the various colleges should get enough talent at short notice, and we begin auditions a week beforehand. Chas has booked the theatre and is getting tickets printed and we confidently expect to raise about two hundred pounds.'

'That's great, I knew you two could get it going if anyone could; but you're wrong about Liz, you know, you've only seen her for a few minutes, I've been with her almost constantly for several days.'

'The poor girl, I'm changing my mind. If she's suffered you for a prolonged period, that explains a great deal. How come she allowed herself to get into a position where she was so trapped as to be with you for several days?'

'I went for a few days to my aunt's in Much Moreham and found that she was there, and not only that, my aunt was dead set on me not only meeting her but

204

making a good impression.'

'So that was where you met her, at your aunt's place?'

'Strangely, no. I first saw her at a cocktail evening at the Boater and had tried to track her down without success. Strange how these things happen what?'

'I wonder if it was just a strange coincidence?'

'I'm not with you.'

'No matter, let it go.'

At this point, there was the sound of a latchkey in the front door lock and Ellingham's voice called.

'Only me sir.'

'I'm in the sitting room Ellingham, talking to Miss Barrington-Ross.'

'I see sir, do you require my services?'

'Yes pop in if you would.'

And a few moments later he did indeed pop in.

'Ellingham, Miss Barrington-Ross has been telling me about the forthcoming concert, and how she has taken a liking to Chas Bestwick.'

'That is most gratifying sir, I hope the young man is equally enamoured, Miss?'

'I think he's as good as on the hook Ellingham. He tells me the concert idea was yours. But what do you think to your young master being hooked by Liz Manson?'

'I'm sure it is not my place to comment on such matters, Miss.'

'Maybe not but I bet you disapprove. I've told all I need to tell this young reprobate, you can dish the dirt as you show me out Ellingham.'

And so saying she got up, leaving my best effort at coffee-making barely touched, gave me a peck on the cheek and was on her way to the door escorted by Ellingham.

'Well, what do you think to your master's new lady, Ellingham?' Jane asked as the sitting room door was closing behind them.

I did not hear Ellingham's reply but I think it would have been noncommittal; he knows his place, and anyway, what is there not to like about Liz? He did seem to take rather a long time seeing her out though.

'She seems to have given you the third degree Ellingham?'

'Indeed the young lady was hard to convince that whatever thoughts I may entertain on the matter they are personal, and not for public consumption sir.'

'Cor; I bet that miffed her a good bit, used to getting her own way is Miss B-R.'

'The young lady was quite forceful in trying to stir me into making a reaction sir, she did however say something that I thought worth noting sir.'

'Really, what was that?'

'The young lady intimated that on meeting Miss Manson, she had the feeling that she recognised her from somewhere else, and that Miss Manson had seemed shy of meeting her eye to eye sir.'

'Nonsense, Jane's never been to Africa, as far as I'm aware, how could she possibly know her from somewhere else?'

'Miss Manson did venture the information that although her mother and father lived in Africa, she had been schooled in England sir.'

'Indeed, and when was this, I don't remember it?'

'It was one of our topics of conversation as I drove her to the railway station sir.'

206

'I see. I'll tell you something strange; you remember that nurse who saw me off from the hospital?'

'Yes sir.'

'Well she said the same, recognised her I mean.'

'Sir?'

'That she thought she knew Liz, Miss Manson, from somewhere else.'

'I believe you did mention it at the time, a very interesting coincidence sir.'

'Yes and I can tell you another.'

'Indeed sir?'

'I had been trying to meet Miss Manson, after seeing her, but being unable to speak to her at the cocktail party at the Boater, and be blowed if she isn't the very person my aunt wants me to meet and impress at The Willow's – how's that for strange coincidence?' I said.

'Strange indeed sir.'

'Could it be divine intervention, do you think?'

'There are no doubt those who would see it that way, but possibly there is a more down to earth explanation sir.'

'Okay, what then?'

'I could not say sir, but I have always thought that true coincidence is far rarer than we think, not by any means impossible, but highly unlikely. I'm sure that if we were in possession of all of the facts in the matter we would see that what at first appears to be pure coincidence has in fact a logical sequence to it.'

'You don't believe in coincidence then Ellingham?'

'I am, I have to say, one of life's sceptics sir'.

And there things rested for a few minutes.

I felt in need of a bit of fresh air and went out to

post the list to Uncle Josh. I met 'Spotty' Bagshaw, still a pedestrian, and stopped for a bit of a chinwag.

'Hi, Spotty, still on foot I see.'

'Hi, you old eyesore, yes, mother is cooling down a bit, but I still expect at least another months enforced foot-slogging.'

'Off to the Boater?'

'No, running an errand for the lady just mentioned, trying to earn an earlier parole.'

'I was going to suggest a quick snifter.'

'You've clearly forgotten the terms of my freedom from incarceration, not a drop must pass my lips until I am off the charge, if you get my drift.'

'Sorry, I had forgotten. Oh well, some other time, give me a ring when you are open for business.'

'Yes, I'll do that, by the way I've not seen you for a while, have you been away?'

'Yes, and burgled for the privilege.'

'You as well, well I'll be jiggered. Half the members of the Boater have been burgled, don't you know?'

'You exaggerate, I trust, there were over three-hundred and fifty members at the last count, so what would a more realistic figure be?'

'Well eight, but with you it's nine.'

'Hardly half, Spotty, but significant none the less.'

'Did you lose anything of value?' he asked.

'The usual stuff you know. They had Ellingham's wireless, and a few nice pieces of china and such, but the real thing that annoys, the blighter snaffled my collection.'

'Really, now that is odd. All of it?'

'Yes, all of it, stamps coins the lot, why is it odd?'

'I remember sitting at the bar at the Boater,

drowning my sorrows with orange juice and soda, not an easy task I might add and I caught one of those odd snippets of someone else's conversation. I thought nothing of it at the time, but I'm sure they were discussing stamps and things and I got the impression they had mentioned you; probably wrong though. You know how easy it is to get things wrong when you're stone cold sober?'

'True, who was it talking?'

'I can't remember, like I said it was just a snippet; went in and out in the same instant. Sorry I don't know. It's odd though, don't you think?'

'Um', another coincidence to add to the queue.'

'Not with you; coincidence?'

'No matter, I've things to be doing, so if you're not able to take a snifter at the moment I'll be wishing you good day. Ring me when you're back on the market, and we'll paint the town if not red a sort of deep pinkish colour. Ring me also if it occurs to you who was taking my collection in vain.'

'Will do, see you around Josh.'

'Yes see you Spotty.'

As you might imagine this new bit of information was still buzzing around the old bean-box when I again entered the flat. Ellingham was there to greet me as usual.

'Ellingham.'

'Sir?'

'I've just been speaking to "Spotty" Bagshaw.'

'Indeed sir, I trust the young gentleman is still in good health.'

'Eh, oh yes, but he's set me thinking,' I said.

'Really sir?' And he moved his head just a little twitch, as though he were surprised, but I let it go.

'Yes, and it's another of those coincidences. He

was in the Boater and overheard an odd bit of conversation and got the impression that they were talking about my collection.'

'That *is* most interesting, was the young gentleman aware of whom it was that was speaking sir?'

'Sadly no, but he's agreed to ring me if he remembers.'

'Although we are unaware of who was discussing your collection, perhaps we should inform Inspector Jackman of this new development. It suggests still further that the crimes are an inside job, I believe we agreed that that's the current term sir.'

'I was thinking along the same lines myself Ellingham. Spotty informs me that with my burglary nine Boater members have been targeted. Get the inspector on the phone, there's a good chap.'

'Certainly, sir. If I might change the subject sir?'

'Change away Ellingham.'

'Thank you sir. I have been made aware of a certain matter that requires me to request a short leave of absence, sir. I am aware that I have already made an application for my annual holiday which you have kindly agreed to allow, and that this new request would be in addition to that already stated. I realise that it is likely to be highly inconvenient sir, but I must request it with immediate effect sir.'

'I have never known you to make a request like this before. It must, therefore, mean that you need to give this matter your most urgent attention. Much as I will find life hard, not to say near impossible without you, do what you must, take as long as it takes, but no longer there's a good chap.'

'You are most kind sir, I will endeavour to

210

complete the task as soon as possible. I anticipate two to three days sir.'

'Go and pack or prepare as necessary, I'll phone the inspector myself.'

'Thank you sir.'

Dashed inconvenient of course, but I supposed even I would be able to boil the breakfast egg and burn a bit of toast for a couple of days, say three at the outside, what?

Well it seems there is a knack to even a boiled egg. Ellingham had obviously put the egg timer, the one with the little chicken on top, somewhere safe, I couldn't find it anywhere, so I had to do it blind, so to speak. I've heard my Aunt E. order a five minute egg, and took that as a guide, making it six to be on the safe side – I had increased this to eight on the second morning but the damned thing was still hard. I made a mental note to ask Ellingham for an explanation on his return. One thing I did find whilst looking for the egg timer, pushed away at the very back of a cupboard, (I suspect the burglars must have pushed it there inadvertently whilst looking for saleable goods,) was my dear old pal Kleeno (large economy size), so I knew that would brighten Ellingham's return to the old homestead. But I'm getting ahead of the scheme of things.

The phone was answered at the other end.

'Inspector Jackman please,' I said.

'Could I have your name sir please?' asked the voice at the other end.

'Joshua Tolson.'

'I'm trying his office for you now sir.'

After a wait that seemed to take about half an eternity, during which there were clicks and mumblings at the other end, eventually a voice materialised.

'Inspector Jackman's office,' said a voice, one I didn't recognise.

'Could I speak to Inspector Jackman please?'

'I'm afraid the Inspector is out at the moment sir, I'm Detective Sergeant Merriweather, can I be of assistance?'

'It's about the burglary at my flat. I'm Joshua Tolson, by the way. I've come up with a new bit of information that may be of use to him.'

'I'm co-ordinating the information on the series of burglaries that includes yours sir. If you wouldn't mind putting me in the picture I'll make sure the inspector is informed; he's due to ring in to report anything new and catch up on developments in about half an hour sir.'

I told the sergeant about the conversation Spotty had overheard, he thanked me and there the matter rested.

As I replaced the earpiece on that hook thing at the side of the instrument, Ellingham was reappearing from his room with what appeared to be a sort of Gladstone bag, he was dressed in a rather snazzy tweed plus-fours suit. Never seen him dressed like that before, quite the man about the country.

'I am ready to leave, if there is nothing further you require of me sir?'

'No thank you Ellingham, hurry to your task, is there anywhere you would like me to run you?'

'Most kind sir, I have already arranged for a taxicab to collect me, it should be here at any moment sir.'

'Well then, God speed and may success attend you in your venture.'

'Thank you sir, I fancy I hear the vehicle now; I will return as rapidly as is humanly possible. Goodbye sir.'

'Goodbye Ellingham.' And with that he went out of my life, for two days, four hours and twenty eight and a half minutes, give or take fifteen seconds or so.

I don't know if you've ever been in the position to notice, but when someone with whom you rub shoulders on a regular basis suddenly removes themselves from your company, so to speak, even if that person is your paid manservant, it leaves one heck of a hole. When you're used to sparking off against another ready intellect, and that other ready intellect is there one minute, and gone the next, well it's rather unsettling.

I considered spending a goodly proportion of my enforced separation at the Boater, but that's just likely to make you blotto. So I decided to ring Chas to see if there was any way I could assist in the concert preparations. But just then I remembered I had another call to make, to the factory to Mr. Fothergill. You'll no doubt remember that I had a plan to outwit Ellingham with regard to Beryl the blue eyesore.

It turned out that planning for the concert was at an advanced stage. Like I said, Chas doesn't let the grass grow.

'So is there nothing I can help with then Chas?'

'Well yes there is something that needs doing, but it needs handling with kid gloves, skill and discretion, with diplomacy.'

'I can be diplomatic.'

'Um, it's out of your league, I'm afraid.'

'Chas, I can handle it, I am discrete, used to handling things with kid gloves and *I'm* also footing the bill remember.'

'Oh, well if you put it that way, and since you'll be able to call on Ellingham for support I suppose you could have a bash.'

'Ah, I think I will be able to handle whatever it is without the need for Ellingham to become involved.'

'Just as you wish. Have a bash by all means, you are the boss after all, but take my advice, have Ellingham in the background.'

'Ellingham will be well and truly in the background I can assure you, so what is this life threatening task?'

'I've arranged for Miss Manson to have a look at the theatre I've found to see if it meets with her approval. I think that at the beginning she might like to say just a few words about her charity, to help with the collection I've arranged at the end.'

'I see no problem,' I said, 'no need for the kid gloves approach.'

'I was hoping to meet her there myself to take care of any problems, or arrange for any changes she might require.'

'So, okay, that'll be me.'

'If only it were that easy. Jane has decided to go in my place and, well to be blunt, they didn't exactly become bosom pals when they met the other night.'

'You think Jane may scupper the exercise?'

'Jane is a lovely girl, as you know, but she's got a real bee in her bonnet about Miss Manson, thinks there's something fishy about her.'

'Jane came to my flat this morning to put me in the picture of how things were progressing, she told me that she was unhappy about Liz, Miss Manson. And I told her, as I am telling you, have a care, you are speaking of the woman I love.'

'Crumbs, I had no idea that there were wheels within wheels so to speak. But if you're sure you can handle it?'

'I see no problem, they will be as putty in my hands,' I said confidently.

'I think wrestling a grizzly bear, or killing a tiger bare handed might be preferable.'

'You overreact old pumpkin.'

'Okay have it your way but don't forget, there'll always be Ellingham in the background. They're meeting at that little theatre down by the Ashmolean Museum - seven thirty tonight. Can you make that?'

I told him I could, and he rang off before I could ask him if he had any idea why Jane had taken a dislike to Liz.

The journey to Oxford would take a little over an hour, which, since it was only twelve thirty, left me with oodles of time to spare. Have you ever noticed that when you've oodles of time on your hands you start to do something to fill that time. I decided to make a list of some of my fellow collectors, so that I might send them a copy of my list of stolen stamps and request their assistance. It took me much longer than I thought without Ellingham to give me his usual timely reminder, "tempus fugit sir", that time is ticking away, I totally lost track of it. A sudden impulse made me look at my watch; it was just gone five o'clock, things could be tight.

It was just before five thirty-five as I got into Beryl, drove up the garage ramps, and was on my way. City traffic was surprisingly light for the time of day, and I was soon making good time, eating up the miles. Beryl might be the wrong colour; but in all other respects she resembles my dearest Ramona, as I suppose you might expect. Slough and Henley on Thames slipped by as I was settling down to enjoy the journey. I missed Ellingham's company of course, but to some extent the pleasant late afternoon made up for it. Wallingford had disappeared into history and I seemed to be getting back on schedule, but about a mile or so before Shillingford, I began to lose power. Beryl gave a hiccup and started to die. If you know a bit about the Tolson Mk14 you'll know that she is fitted with a reserve fuel tank, operated by a tap on the dashboard. I thought Beryl was running out of fuel and tried to turn the tap to reserve but it was already there, so both Beryl and yours truly were out of fuel, HA. I was left with little option but to walk to Shillingford and hope it was endowed with a garage selling petrol. So I hitched up the old trousers and put my best foot forward, as the saying goes.

I remember thinking that it would have been a lovely time for a walk, if only I had been a more free agent to time than was the present case. I don't know what Ellingham would have made of the sequence of events that followed, but yet another coincidence occurred. The road at that point is fairly straight and I had walked but a few hundred yards, when I noticed travelling towards me, going at a goodish rate of knots was a Rolls Royce. I started to jump up and down and wave my arms madly in the air, must have looked a bit like a demented windmill, to attract the drivers attention, the vehicle began to slow and eventually came to a stop beside me. Imagine my surprise when the driver of the aforesaid vehicle turned out to be none other than my acquaintance of the other day, the man who thought I owed him lunch. I suffered a turmoil of emotions as you might expect, here was my

216

saviour, my knight in shining armour so to speak, but the very man I had made a mental note to grind in the dirt if we ever met again.

'Hello, we meet again my friend,' he said with a winning smile.

'As you say we meet again,' I replied keeping a lid on my wish to tear out his gizzard and boot it over the nearest hedge.

'Has the Tolson broken down old chap?'

'Just out of petrol I think.'

'You've tried the reserve?' he grinned.

'Of course, only to find the tap was already on reserve so I guess I'm well and truly out.'

'Hard luck old chap; bet you're in a bit of a hurry too, what?'

'I have an appointment in Oxford in a short time, so I would be most grateful if you'd run me to the nearest garage.'

'Normally I would be only too pleased, being in your debt so to speak, but I'm in a bit of a rush myself.'

'Could you drop me off back in Wallingford? I noticed a garage there, and I'll make my own way back.'

'I'll do even better than that, I've a spare two gallon can in the boot, you could have that.'

I have to say my opinion of the chap began to brighten somewhat, and at this point I would probably have settled for flattening his nose.

'That's very decent of you,' I said, even if it was a little bit through clenched teeth.

'Yes, isn't it,' he grinned, 'jump in.'

I did as requested and we were soon back at the Mk14. We climbed out, me to go to the Tolson to open the filler cap and him to collect the can. It turned out to be about half full, so say it contained about a gallon of fuel. Enough to get me to Oxford, that's for sure. He set the can on the ground without opening it.

'Shall we negotiate a price?' he smiled.

'Shall we say the cost of a lunch?' I replied.

'Ah, water under the bridge old chap, in the present situation I'm in control of a sellers market.'

Back to the gizzard tearing and kicking feeling, but what could I do?

'I see it's like that is it?'

'Favours always come at a price old chap.'

I felt in my pocket and fished out a two-bob bit, which considering a gallon of juice costs about one and a penny, I thought more than generous.

'I was thinking more along the lines of a pound.'

'I'd rather walk.'

'Fine by me.' he said and picking up the can began to walk back to the Rolls.

'Okay, a pound it is, pour it in.'

'I've been thinking, a Guinea would seem a nicer figure, more the sort of figure two gentlemen would agree on, what?'

'Pour it in, a guinea it is blast you.'

'I think I'll have the guinea first if it's all the same to you, once the fuel's in your tank, you might see fit to fail on the deal, and I can't get the stuff out again can I?'

He must have read my mind. I felt in my wallet and extracted a pound note, and added a shilling from my pocket.

'One guinea as agreed.'

He handed me the can and I poured the contents into my tank, then put the can in the gap behind the seats on the Mk14.

218

'I say, that's my can,' he said.

'Well I'll fight you for it, and I must warn you, I intend to win if we do.'

'Ah, okay, keep the can with my compliments,' and he was off.

Met his match I think what?

Back on my way having lost about half an hour; much less than if I'd had to walk to Shillingford and back; so not too bad even if I was well out of pocket. Just on the outskirts of Oxford there's one of those little shops that sell everything from safety pins to petrol, and I made the owner's day by filling Beryl to the brim, all fourteen gallons. I remembered to turn the tap on the dash to main tank, and was on my way being only a few minutes behind plan.

I found the theatre in question just as Jane B-R was pulling up in her bright red little Swift 7. We waved and I walked across to meet her.

'What are you doing here, fathead?' she cheerily greeted.

'Chas asked me to give you a hand, take notes, that sort of thing I suppose,' I replied.

'Act as referee, I think you mean?'

'Something like that maybe.'

'No need, I've become very philosophical about the whole thing. I understand we use the side door.'

We found the door and let ourselves in. Liz was already on stage looking around. I guess she must have heard us entering because she turned and gave us a little nod.

'Hello again,' said Jane.

'Hello Jane,' she said, then more warmly, 'Josh, what a lovely surprise, what brings you to Oxford?'

'Chas asked me to assist Jane, and help with any

219

suggestions I might have.'

By this time we had met up and I had kissed Liz on the cheek.

'This is a lovely little theatre, how clever of you to find it Jane, and with a ready-made talent supply, it's just the job.'

'It took no finding, it wasn't lost. And it was Chas who arranged it, though I have to agree he was clever securing it.'

'Strange it was free at such short notice,' I commented.

'Yes I wondered that,' Liz said.

'It's closed for re-decoration, they have agreed to have it finished for our evening. I think the manager is glad of the free publicity Chas has offered him,' Jane replied.

'I have only one tiny reservation. Is an audience of students going to raise enough money to make it a success?' asked Liz.

'There are some tickets at student prices, but Chas has very cleverly I think, asked for a donation rather than a fixed price for the prime seats,' Jane replied.

'That seems to scupper any appeal I might make to the audience if they have already donated, as they see it, for their ticket,' Liz pointed out.

'Possibly,' Jane snapped.

'I see Liz's point,' I added.

'No doubt you do, but perhaps she feels that the estimated two hundred pound we expect to raise is hardly worth her bothering to turn up.'

'I didn't mean that, of course I'll turn up, but if you've already taken the crowd for all it's worth a further appeal will not go down too well.'

'A fair point,' I said, which gained a smile from Liz and a scowl from Jane.

'Come on then you woolly headed waste of space, what do you suggest?' Jane sneered.

'Don't make a further appeal stand up and thank everyone, audience, performers and theatre management, for their support. Tell them briefly about what the charity does, and thank them again for their generosity,' I offered. 'Those who feel they've been a bit mean could well dig a bit deeper.'

'I like it,' said Liz.

'Then what if Josh goes up on stage at the end, says how much he's enjoyed it and pledges say fifty quid, and requests everyone to dig deep?' said Jane.

'Ah,' I said.

'We'd need to rehearse him a bit on what to say, he went down like the Titanic a few days ago saying much along those lines,' Liz grinned.

'Oh what happened?' Jane asked looking at me.

I gave her a brief outline.

'You really are a chump, Josh; you should have seen that one coming.'

'It wasn't his fault, I asked him to speak on the spur of the moment and he assures me that given more time he could have excelled,' said Liz.

'Apparently Ellingham had suggested that I spoke better when given the task unexpectedly,' I said.

'Oh, Ellingham suggested it. I see,' said Jane.

'What do you mean by that?' I asked.

'Oh nothing er, had we better look at dressing-rooms and things and see if we need to sort anything out?'

Over the next half-hour or so lots of minor details were discussed and ironed out, not always with mutual agreement, and that was where I used a casting vote, you could see why Chas had asked me to be there. Occasionally the ice in the air would melt, then re-freeze with a vengeance. Those two girls really didn't hit it off, beats me why.

Eventually we'd finished and shouted the old boy in charge to come and lock up, and we stood outside for a moment. Jane gave me a peck on the cheek, said goodbye to us both and buzzed off with a roar in her Swift 7.

'I hope you didn't mind me siding with Jane every so often? I asked.

'Of course not, she obviously has some sort of hold over you.'

'Did have, we were engaged for a while, but it's done with. Dead history.'

'I don't think she thinks so.'

'Well she can go boil her head, not on, dead and done with. Though I still love her as a brother, an idiot brother perhaps.'

'Ah, well in that case you could have taken my side a bit more often.'

'I could see both side of the argument and made my decision as I saw fit, in the best interest of your charity.'

'Yes, I know, in my heart of hearts I know your decisions were fair. I think it was just me wanting to be contrary to upset Jane, so thank you for being a calming influence.'

'My pleasure. Talking of pleasure, have you time to have dinner with me, there's a nice little restaurant just around the corner?'

'Lead on kind sir, I'm in a hotel at the end of King Street, so the evening is ours.'

'Oh spot on, I've something rather important to ask you.'

'Sounds interesting,' she said, and gave me a little quizzical look.

'Oh, it is, shall we go?'

When you've said something like that it sort of hangs in the air until you actually come to the matter, and such was the case in point. Although we prattled a bit of this and that through the meal, it was always waiting in the wings.

'You said you have something important to ask me, have you forgotten or are you just unable to get round to it?' she prompted.

'Oh, I've not forgotten, and it's about as important as things get,' I replied, my insides turning to jelly.

'Then for goodness sake, say it, the worst I can say is no.'

'That's it, I suppose; if you say no, I don't know what I'll do.'

'So ask you silly chump.'

'Well, erm, I think you like me, and I like you. Oh dash it, I love you, will you marry me. There I've said it.'

'Wow, that was a bit of a bombshell. Gosh. Do I have to answer now?'

'Now would be nice, but I remember Jane took a couple of days to come around to the idea.'

'I don't think mentioning Jane at this point was a good idea.'

'No, you're right, I just threw it in to show I can wait for an answer if I really have to. I did rather drop it on you, what?'

'You are sweet, do you think I didn't know you

were leading up to it, have been for a while? I just didn't expect it to come out all in a rush like that.'

'You knew?'

'A girl always knows, the dreamy way you look at me sometimes. Others have noticed it as well you know, your aunt and the major, to name but two.'

'Well I'm dashed.'

'No you're not. Not really, you just think you've come up with something earth-shatteringly new. I have been asked before you know.'

'Oh, yes I suppose men must be queuing up to pop the question,' I said a bit down-hearted.

'Well yes, I suppose at the current count you stand about twenty-seventh in line for an answer. I'll get around to one for you about July next year. Of course I've been asked before, and I'm very flattered that you've ask me and I think you're the nicest, sweetest, man who's ever asked me, but the problem is, if I were to say yes, I come at a price.'

'Your charity work in Africa?'

'Yes.'

'Understood, and I can think of nothing nicer than to spend the rest of my life helping you with that,' I said.

'Even if it means the hardships of eating out of doors?' and she grinned.

'I'll learn to cope.'

'But would you? I'll ask you a question in return. Think overnight about the differences life out in Africa would make to your life; ask yourself if I'm really worth it, then if you still feel the same, ring me and ask me again tomorrow. And I'll think about it too. If you decide not to ring I'll be disappointed, but no hard feelings,' she smiled.

224

We walked back to her hotel in silence, each of us thinking, I suppose, on the question I had raised. As we lingered at the entrance, she said -

'Please do think very carefully. When I'm in Africa, my whole existence is about my work. You might hardly get a look in, you know.'

'Playing second fiddle to schools for little African kids but married to you, seems good enough to me,' replied.

'But would it be? There's no clubs out there like yours, what clubs you'll find are all stiff upper lip and pink gin. They are nearly all for people with a military background, or people who constantly chatter on about "the old country" with no intention of ever returning. You'd be like a fish out of water.'

'I think, then, I will become your Ellingham, I will be at your beck and call and wait upon you hand and foot, that sort of thing.'

'You'd soon grow tired of that, anyway Mumbo already does that now.'

'Well then, he'll golly well have to go.'

'He's my bodyguard when things get tough, he recognises animal tracks, that I often can't see even when he has pointed them out to me. Much as I love you, and yes I admit it, I do love you, you'd never be able to do that.'

'Oh well, I suppose he'll have to stay on in the bodyguard-in-the-jungle role but I'll do things around the house.'

'And put two girls out of a job?' she asked.

'It seems you don't want me to marry you, you say you love me but you just keep on raising doubts.'

'I do love you, I've known it since the time you

dragged me back to the bridge, when you thought Ellingham was going for an illicit evening drive.'

'Oh yes I remember, the night we saw the kingfisher.'

'Heron.'

'Oh yes, that's right. But you are, you know, putting pitfalls in my way, as though you are testing me.'

'I suppose I am. I don't want you to find that you're dreadfully unhappy about twenty minutes after you've married me, so do as I say, think it over overnight and ring me tomorrow, even if it's to say that you're still thinking it over.'

'I won't change my mind.'

'You changed it over Jane and you were already engaged to her.'

'Ah yes, but Jane wanted me to get a job, and anyway she broke it off.'

'That's my very point. Could you accept a change in you life as drastic as Africa, if getting a job was out of the question?' she said and began to scribble something on a bit of paper.

'I see your fears, but I'll manage.'

'Well think it over. Here's the telephone number that I'll be at tomorrow. Ring me at about two o'clock, I'll be available then. As I said, even if it's to say you're still thinking it over.' She smiled, gave me a kiss on the mouth, turned and she was gone.

I walked back to the Tolson in a blue mood, just about four shades bluer than the blasted car. I could see her point of course, and she had raised doubts in my mind. Not about if I loved her, that was never in doubt, but could I love Africa, that was a different kettle of fish. Though why fish should be put in kettles I've never really understood, must give the next few cups of tea a funny taste what?

Have you ever run a sort of balance sheet in your mind, trying to come to some sort of answer? I bet you have. Well I did it that night on the way home.

Against She has a point you know; you know nothing about Africa.

For Yes but I love her.

Against She'll be all wrapped up in her work, you may not see her for days.

For Yes but I love her.

Against She thinks a lot of this damned Mumbo.

For Yes but I love her.

Against There must be a thousand and one things you've not thought of.

For *Yes but I love her*.

Pretty much cut and dried, I'd say what? I arrived home with that funny feeling you sometimes get, you know, where you suddenly find yourself at journeys end wondering how the heck you got there, the whole journey a total blank. Perhaps I'm the only person it happens to. Once inside Tolson Towers I picked up the evening paper, locked the door for the night and put the kettle on.

Without Ellingham to edit the rag for me, I had to look at it myself. The only things that seemed of interest were both on page four.

Police Still Struggling

The police are still no further forward with solving the string of burglaries that have been plaguing our local citizens.

A spokesman for Inspector Jackman, the detective in charge of the case, said:

"We are still looking into several new leads that we are hoping might culminate in us apprehending the villain or villains responsible."

As we all know, that's a police term for; we are completely baffled.

The second bit was much along the same lines, if only they knew. I drank my tea, having suitably laced it with whiskey, and turned in for the night.

I had consumed the breakfast toast and the six-minute egg of which I have already made mention. I was amazed at the multitude of things that needed doing; things that Ellingham always did in the background. It makes you realise just how much you depend on a good manservant. I remember thinking, I will certainly miss him when I marry Liz. I have to admit the rest of the day was as good as uneventful except that at about two o'clock I rang Liz, or at least tried to, only to find long distance calls were stacking up and by the time I was able to get through it was about four-thirty and she had moved on. So Friday was all but a washout.

Saturday morning's egg was, as I said, no better, though I hardly noticed due to thinking about how I was going to get in touch with Liz. I was brought out of this train of thought by the ringing of the doorbell, not just any old ring, you understand, but the type where either the button has stuck, or the person without is leaning on it intentionally. Being barely half past ten, I was still in the jolly old dressing gown. Being summer it was my bright red silk one, with an enormous golden dragon on the back, hardly the thing to be wearing when opening a door. However I had little choice but to do so since the bally doorbell looked like blowing a fuse or something.

228

'Mr Joshua Tolson?' asked a tall man wearing a trilby hat, the taller of the two men standing there.

I took them to be policemen.

'Yes I am,' I said.

'I am Detective Sergeant Merriweather, and this is Detective Constable Brice.'

' Ah, yes, we've spoken on the phone I believe,' I said.

'That's correct sir, I wonder if you'd be kind enough to come down to the station with us, there's a matter you might be able to assist us with.'

'Lummy: am I under arrest or something?'

'No sir, and you can of course refuse, but you could be of great assistance to us sir.'

'Always willing to assist the police with their enquiries. Give me five minutes to get dressed and I'll be with you. The kettle has just boiled if you'd like to make yourselves a cup of coffee or tea.' One likes to be civil what?

'Thank you sir, that would be most welcome.'

As you can imagine I would have much preferred to have Ellingham on hand to chew this latest development over with. But as you already know he wasn't, and so I dressed with my mind in a whirl. Having suitably attired myself I returned to find the two coppers enjoying the last drops of their respective drinks.

'If you're ready then sir?'

'I am, do I need to alert a solicitor or someone?' I asked.

'I don't think that will be necessary sir, it's just your assistance we need.'

'Can't give me any idea what it's about I suppose?'

'All will be revealed at the station, sir.'

I imagine it must be a sort of game they play, cards close to the chest and all that, what?

The police car rolled to a stop in the police station yard and the three of us got out. I have to my discredit had occasion to frequent police stations for a couple of minor misdemeanours which have no bearing upon the situation in hand, but I was struck as previously by the police station pong. I remember thinking that if hospitals and police stations occupied the same building, the combined effect would be a sort of neutral smell. I was taken into a small room, a bit like those you see on the films; a table bolted to the floor, a chair bolted to the floor, and dark green paint. I'm sure it had once been dark green in it's dim and distant past, bolted to the walls. The room would have been lit only by a barred window high up in the wall if the electric light had not been switched on. A bit depressing as I'm sure you can imagine. I sat in the fixed chair and Sergeant Merriweather sat on one of the two movable chairs at the other side, Constable Brice did not enter with us but went off somewhere else.

'Could I offer you a cup of tea sir?' he asked.

'Just a glass of water please.'

He disappeared for a few moments and returned with a glass, clean and sparkling much to my amazement, filled to the brim with fresh clean water, quite refreshing actually.

'You told us that your collection of coins and stamps had been stolen in your recent burglary, is that correct?'

'Absolutely, the whole job lot, albums, little flat wooden display boxes and all.'

'I see. You haven't within the recent past, sold

any of your collection to a dealer?'

'I do sell them from time to time, but collectors tend to buy rather than sell, Sergeant.'

'When was the last time you sold some of your collection sir?'

'Gosh, now you're asking, er, must have been the best part of a year ago.'

'Can you remember who you sold them to?'

Awful grammar, but I let it go.

'I certainly can, one of the members of my club.'

'Would that be the Straw Boater Club sir?'

'None other, Sergeant.'

'Would you give me the person's name sir?'

'I can't see what that has to do with my burglary?'

'Maybe nothing sir, but it's strange how many times your club keeps popping up among the facts of this case.'

'We're a close knit group Sergeant, whilst we don't exactly live in each other pockets so to speak, we do have a great camaraderie.'

'I see, sir, but bear with me, I merely want to eliminate this person from our enquiries.'

'Willy, that is William Dixon. Don't know his address, but I've his number here in my diary,' I said, reaching into my inside pocket.

'If you would sir.'

'Marble Arch 61398.'

'Was it common knowledge at your club, that you are a collector, sir?'

'Other like minded members would no doubt have known, but hardly common knowledge Sergeant.'

'Thank you sir; you're sure you've not sold any or all of your collection in the past three days?'

231

'Be bally hard when the blasted things have been stolen what?'

'I agree *if* they had been stolen, it would be most difficult, sir.'

'What do you mean, *if* they had been stolen?'

'We have been questioning a certain stamp dealer who swears that you sold him a certain item, which seem to have come from your collection sir.'

I was fortunate in that I had just put the glass of water back on the table, but it did rather spoil my hither-to unbroken record of spilling stuff over myself when confronted with startling statements.

'He says *I* sold them to him?'

'Swears it sir. We did not detain the man and he should be arriving here again any minute.'

'When was this supposed to be? I ask because I have been away in the country until midday Wednesday.'

'I assume you can verify that, sir?'

'I say this is getting a bit thick, am I a suspect or something. As it happens I was away at my aunt's place in Gloucestershire.'

At this point Constable Brice entered carrying a large leather-bound book exactly like the ones I used as my albums.

'Do you recognise this album, sir?' asked Brice, after a nod of approval from Merriweather.

He passed it over the table to me and I opened it.

'Yes, it's mine. At a quick glance I'd say it's complete.'

'If, as you say, it was not you who sold them to the dealer, why would the thief pretend to be you?' he said with a sarcastic smile.

'Perhaps *he* had noticed that I have taken the

precaution of writing my name inside the cover Constable?'

'Ah, yes I supposed that must be the case, sir.'

I let it go, having scored in this way. I felt elated, but not stupid enough to rub his nose in it so to speak.

'You had noticed that I assume Brice?' asked Merriweather.

'Just wanting confirmation from Mr Tolson, Sarge.'

'So, let's get this straight; you confirm that these are your stamps, in your album, but you deny selling them to a stamp dealer?'

'Absolutely.'

'And you've never met this stamp dealer before?'

'It's hard to say that until you tell me who he is; are you trying to trip me up, Sergeant?'

'Forgive me sir, I thought we had told you, it's a Mr Carter Noakes sir.'

'Never heard of him.'

'You've never dealt with him in the past then sir?'

'Not knowingly, certainly.'

'Not knowingly sir?'

'I'm a collector, I buy for my collection. I've been buying stamps and coins for over ten years; it's not beyond the bounds of possibility that I may have purchased from him in the past.'

'But not sold to him?'

'That, I would remember, Sergeant.'

'So you would have no objection to meeting this person, sir?'

'Wheel him in, Sergeant.'

'Is Mr Noakes back yet Brice?'

'I believe so, Sarge.'

'Bring him here then, Constable,' said Merriweather.

'Right-ho, Sarge.'

There was a wait for a few minutes during which time I lovingly turned the pages of the album. The door opened and admitted a man who looked a bit careworn and tired.

'Is this the man who sold you the album you see on the table Mr Noakes?' asked Brice.

'No, nothing like him, that chap had a beard. Who's this then?'

'This *is* Mr Joshua Tolson.'

'The real Joshua Tolson?' the poor chap asked.

'None other,' I said.

'I'm terribly sorry Mr Tolson, I really took the other fellow to be telling the truth. I had no reason to doubt him.'

'Alright, assuming you bought them in good faith as you suggest, is it your normal practice to leave them together as a collection, or break them up?' asked Merriweather.

'I did buy them in good faith Sergeant, but as to how I would have disposed of them that's a matter I was still deciding on. It's a fine collection by the way Mr Tolson,' he added looking at me.

'Thank you,' I nodded.

'The chap said he had some coins as well?'

'That's right they were stolen at the same time,' I replied.

The constable fetched another chair and Mr Noakes seated himself on it, my side of the table.

'So you might have broken them up, sold them off piece-meal?' asked the sergeant.

234

'About twice a year there are stamp auctions, it sometimes works well to sell the whole lot as a collection. As I said, I was still trying to decide which avenue to proceed for the best.'

'All told Mr Tolson claims to have lost four similar albums and some coin trays, is this the only one you purchased from the villain?'

'No, well yes, that is, I agreed to buy another three and look at the coins, subject them being to the same quality and a price being agreed.'

'Why didn't you tell us that before?'

'I told the constable who brought me in, but he seemed only to be interested in the one album I'd actually purchased.'

'If it's such a good collection, why didn't you buy the whole lot on the spot?'

'I probably would have but I hadn't the necessary cash. This one took me to the limit I had available, and as it was I took about an hour to come to my decision.'

'Was the chap standing around for that long waiting for you to value it?'

'No, of course not, he left it with me, did something else and came back.'

'He took the other albums with him then?'

'This is the only one I was shown, and yes he left it with me.'

'We circulated all stamp dealers with details of the theft, why did you still continue to buy the album?'

'Your letter arrived in the post this morning, having been redirected from an address I left five years ago, Sergeant. I contacted you as soon as I realised they may be what you were looking for.'

'Ah, I see. So when he returned he accepted your valuation?'

'Not immediately, he suggested a figure slightly higher than my valuation and we agreed to a mid-way figure.'

'You haggled?'

'Hardly haggled exactly; we each had an idea in mind. I tried for the best price as a dealer, he as a seller, we made a gentleman's agreement, as I said about half way between the two.'

'You say you paid in cash, is that normal?'

'Look I've already told you all this, about fifteen times. I bought the bloody things in good faith. I paid cash because the chap said he needed cash urgently, he didn't want a cheque. It is a valuable collection, I could see a good profit in the transaction, so yes, I agreed to pay cash.'

'Mm, so what arrangement was made about the other three albums?'

'He said he would be bringing them in this morning but I can't see that happening now, me being here, can you?'

A thought occurred to me; and I asked -

'Why are you questioning us together Sergeant, isn't it more normal to keep us apart? It's always what they do in the films.'

'Once Mr Noakes said you weren't the man who sold him the album it became clear that you were both innocent parties, and I took the chance that we might better be served by letting the two of you spark off each other.'

'Does that mean I'm free to go?' we both asked together.

'I've no reason to keep you, but give me another few minutes please gentlemen. I'd like to ask...'

He was interrupted by a knock at the door.

'Yes, what is it?'

The door opened and a thin-faced policeman poked his head around it.

'Phone call for you Sergeant, says it urgent.'

Merriweather got up and asked who was calling as he walked through the door.

'The gentleman said his name was...'

The blasted door closed, so I couldn't hear the name.

The door opened and the sergeant re-entered and asked me.

'You have a man servant by the name of Ellingham, is that correct, sir?'

'You know I have, you met him at my flat. He reported the burglary.'

'Inspector Jackman came to your flat sir, but that agrees with his notes.'

'Trying to get me released what?'

'Not exactly sir, a name has been suggested and we're taking it very seriously.'

'What, you're not suggesting Ellingham is in anyway connected with all this?'

'At the moment I don't think so, sir.'

'Well don't think it at all, the man has been with me for years, he's as honest as the day is long sergeant.'

'Just so, sir. As I said, a name has been suggested, and it looks very promising.'

'Are you going to tell us or keep us here all day Sergeant?'

'The person is known to us as "Charlie Charity".'

'Never heard of him,' we both said together.

Quite a double act we were becoming, this stamp dealer and me.

'I didn't suppose you would, but he's well known to us, well the Scottish police to be precise. In fact we have a picture of him. We're just looking it up now.'

'Has he got a record then Sergeant?'

'If he's our man he got out of prison about a year ago. Supposedly gone straight, but in my experience they seldom do.'

'If he's known to you why don't you keep an eye on him?' I asked.

'If we were to keep an eye on every known villain we'd need a police force about twenty times bigger than it is now. Anyway he's not from this patch, comes from way up north, though they say you'd never know it from his accent. Real posh they reckon.'

'If he's from up north, how come you have a photograph of him?' I asked.

'I'll explain that if he's our man.'

At this point the door opened and the thin-faced copper handed the sergeant a large brown envelope.

'Thank you, Constable. Now Mr Noakes, in this envelope there are several pictures of men with beards; look carefully and tell me if you recognise one of them as the man who sold you Mr Tolson's stamps,' he said and passed the envelope to the stamp dealer.

Noakes spread the pictures on the table, and straight away without a moments hesitation pointed to the very one that had instantly grabbed my attention.

'That's him; that's the man who sold me your stamps,' he said turning to me.

'Yes – "Charlie Charity",' said the two coppers

together.

'If you knew this man was in the area, why haven't you had him in for questioning?' asked the stamp dealer.

The poor chap had a point.

'Common burglary is not his style, he's into other things, clever things. Confidence trickery. I believe, the Americans call them scams, sir.'

'Selling Nelson's column to the Americans, or shares in non-existent gold mines, that sort of thing?' I ventured.

'Oh, no, nothing so grand as that sir. Glasgow people are a bit too wary to fall for anything that dubious.'

'You said you would explain how you happen to have a picture,' I said.

'That's a strange one. It happened by accident. There was a photograph in a newspaper a few weeks ago and one of our officers has recently transferred to us from Edinburgh or Glasgow or some such place. He noticed "Charlie Charity" in the background. Realising he might have moved down here we approached the newspaper for a close-up of him, which they very kindly supplied; it's a bit grainy, you couldn't use it in a portrait exhibition, but you can see the man clearly enough.'

'A stroke of luck then, Sergeant?'

'We prefer to think of it as diligent policing, sir.'

'Ah, of course.' I let it go.

They must have noticed the look on my face, after all they are trained to look for that sort of thing aren't they?

'Do *you* know this man Mr Tolson?' asked Merriweather.

'Yes, but there must be some mistake; that's John

239

Manson from the Boater,' I corrected them.

'That may be what he's calling himself now, sir.'

'I can't believe it, there must be some mistake. His cousin is running a schools charity in Africa.'

'Now that is interesting sir. "Charlie Charity" as his name suggests, likes to set up charities; easy to collect quite large sums of money from small donations. No-one's going to press charges for the odd half-crown.'

'You're wrong Sergeant, I'd stake my life on this man,' I said.

'How long have you known him sir?'

'About a fortnight I suppose.'

'He must have a very winning personality to have gained your friendship and trust so quickly sir.'

'I say, you think that's what he intended?'

'Indeed so sir, but you said his cousin runs the charity?'

'Yes, a lovely girl, totally above suspicion. In fact I've asked her to marry me; wouldn't do that if I was unhappy about her credentials what?'

'Her name sir?'

'She can't have anything to do with all this, she's been in the papers with her charity work; you're barking up the wrong tree in her case I'm certain,' I said.

'I hope you're right sir. Is she the young lady who was in the newspapers recently?'

'Yes, Elizabeth Manson.'

'Do you know her whereabouts at the moment sir?'

'Look here, she was at my aunt's place in the country a few days ago. My aunt is most particular about whom she invites as guests.'

'I don't doubt it sir, but do you know where we

can contact her?'

'She gave me a list of all of the charity events she's organised, it's at home, but she's innocent Sergeant, I'm convinced of it.'

'Tell me, was she promoting her charity work whilst at your aunt's, sir?'

'Well yes, but it's what she does.'

'I'm guessing that the donations were a little more than a half-crown from your aunt's guests, sir?'

'Look here Sergeant, as I've already said, I would stake my life on this young woman.'

'Clearly so if you've asked her to marry you sir. But I must ask you for the list she gave you. I would also be obliged if you didn't contact her in the meantime.'

'I say that's a bit thick, I'm supposed to be asking her for her answer at this very moment.'

'I repeat. Please don't contact her sir, it could be seen as interfering with the course of justice,' he said giving me a "be-careful-my-lad" look.

Well I mean, damned awkward what?

'Put that way I have no choice, I just hope she won't think I've gone cool on the idea.'

'No I'm afraid you don't have a choice, sir. Right gentlemen, you're free to go. Mr Tolson that list as soon as possible please.'

10

The police were kind enough to give me a lift back home again, and I was surprised to find out that it was nearly two thirty. In my haste I had forgotten my pocket watch, no wonder I felt a bit peckish. The police driver waited for me to find the list Liz had given me and went off with it back to the police station. Somehow the thought of eating at the Boater gave me the colly-wobbles, but I needed to reassure myself that it was not a seat of crooks and villains. A few minutes later I rang Walters to ensure there would be a table available for lunch.'

'I'm afraid luncheon has finished, and the kitchen staff have all gone off duty until five thirty sir. We do have an arrangement with the Alexandra Hotel across the road on these occasions, they should be able to accommodate you sir. I could ring them and make arrangements, if that would be suitable sir?' said dear old Walters, helpful as ever. But having dined on occasions at the Alexandra and never felt quite comfortable it's one of those places that have the ability to make you feel that, "the only thing wrong with the hotel business, is, all those damned customers" so I decided to cheese it.

'Any chance of a few sandwiches or something to tide me over until dinner? I asked.

'I'm sure I could arrange that for you Mr Tolson, could you give me an idea when you are likely to be arriving sir?'

'About half an hour, I should think.'

'I'll see to that sir. Excuse me for taking the liberty, but the young gentlemen have arranged an impromptu snooker tournament. Perhaps you would like me to enter your name? There is an entry fee of five pounds, winner takes all sir.'

'Rather, a bit keen on a spot of the old snooker. Skinning a few of my fellow members is just the thing to take my mind off life's cares.'

'Am I to enter your name then sir?'

'If you'd be so kind, Walters, what time does it start?'

'One of the preliminary matches is already underway sir, but I expect, since there are several young gentlemen already entered, you should have time to eat and still be in time for your game sir.'

'Right, I'm on my way now, and thank you Walters.'

'My pleasure sir.' And we rang off. This might just be the boost to the dear old system that was needed.

At the Boater things were already well underway, amid much horseplay and friendly banter. I had time to eat in a leisurely way as I watched the first few games, so that when my turn came to strut around the glorious slate bed I felt much restored to the old Joshua Tolson, of myth and legend. So much so that I wiped the board with one Daniel "Dinkie" Hoskins, much to his general disgust. Dinkie rather thinks himself a bit of a snooker wizard. With only three frames per game it was soon time for semi-finals, and though I would have been willing to play my little heart out, I lost to a player who twice allowed me to break off, then commenced to clear the board, all but blue, pink and black, thus leaving me no alternative but to concede victory.

I'm getting ahead of things again; between the games I sat chatting to Spotty Bagshaw.

'Hello Spotty you old duffer, still on Shanks's Pony?'

'What ho, Josh, yes still wearing out the old shoe leather. Costing me a damned fortune in cab fares. The money those guy's must make, I've a jolly good mind to buy one and start up in competition.'

'No let up then in the parental sanctions?'

'Not even on the horizon. That reminds me, I never thought to ask when we met the other day. Was that your nifty little red Tolson I saw about a week ago?'

'Probably, her name was Ramona. There is much to tell about her, but I prefer you didn't ask.'

Well you know how it is when you say don't ask, that's the very next thing they do ask.

'Pore out your heart to me dear pal, solace and comfort are my middle names.'

Strange really, I thought it was something like Gerald or Deryk, or that sort of thing, but I could be wrong.

'It's a long story, but if you've got about a week or so I'll let you in on it.'

'Time has little meaning for me at the moment. Without the old mechanised wheels I'm in a sort of pointless limbo. So cheer up your old buddy by telling him your woes. Make him see that the lives of others are not all sweetness and light, that others also suffer.'

Well, put like that what could I do? But you know how it is, when you start to tell a complicated story you find that there's a bit you've left out and have to go back again to try to put things straight. Then they ask you why the princess had dyed her hair, or why she had found it necessary to kiss the frog in the first place, and you have to start long explanations. You must have had it happen, and so the long afternoon drew on into early evening interrupted by me being slaughtered on the billiard table, as the previous account. But I have to say there is some meaning to the old saying get it off your chest. I could feel the burden lightening with every word. I was just coming to a close when the dinner gong rang, and we toddled off to the dining room.

We had seen off the preliminaries, and as the main course arrived Spotty said -

'I say, I've remembered who it was I heard talking about your collection.'

'Really?' I said already half aware of the name he would suggest.

'Yes, it was that new chappie, Manton, I think.'

'Manson?'

'That's it, Manson, John Manson, he's the one. I've only met him briefly myself but he seems alright by all accounts.'

'I'll inform the police first thing in the morning.'

'Inform the police? I say that's a bit thick, the chap's a fellow member; below the belt Josh old pal, below the belt.'

'Between you and me, and this must not go further, at this stage they think he is somehow behind the theft of my collection and possibly the other thefts at the club.'

'I say old thing, shouldn't say that sort of thing even in jest, yer know.'

'Deadly in earnest. They had me at the station this very morning, and that was definitely the direction the

245

thing was taking. So no further, understand?'

'Strewth, when this breaks the manure will fly everywhere.'

'You speak the truth.'

'I hardly think that he's the one, I gave him fifty quid for that schools thing his cousin is raising funds for.'

'Ah.'

'What do you mean, ah?'

'Nothing as yet, and I hope it's all above board, but I have my doubts.'

'I only gave it on the understanding that he would arrange a meeting with her, rather taken with her don't yer know.'

I reeled, as you might imagine, quite put me off the dear old nosebag.

'Did he agree to arrange a meeting with Liz, er, his cousin?' I spluttered.

'Yes, he's arranged for me to go and meet her next Friday, in Melksham.'

I didn't like the look of this thing at all, as you can probably guess.

I couldn't believe that I had been so badly swindled. And to think, this wonderful girl was being used by this bounder. I bet his plan is to nip off with all of her funds as soon as she's finished collecting them. To think, doing that to his own flesh and blood. If I ever see the swine again I'll tear him limb from limb, and beat him judiciously with the soggy ends.

That Liz returned my feelings I had no doubt, that her cousin was swindling her seemed pretty obvious. The police had warned me off contacting her, whatever was to be done? Ellingham, that master of the impossible was off on some errand of his own, leaving yours truly with a blockbuster of a headache from trying to sort it all out. It was an even more depressed Joshua Tolson than ever who turned the key of the flat later that evening.

'Good evening sir.'

I nearly jumped out of the dear old skin.

'I'm sorry if I startled you sir.'

'Ellingham, when did you get back?'

'I only arrived a few moments ago myself sir.'

'Glad to have you back Ellingham, I have much to tell you but it will have to wait until morning. I'm just too tired to get it all into any sort of order,' I said.

'I too have much to inform you about, and a clear head on my part would also be an advantage to get the true picture sir.'

'Then I suggest we both sleep on it and exchange our news in the morning.'

'Very wise sir, if I may say so.'

'Say away Ellingham, just a night-cap I think.'

'Very good sir.'

I had a whiskey and soda, going a bit light on the soda, and went to bed.

11

I was awakened, by Ellingham's gentle cough. The old brain box seemed to have cleared a good deal overnight, so that I was aware that it was raining.

'Forgive me awaking you sir, a telegram has arrived from Much Moreham.'

'Oh lord, now what?'

'I could not say sir, but since the boy is still waiting in case you wish to reply, perhaps an early appraisal of the contents could prove judicious.

'You mean read it now?'

'Exactly sir.'

I tore it open and as anticipated it was yet another of Aunt E's messages.

> *HELLO YOU YOUNG BLOT ON THE*
> *ENGLISH COUNTRYSIDE. WE'VE BEEN*
> *BURGLED OVER NIGHT AND CAUGHT*
> *THE BLIGHTER RED HANDED. THAT NEW*
> *BUTLER CHAP OF OURS – SORRY CAN'T*
> *THINK OF HIS NAME AT THIS INSTANT*
> *BUT YOU MET HIM WHEN YOU WERE*
> *DOWN HERE – HE HAPPENED TO BE*
> *AWAKE AND HEARD NOISES AND WENT*
> *TO INVESTIGATE AND COLLARED THE*
> *BOUNDER. JOSH SAYS HE'LL REWARD*
> *THE CHAP SUITABLY AT A FUTURE DATE*
> *– WE CALLED THE POLICE AND HE'S*

GONE OFF TO THE CELLS – THE
BURGLAR OF COURSE NOT JOSH OR THE
BUTLER. BUT HERE'S THE BIG NEWS –
THEY THINK IT'S THE SAME CHAP WHO
ROBBED YOU. WHAT DO YOU THINK TO
THAT? LOVE AUNT E.

I handed the telegram to Ellingham to read.

'I had feared that this might be the case sir.'

'Really Ellingham - why?'

'It is part of the information I need to give you sir, but if I might suggest a reply would be wise.

'Gosh, what should I say?'

'Perhaps, something along the lines of – "Well done every one, will telephone later" and your initials sir.'

'Do you think that will do?'

'I would think that adequate if you then follow it up with a telephone call later this morning sir.'

'Why, what time is it?'

'Seven-thirty sir.'

'Good lord, on a Sunday?'

'Indeed sir.'

'Then send that, and wake me at nine.'

'Very good sir.'

And I turned over for that last little bit of shut-eye that tops the old batteries to the brim.

About ten seconds later, or so it seemed, there was Ellingham awaking me with a cup of tea and the news that it was already nine o'clock.

'I have taken the liberty of running a bath sir.'

'I trust you beat it Ellingham?' I quipped.

'Most amusing sir. I have laid out clothes of a casual nature and others more formal; I was unaware of

249

your plans for the day, sir.'

'No plans Ellingham, casual will do quite nicely, I intend to take it easy and mull things over.'

'Very good, sir, have you any particular request for breakfast sir?'

'I think a bowl of those corn things and an omelette.'

'Certainly sir.'

I lowered the cherished personal frame into the soothing water, and said good morning to the quacking duck. I was out and dressed within about ten minutes feeling almost back to midsummer condition. The thing that had bucked me up more than anything was that for once I had got the drop on the blighter. I was about to pull a masterstroke; at two thirty something would happen that would have Ellingham rocking back on his heels.

With breakfast over and the first gasper of the day about half consumed, I poked my head around the kitchen door.

'Leave the washing-up Ellingham, we have much to discuss.'

'As you wish, sir.'

'Sit down faithful servant,' I said indicating the other armchair.

'It is hardly my place to take such a liberty, sir.'

'Sit down damn it, we need to talk man to man.'

'Thank you sir.'

'Cigarette, Ellingham?'

'Thank you sir.' He took a gasper from the box on the little table between us and lit it.

'Pour yourself a coffee, Ellingham.'

I was trying to soften the blow that was to fall at the said hour.

'Thank you no sir, I have this moment consumed a cup of tea in the kitchen.'

'As you wish. So, you said this morning, if I recall correctly, that you were not surprised that my aunt had been burgled?'

'Indeed so, sir; I have to admit to a certain clandestine activity in my absence from your employment sir.'

'Tell all then Ellingham.'

'I am as you know sir – indeed I think you have yourself commented upon the fact – somewhat sceptical when it comes to coincidence. It seemed to me that too many of them were presenting themselves. I decided to try to investigate the matter to see if there was, as I had begun to fear, some ulterior motive behind them.'

'Is that the reason for the days off?'

'Yes sir.'

'Then you shall be paid for them.'

'That is most generous. However you may wish to revise that kind offer when I inform you of my findings and my motives sir.'

'Not good, what?'

'I fear you may not be altogether happy with my motives, sir.'

'Oh, well proceed anyway.'

'Thank you sir. I have to admit to less noble reasons before the point where I took time off sir.'

'Less noble, Ellingham?'

'I fear so sir. I did not wish to have to leave your employ, a situation I have always thought myself most fortunate to hold, and to this end I engineered certain things to discourage the young lady from forming a marital alliance with you sir.

'Engineered – what do you mean?'

'Whilst taking the young lady to the station in your car, I suggested that she invite you up on stage to speak for her charity, a thing she seemed quite agreeable to. I did not of course tell her that I would ensure that you were heckled sir.'

'I bally well was too, how could you have engineered that?'

'You were unwell at the time and so I took my time returning with the replacement vehicle that same afternoon to delay you until the following evening. The young lady said that Buxton was to be the next venue and by coincidence my second cousin lives very near by, he owed me a favour and was pleased to take part, sir.'

'So you were responsible for that eh?'

'I fear so sir, my hope was that the young lady would be most upset and be unwilling to continue the relationship.'

'Well it damned near succeeded, she was not nature's happiest little bunny, the meeting broke up in disarray and she saw red.'

'I had anticipated such might be the case sir.'

'That was your original motive. Can't say I like it, interfering with and trying to upset the young master's plans and all that. Not the line expected of a manservant, but what set you working on other lines?'

You'll notice I didn't say gentleman's gentleman; put the blighter in his place, what?

'The alarm bells began to ring, if you'll excuse the colloquialism, when two people seemed to remember Miss Manson but were unsure from whence. I took the liberty of tracing the young nurse who had seen you out of the hospital.'

I didn't like the way this was heading.

'Checking up on Miss Manson?'

'I used it merely as a starting point sir. The young lady suggested that she thought that Miss Manson was in fact Phylis Hargreaves. She told me so convinced was she that she was right that she had looked out the old newspaper to have another look, and was even more convinced that it was a photograph of the girl she remembered.'

'Surely your schooled-together theory still holds water?'

'As you say sir. She, the young nurse, was schooled in Newcastle-upon-Tyne and had played in a hockey match with a school from over the border in Scotland. The other schools star player, she remembered, was none other than Phylis Hargreaves.'

'So why would she change her name if she was indeed Phylis Hargreaves?' I asked.

'There is of course a very common reason why a young lady changes her name, sir.'

'When she marries, of course, but that not being the case why change it to the name of your cousin?'

'You are assuming, sir, that Miss Manson *is* Mr Manson's cousin.'

'What else – I say you are not suggesting she's *Mrs Manson*, his wife?'

'I fear that is in fact the case, though there is a further twist, sir.'

'Ye gads, hell's bells, I asked her to marry me the other night.'

'I assume the young lady declined, sir?'

'Delayed me, rather than declined.'

'Just so, sir.'

'How on earth did you find out that they were married?'

'I remembered that whilst at The Willows, Miss Manson had been in conversation with your uncle. I assume she must have enquired in a roundabout fashion into the house security sir, for he was at the time I chanced upon them, imparting certain, if not classified, at least sensitive information with regard to the site and operation of specific features of the burglar alarm system. This, together with your young friend Mr Bagshaw remembering a conversation about your stamp collection, between other members – yet another coincidence? I thought not, sir.'

'So the old duffer had inadvertently shown her the way in?'

'It seems so, sir.'

'Carry on.'

'I suggested to Inspector Jackman that it might be worthwhile investigating whether a Phylis Hargreaves had at some point married a John Manson, possibly in Scotland. I understand that through a young constable who had moved down from Scotland a certain known criminal had in fact got married; it took only a small investigation to find out that Elizabeth Manson – Phylis Hargreaves – Married one Angus McCleod and is in fact, Phylis McCleod, sir.'

'Mrs 'Charlie Charity?'

'Indeed, sir. At that point I contacted Thornton, your aunt's new butler you may remember, and suggested that he be alert to a possible burglary. That really concludes my story other than to say I am most sorry to have been instrumental in bringing about this sad state of affairs, sir.'

254

'Could never have been if she is already married. Oh well, I suppose I'll get over it?'

'I sincerely hope so, sir.'

'One thing's a puzzle though Ellingham, how come she happened to be at my aunt's place, at the very time I was there?'

'I understand from your uncle's secretary, that she wrote asking for help with her charity. It was a fluke I suppose that your aunt fell so in love with the idea that she invited Miss Mans… the young lady in question, to The Willows. Apparently your aunt told Miss… the young lady, that she would also invite you since you had connections to the motor industry, and therefore the possibility of large donations, sir.

'It just fell into their combined lap?'

'Very much so, sir.'

'Fooled the lot of us, what? My aunt will get the screaming willies when she realises that she egged me on to marry the girl. Coo, I'd give a hundred pounds to see Aunt E's face when she finds that out. '

'As you say sir, a most convincing ploy.'

'And all sorted out by a few albums of stamps, and boxes of coins.'

'It has long been an interest of mine to read up on crime, and such is often the case.'

'Sherlock Holmes, and all that?'

'No sir, reports of real crimes. There is often one simple mistake that leads to the person being found out.'

'Drop a bit of a clanger, what?'

'Indeed sir.'

'One bright outcome though.'

'I'm pleased to hear it sir?'

'You'll still be able to stay with me, continue as

255

my gentleman's gentleman, if that still suits you?' I asked.

'I would find that most agreeable sir.'

'Reserve your judgement Ellingham, I have a bombshell for you which might well be more than you can take.'

'What is the nature of this difficulty sir?'

Before I could answer the telephone rang, and Ellingham excused himself to go off and answer it.

'A Mr Dyson on the telephone, he says you are expecting his call, sir?'

'Indeed I am.' I said as I arrived at the instrument.

'Mr Dyson, hello, is all set for two thirty?'

Two thirty arrived, at about half-past-two in fact, much as anticipated. I had told Ellingham that that was the time that all would be revealed.

'It's half past two Ellingham, would you accompany me to the garage please?'

'Of course sir,' he said with slightly raised eyebrows.

A few moments later we stood at the bottom of the steps.

'What do you see before you, Ellingham?'

'A number of various motorcars, and in your allotted space is the motorcar loaned to you by your father's company, sir.'

'Correct, but over in the corner, the one under that dust sheet.'

'It had not escaped me sir, but the more fastidious of the tenants will often cover their respective vehicles if they are away for lengthy periods.'

'You speak the truth, but we need to raise that cover to reveal all.'

We walked over to the said drape, and I whisked

it off with a flourish.

'A red motorcar, similar to the one you had originally. One of the tenants has bought a car like the red one you had on loan, sir?'

'One of the tenants indeed, Ellingham.'

'I can see that that would be upsetting to you, but how does it affect our relationship sir?'

'The car is in fact none other than my estranged "Ramona".'

'Ah, I see sir.'

'You only think you do. The tenant who owns her found out the person who had purchased her and offered a sum of money, well in excess of the price paid, in short made an offer the then owner could not refuse.' I had the blighter's attention now.

'Then the owner is – *you*, sir?'

'Bulls-eye, first arrow, the fair "Ramona" is mine. Bought and paid for. This is why I suggested you might want to revise your decision to stay on?'

'I am pleased you have been reunited with the vehicle. I know it means much to you, and I will still be most pleased to accept your offer of continued employment, sir.'

'The redness still offends though Ellingham?'

'A very small price to pay sir,' he said and the corner of his mouth twitched a little.

About the author

Dennis Talbot was born and bred in Derby and loves to walk with his wife Pauline in the beautiful English county of Derbyshire.
Dennis wrote his first novel 'A Small Price to Pay, Sir' at the age of 70. With his lifelong love of the novels of PG Wodehouse, this was bound to be a humorous offering. It reached the finals of 'The People's Book Prize' 2016. Two further novels using the same characters, Josh & Ellingham followed.

Best Foot Forward, Ellingham

Look Lively, Ellingham

During a spellbinding holiday in America and Canada, the seeds of a detective story set in the 1930's began to take shape.
"The Killing of Cristobel Tranter", the first in the Whitecross Yard Murder series was the result.

www.dennistalbot.co.uk

Books in the

Josh &
Ellingham

humour series in order are:

A Very Small Price to Pay, Sir

Best Foot Forward, Ellingham

Look Lively, Ellingham

One Has to Smile, Sir

The Best Laid Plans, Sir

All available from Amazon as
Paperback – eBook

or free to read on Kindle unlimited

www.dennistalbot.co.uk

Printed in Poland
by Amazon Fulfilment
Poland Sp. z o.o., Wrocław